Also by N.E. Lasater:

Farmer's Son

"A powerful drama with a conscience"
Publishers Weekly

ALTERNATE ENDINGS

N.E. LASATER

Alternate Endings/N.E. Lasater – 1ˢᵗ ed.
ISBN 13: 978-0-9903069-5-5
ISBN 10: 099030695X

CONTENTS

It's not the load that breaks you down, it's the way you carry it."

— Lena Horne

She couldn't catch her breath. She gasped and gulped the air, her chest pumping the dry wind that had robbed the wet from her mouth an hour before and a thousand feet below, where the canyon floor met the first long climb.

Far above her, so high she had to jam her head back onto her sweating shoulders to see it, a red chunky peak scratched the turquoise sky. It topped a peninsula of sheer cliff that rose 1,500 feet in a shark's fin whose ridge in spots was less than two feet wide. The moody river carving a rusty groove had so far lost to this great stone altar, for the flash floods that routinely killed hikers still swung wide in a respectful bend around its feet.

She saw them ahead of her still, laughing, their voices young like the perfect day. At first they had included her, walking alongside in the freckled morning as they crossed the shady metal footbridge and began what started as a level stroll. Once the trail had steepened to leave the cottonwood trees, though, the pack of happy teenagers had moved ahead in the basking sun. By the time they arrived at the long dusty switchbacks up the bright west wall of the valley, they had stopped calling back to her.

"I'm all right!" she yelled to them anyway. "Go on ahead!"

She was panting now, her chest aching, and her heartbeat way too fast. She peered ahead but could only hear them. They had turned a steep corner and were gone. Lightheaded now, with both legs shaking on the sharp incline, she stepped back to the hard wall, her daypack between her spine and the rock. She bent her twitching knees and put her hands on them, then willed her arms to straighten to brace her as she struggled to find her breath.

SEPTEMBER

"Five. The plane's at five."

Calyce Tate pressed her phone to her ear as she drove south on the George Washington Parkway toward National Airport.

"Nina won't come. She wanted Labor Day at her place this year, but how could we all fit in her one-bedroom? And how were we all supposed to afford the trip to Chicago? I know you and Greg could do it. Me too, but what about Damion?"

Calyce leaned left to feel the steam heat rushing in through her open driver's side window. She had rolled down all the windows on her old Camry, though the air-conditioning still worked fine.

"Let Nina stew," Calyce said. "But you'd think she'd want to see her own mother. No, I'm all right. Just hoarse."

Through flashing breaks in the summer trees, she saw far below to the languid Potomac River and the rock cairns of Three Sisters Islands clearing the surface by only a few feet. A huge tree had come hurtling downstream sideways in the last big thunderstorm, and its long trunk had caught between two of the tiny islets a child's height above the water. Browned debris hung in flags from the bare wood.

She coughed and it hurt her.

"You can bring red cole slaw. I've got the rest." She smiled. "Tell Jimmy I'm making his cuppie cakes."

The call over, she dialed the next one with her right thumb

and waited with her ear to the phone as cars darted sullenly by her. When no one picked up, she dialed it again, punching the same digits with irritation. When her son Damion finally answered, she pounced.

"Were you sleeping? No, I don't know when you came in. I want you to clean the powder room. I've been asking and you haven't done it and we have people coming. No I can't. I'll have your grandmother. Today. I told you. Four fifty-six."

Across the slow river, Georgetown University crenellated the ridge with its two steeples and its odd, massive, square croquet arch through which she could see the sky. On the wooded shore below, a clover green and white boathouse had launched student-rowers on two long boats that sliced the glassy water. She watched their rhythm as they moved as one in the bright sun that strobed their white skin.

"Steak like you like it," she told Damion. "And barbequed chicken. Yes of course she's welcome."

Key Bridge skipped over the river, its ribboned arches light. She moved to the right to avoid the slow traffic turning left to head north into D.C., and she continued south along the Virginia side through Rosslyn.

"Seven? Can't she get there earlier? That's too long for Jimmy to wait."

But then she laughed at something he said to charm her. "Just tell her to come as soon as she can," she said. "Did you update your resume? Then do that too. Starting Tuesday everyone will be back at work."

Once she hung up, she hitched her thin hips to inch her long legs back from the steering column that hit both her knees, and she reached again for the typed papers in her lap. She found her half-glasses in the cup holder and pushed them to the bulb of her nose, then swung her eyes between the sheets and the busy road, flipping the pages with growing annoyance as she drove.

She had been standing at the end of Terminal B for half an hour but her mother hadn't showed. Calyce had gone from standing, to standing with her arms crossed, to leaning against a round pillar opposite the short guarded hallway that led in a jog to the gates. She had finally put her heavy shoulder bag on the glossy floor. Above her, honeycombed arches made angles of origami steel, folding into one of the many high cupolas that ran the length of the new building. After twenty minutes, her left black pump had begun tapping.

After thirty, she picked up her bag, slung it over her tired shoulder, and turned to look behind herself once again up the long main hall toward the other concourses, but her mother still wasn't coming from that direction either. The plane had landed on time, the signboard said, and had long ago docked at Gate B 32.

She ascended the escalator to the ticketing level, where the line was long, so it took another twelve minutes, according to her watch, to finally step to the counter. All the while, Calyce continued scanning.

Flight 250, from Tampa.

"Name?" the young ticket agent said.

"Effie Guthrie."

The blonde typed at a screen they both could see.

"Not here."

"She must be. Is that the final manifest?"

The woman's eyebrows walked up her forehead. "I'm telling you. She's ticketed but she never checked in."

Calyce looked around for someone older. Maybe a man. "Is there a supervisor?"

"I *am* the supervisor, and she didn't board. The seat stayed empty."

The young woman looked at the person next in line. "Can I help you?"

⋀⋀

She dialed, getting no one. Into voicemail she said, "Simon, it's Calyce. Mom didn't get on the plane. Has she called you? It's six o'clock on Sunday. If you hear from her, will you call me? I'm calling Nina."

She dialed as she walked to her car in the parking structure behind the terminal, her heels clicking on the gray cement.

When her sister answered, Calyce said, "Mom didn't get on the plane in Tampa and she's not answering her phone. Have you talked to her? ... No, Chicago is not easier. Not for anyone."

She pinched her arms against her slender body. "You know how she is. Yes, Nina, she treats me like that too."

⋀⋀

She came downhill on the narrow road that pretzeled through her tight neighborhood of fifty wooden-slat townhouses. After making one left and another, she descended in the twilight past a last row of mailboxes and pulled up at the bottom, at the curb just beyond her one-car driveway, two houses up from the end of her particular cluster. Her white multifold garage door was closed.

She opened the two doors on the sedan's passenger side and pulled out six bulky white plastic grocery bags, which she loaded, wincing, onto the crabbed fingers of both hands. She bobbled duck-like over a short, elbowed walkway of fake-brick to her no-glass, solid, blood-red front door, which was the only noticeable color on the home's exterior. She struggled with the key then twisted herself sideways to step into the tiled entryway. Despite the warm day it was cold, ice-cream cold inside.

"Are you home?" she stage-whispered, her mouth to one of the two identical closed doors immediately inside. "There's more in the car."

But no one answered. She sighed, then climbed the narrow staircase up the right-hand wall with one arm's heavy load knocking the other. She thumped the bags onto the linoleum kitchen floor and went to the thermostat on the wall around the corner to turn off the air-conditioning. She switched on the old can lights in the low ceiling and began unpacking the groceries, which she inventoried out loud as she opened the behemoth stainless steel fridge whose French doors curved far beyond the front edge of the laminate counter.

"But where's the mayonnaise?"

She looked again on the door, then checked the cupboard. "I had mayonnaise this morning. And what happened to the eggs?"

The kitchen occupied the main floor's far back left corner. The refrigerator faced right on the long left wall while the much older, shallow, single-bowl metal sink was mounted on the short-er rear wall under the one small sash window that slid up only halfway, a floor above the fenced pen of the back yard. On the ground, twelve feet beyond the house, a six-foot spear-point-ed fence stood in military precision, beyond which loomed the identical gray-blue backside of an identical cluster of six town-houses on the next street. Calyce and her directly-behind-neigh-bor watched each other wash dishes every night.

The small kitchen ended on the right with an interior wall,

on the other side of which was a twenty-year-old brown corduroy loveseat with sewn-on cushions like bustles behind the head and over each round arm. Into the corner on the side of it was shoved a square pine coffee table that had been purchased originally for a much larger room. On it, a small square-box TV faced out diagonally with its remote placed exactly parallel to the screen.

Along the long back wall, between the corner table and the top of the stair landing, a matching second brown corduroy loveseat had a pink plush snuggie draped over one arm. Two padded tan faux-leather ottomans sat in the middle of the beige wall-to-wall carpet. On one of them, a woman's small yellow shoulder bag lay open.

When she had finished with the groceries, Calyce picked up the purse. She latched it without looking inside and headed downstairs with it. She hung the bag on the same interior door she had spoken to, and she went out again.

Four minutes later she charged back through the front door with the mail in her hand. On top a white business envelope blared a red banner in alarming lettering. She knocked hard on the same door, the yellow purse still dangling.

"Damion! Are you up? Selene, are you in there?"

She put her ear to the door. After a moment, she opened the door next to it and peered into an empty garage. Her son's car was gone.

Calyce heard them downstairs finally as she was getting ready for bed. The chime of china plates rose to her overhead in the small bathroom of her small master bedroom. She heard their low conspiratorial voices and their shushing and muffled laughter.

She cinched the belt of her blue chenille bathrobe and slid her feet into her matching backless slippers. Holding the wooden railing she carefully went down, clearing her throat at the bottom so they would hear her.

She heard the door to the powder room close suddenly and the ceiling fan inside it start to hum as she smelled the warm, inviting smell of oregano in tomato sauce.

In the kitchen her son Damion stood eating her leftover lasagna. He held the plate near his mouth as he shoveled with a fork. He was shorter than his very tall mother but undeniably beautiful, with close-cropped hair and pecan eyes under lashes so thick they looked false. He wore a neat goatee that focused attention on his lush mouth. His full-face smile could convince anyone of anything.

"Is she asleep?" He looked at the ceiling, to where the guest-room was above them, next to the master bedroom.

"She didn't come. She said she decided to stay home."

"You went to the airport?"

"It was two hours before she answered her phone. She said she was out walking the beach like always."

Calyce pointed to the envelope she had left on the counter, inches from the glass lasagna pan whose foil top was now gaping. "Did you see that notice?"

Damion shrugged.

"It's addressed to you," she said. "May I open it?"

She tore carefully. "It's what I thought. They're canceling if you don't pay within the next five days."

She heard the fan stop in the powder room and the door open, so she hurriedly whispered, "You need to call our insurance agent first thing tomorrow. They may want a certified check. I don't know. This has never happened before."

Selene wandered in, transparently pale with long, fine blonde hair that sat limply on the curve of her bony upper back in her gunmetal summer halter. Her makeup-less eyes were the merest sigh of blue and her eyebrows so blonde they disappeared. She smiled at Damion as she greeted Calyce, and he smiled back, his wet lips pulling his cheeks into four unequal signs, one pair each of less-than and greater-than bracketing his perfect teeth.

Selene took his now-empty plate and put it in the sink along with his fork, then moved in under the arm he offered. They both leaned against the counter facing Calyce, who had stopped talking. She looked from Selene to Damion and back again as they regarded her.

"Sorry to wake you," Selene said. "We'll be quieter so you can get back to sleep."

They stared at her, mute now, but still she didn't leave. She cleared her throat.

"What is that?" Damion said. "You do that a lot now. It's annoying."

Calyce looked significantly at Selene but still the young woman didn't move. "There's something I need to discuss with my son."

Calyce bent her right leg and propped the foot on top of her left slipper, stork-like. Selene said she was going to take a shower and politely wished Calyce goodnight.

When the door closed to Damion's room beneath them, he said, "'My son?' What am I? Twelve?"

"I'm sorry, but you were supposed to pay this."

"I've never paid it before."

"You know I changed it so you'd have your own policy."

"Which costs way more. And it moves all the cost for my car to me. You drive it sometimes. You know I don't have the money."

"Which is why you're looking for a new job, something that fits your degree. Not that bartending."

The siren woke her from her light sleep. Calyce jerked as the throbbing wail raced along the dense blocks of streets.

She felt a sharp lump in her throat and sat up. She tried to swallow but had to cough. She forced a gulp to clear it, moving her neck like a bird.

The only light glowed red from the squared digits on the plastic clock that faced her from the end table on the other, empty side of the bed. It was 3:12 a.m.

From her pillow, she saw out the open glass single door to her Juliet balcony, which wasn't an actual balcony despite the realtor's name for it but an outside railing waist high.

She found a full moon fuzzed by streamers of cirrus clouds as she felt the damp air, which was being chopped rather than moved by the whirring ceiling fan.

She untied the silk scarf she wore knotted below the knob of bone in the back of her skull. She tied it again, tugging on the rabbit-ear ends. She lay back once more and tried to sleep, feeling on her cheek the slick kiss of her satin pillowcase.

Calyce held the basket in the doorway as the high school seniors shuffled in, heads down and backpacks hung by one strap over slumping shoulders. She blocked each teenager from entering until a smart phone had been relinquished. The new kids who had never had her mewled but the veterans told them to "just give it up, already." She didn't slide the basket under her desk until she had collected all twelve.

"And your computers," she said as they took their seats around the three outsides of a square U made with long tables, whose open top faced the virgin whiteboard where she stood. Like the rest of the building, everything in the classroom was nearly brand new.

"You can keep them, but you can't have them out. Only paper. You remember paper."

Of her dozen Senior Creative Writing students, she saw that three were black and four were boys. All were privileged to attend the private high school in Upper Northwest D.C. whose college placements danced like sugarplums in the heads of their overweening parents. Room 2860 was on the top floor of the high, white-clad building. Two more floors, which included a full-sized basketball court, hid underground at the insistence of the plush homeowners in the surrounding neighborhood of 1920s Craftsman bungalows.

Each day they would discuss two original pieces of student writing, Calyce told them, which meant that each week, over three classes per week, they would discuss a total of six pieces they would write. This in turn meant that each of the twelve students would be critiqued once every two weeks. The assignments would flow from well-known short stories she would give them.

"So you're responsible for always having a piece ready. No excuses. I want them distributed in hard copy by the end of the class before. And once we critique yours, immediately start the next one. I also expect you to know how to use proper grammar. You chose this course. It's an elective so I expect you to know how to write."

"Calyce, are you doing the assignments too?" a black girl with long twists asked her. "John DeGroot always does. That's what my friend says."

"Yeah," a gangly boy said. "John doesn't care about grammar."

"Well I do, and it's Cal-iss, like Alice with a hard C. Not Cal-lease. And be sure to spell it correctly, even though it sounds like that hard thing on the bottom of your foot."

She didn't smile. No, there would be no poetry, and no non-fiction. "Use your imaginations, starting with today's assignment."

She picked up some printed sheets to distribute. "Read *The Monkey's Paw* and use it to write your own piece focusing on setting, which –"

"Is that it?" A white girl cut her off. "You don't want plot?"

She waited, staring. A full beat. "We'll get to plot."

"But setting alone isn't impactful."

One of her veterans groaned as Calyce crossed her arms and said, "'Impactful' is not a word. It's a trendy absurdity, like 'incentivizing' and 'reach out.' He reached out to me, instead of he wrote me an email. You may not use such words in your stories. They are what? Anyone?"

The groaning veteran had to say it when Calyce finally pointed at her, but she rolled her eyes as she did. "Index expurgatorius."

"And that's not Harry Potter," Calyce said. "Madison, tell us what that means at the beginning of next class and bring in a poster board so we can write words as they arise."

"Seriously?" rookie Madison said. "A poster board?"

When they filed out at the end of class, a shy girl lingered, pretending to arrange things at the far bottom of her pack. Once Calyce knew they were alone she quietly asked, "How's your mother? Any better?"

The child didn't look up as she shook her head.

"Do you want to talk about it? I've got a few minutes."

The girl nodded.

As Calyce tried to make her way through the throng of rushing teenagers shouting and weaving, Roger, the freckled science teacher, came abreast of her in the hallway. They maneuvered shoulder-to-shoulder to create a wedge that diverted the flow.

"I got that map for you," he said loudly so she could hear him. "To show you the topography, remember? I'll bring it in."

Then he was gone, having stepped ahead of her as the tide took him. All she could see was his red hair that curled like peaked whipped cream, but soon even that was swallowed.

Twenty minutes later she was squeezed into a chair at a small round table in a little room next to the English Department faculty office. The space was only as large as a walk-in closet, but served as storage unit, winter coat rack, book depository and conference room. If four people met, the table had to be pulled away from the wall, where the whiteboard was, whose ribbed metal bottom lip poked now into her left shoulder.

She waited with her papers lined up neatly on the fake wood tabletop as she squinted through her reading glasses to text on her phone, holding it with her left hand and stabbing letters with her right index finger.

John DeGroot, the head of the high school's English Department, returned finally. "Everything okay?" he asked as he shoved a stack of books on the floor out of the way with his foot in order to close the door.

"It's my sister." Calyce clicked the phone off. "There's something wrong with my mother but Nina thinks I'm crazy, at least that's what I'm getting from these texts. Three words. Why doesn't anyone talk anymore?"

DeGroot had fine white hair in gauzy tufts and small, close-set eyes straddling the narrow bridge of a beaked nose above a strong jawline parallel to the accordion ridges on his neck. "Why does she think you're crazy?"

"Mom didn't come for Labor Day and she was supposed to stay for two weeks. I went to the airport but she didn't show. She says she just changed her mind."

"Has she done that before?"

She nodded. "But you know that feeling when something's not right?"

"I do," he said as he scrolled on his laptop.

Calyce still had two more things to discuss. First was the new teacher, a young black woman who had already sent around a multitude of emails with her "thoughts" about the curriculum.

"Who is this child?" Calyce said.

"It's Amita's first teaching job."

"She doesn't understand politics."

He smiled. "And you do? She reminds me of you all those years ago. I want you to be nice to her."

Second was the Senior Creative Writing class Calyce was teaching for the first time, and she told him she was nervous because she wasn't a writer. DeGroot told her to relax. She didn't have to use the same short story prompts he had used for years but should find pieces that spoke to her. And yes, he confirmed, he had done the assignments along with the kids, though he hadn't always shared them.

"It kept me attuned to the process of writing."

"I'm not a writer," she said again. "Grammar I know but imagination eludes me."

"Life's not as empirical as you make it," he said warmly.

He thanked her again for being willing to teach his class at the last minute and in addition to her English 9 for freshmen. He said it meant a great deal to him, that she would cover for him, particularly since he hadn't given her a reason.

"I figured it was Steven," she said. "And you would have done the same for me."

He said she still deserved to know why he had asked her to do it. He hadn't been able to say before, it was all in flux, but he had finalized things that morning with the school's Head of Academics, so he could tell her.

"I'm retiring."

Calyce blinked as he hurried to say, "Don't worry, I'm not leaving until June, but I can't do it anymore, not with my brother institutionalized. What Steven did really threw us and he's alone out there."

"But you promised."

"You've got Belinda."

"She's a history teacher. Can't you work part-time?"

"He nearly died, Calyce."

She finally registered the reason for the closed door.

DeGroot said, "I know we promised each other another five years, but I can't do that now. I'm here all this year but with time off whenever I need it. You'll be head of the department next year like you've always wanted, and I'm asking Hank's approval to make you Interim Head immediately, so it'll be a *fait accompli*. You're younger than I am. You'll have years to run all these pain-in-the-ass people we hired."

"Did he say what Janice is going to do?" Belinda asked as they walked into the noisy faculty lunchroom at first-period lunch that same day.

"Only he's retiring, not her. She's staying on as Vice Principal." Calyce lowered her voice as she talked about DeGroot and his wife. "He said they need her salary."

Not all the tables were occupied. At one, next to the double row of small windows that punched holes that looked like an ice tray in the school's outside wall, three English teachers sat talking and eating. One of them was the young black woman, Amita, who had sent all the emails. She was flanked by a white woman in an olive sweater set and a broad-cheeked white man in his thirties. The other three chairs at the table for six were empty.

"Is that the new teacher?" Belinda whispered.

Calyce nodded but didn't lead them over, choosing instead an empty table by the entrance, near short cabinets on which a microwave sat with its door open. She smelled the aroma of canned chicken noodle soup.

"He likes her. I don't," Calyce said as she sat.

"Who's 'he'?" Belinda scanned the other table. "Dan?"

Calyce nodded. "Let him deal with her. I like your new 'do'."

Belinda pulled plastic containers from her neoprene lunch bag. "I had to stop paying all that money."

Calyce was doing the same, laying a place for herself with her fork on her napkin on the left and a knife and spoon on the right. "It's shorter but I like it. The big earrings help."

Belinda jangled them, bouncing her gray spirals. "You know the best part? I can scratch my head."

The lunchroom's ground-level portholes faced the school's

long entrance driveway, down which boisterous teenagers streamed like fire ants to the quick eateries they sought in their daily flight from the school cafeteria. Calyce saw a car trying to edge its way through the mass of young people.

"All the girls have the same short shorts," Calyce said. "Their backsides are falling out."

Four tables away, the three English teachers laughed as a math teacher joined them. The perky young man had curly hair and earnest brown eyes. Unlike the others, who dressed casually, he wore a short-sleeved white dress shirt and a red-striped tie.

"That'll wear off," Calyce whispered to her friend.

"Are you okay? You're in a mood today."

"It's Damion. What's he doing bartending?"

"That again?" Belinda took a bite. "Cut off his internet."

"What?"

"Cut it off. You know, intermittently. Turn the Wi-Fi on and off when he's home, secretly, so he doesn't know. 'Gosh, honey, I don't know what's wrong with it.' That'll make him get his own place."

"I don't want him to get his own place. I just want him to get a career. He spends money like water."

Belinda waved goodbye at a woman leaving. "So show him how much it really costs to run a household and show him he spends more than he earns. He's a business major. He'll understand."

"May I join you?" said a deep voice above them.

It was Roger, the redheaded science teacher, who looked and dressed like a Brawny commercial.

Belinda made eyes playfully at Calyce, but the towering man didn't see it.

Shocked, Calyce didn't speak, so her old friend said, "Sure."

But he didn't sit down next to Belinda. Roger stepped over quickly to claim the seat next to Calyce.

Two Sundays later Calyce stood impatiently in her kitchen holding an armload of clean folded clothes and a ceramic mug of fast-cooling coffee. She had made brunch just an hour before, but her son already had his close-cropped fade deep inside her refrigerator.

"You think if you stare long enough things will start dancing?" she asked Damion's back. "Electricity costs money."

But he didn't move. Finally, he opened the crisper to select a nectarine as big as his fist. He bit and sucked at the sudden spurt of juice as he walked from the kitchen through the small brown sitting room with his mother padding behind him.

"I'm glad we're doing this," she said. "Did you print out your bank statements and your credit card bills?"

Damion suddenly stumbled, catching one foot behind the other. He flung out his hand to snatch at the banister so he wouldn't fall down the stairs, which sent the fruit flying. She heard it thump on a step, then bounce on the tiled floor below.

He was shaken but unhurt.

She turned back to the kitchen. "I'll get a paper towel."

Damion didn't wait for her but headed down, his sullen feet bumping. "If I had a fridge in my room, I wouldn't have to keep coming up for food all the time."

He had gone inside already when she arrived at his closed door. She had to knock.

Damion let her into his living room with its black leather corner sectional on her right, from where a tall chrome floor lamp arced nearly to the spot-lit ceiling. Under the lamp's silver globe a black coffee table sat on a rug whose furry white pile matched the two fake-fur throw pillows, one at each end of the sectional's arms. In the corner was a fake-chinchilla Afghan she hadn't seen before. whose long hairs riffed in the icebox breeze that fell from the ceiling vent.

The side of sectional along the long right wall of the house faced a flat-screen TV mounted on the room's left wall shared with the garage. The TV was on and the remote was on the couch where Damion usually sat. A *Fast and Furious* movie cast the only colors in the monochromatic room. Even his clean clothes in her hands were all dove grays and blacks.

Beyond the TV a short hall led to the full bath and dim bedroom, where Calyce at the door saw the unmade edge of his queen-sized bed. On the new bedroom carpet that Calyce had paid for lay a balled up and surely wet white bath towel.

"Let's start with inflow and outgo," she said as she sat. "I don't want to have to pay your car insurance again like I had to last week."

"Careful of the mug." Damion pointed, then went into his bathroom and closed the door.

She waited, eyeing the towel on the floor but not moving.

When he emerged minutes later, changed and patting his hair, she said, "It's like ice in here. And dark. Do you still have the bedroom blinds closed?"

He pinched the razor creases of his charcoal slacks as he sat.

"Where are your papers?" she asked.

"I don't need them because I know what happened. It was that blue suit you had me buy for Jay Jay's wedding. Plus that shirt and tie. And these shoes. Altogether, it cost me a thousand."

"A thousand dollars? That's my mortgage."

One shoulder moved. "You said you wanted me to look good."

"I told you to shop at Macy's. Where did you go?"

"You said I looked 'better than every other cousin there.' Plus I need it all for interviewing."

"But a thousand dollars for a suit?"

"You haven't bought men's clothes in twenty years. That's what a barely decent one costs. But that's why I can't pay my minimums, and by tomorrow there'll be late fees."

She shook her head at him. "You can't keep waiting until the last minute. What are the balances?"

He lifted his right ankle onto his left knee, where she saw a matte black sock above a polished black dress shoe.

"The minimums aren't much," he said. "A hundred each for the two of them."

He paused, then said, "I could always work a day shift."

"No. I want you –"

"To have my days free for interviews, I know, but you can't have it both ways, Mom. I can either be available during the days or be able to pay my credit cards."

He tilted his head at her, waiting.

She said, "I want you to focus on your job search, of course."

"Of course, but these bills distract me. I don't need the whole thousand. I could ask for that. After all, you're the one who wanted me to look good for that wedding. But just a couple hundred. Oh, and maybe some cash too. So make it four. Five."

"I don't have five hundred dollars."

"Sure you do. Not in your checking but I went over all your bank accounts like you told me, to see how you manage your money." He smiled. "See, I do do my homework, and you say

I sleep all the time. You've got two thousand in savings. Take it from there and it won't affect your cash flow."

She frowned as she thought about it.

"Or I could start working a day shift," he said again.

"No, I don't want you to do that. But you'll pay me back? This is just a loan?"

"Like I always say, I'll pay you back as soon as I get that big job you want me to find."

Calyce was on the phone as she drove to school early the next morning. It was Maryland, and the Beltway, and she was holding the phone to her ear, which was illegal, so she was looking for the police all while she was trying to breathe. A sudden coughing fit had stolen her wind.

"I've got a job, Nina, an actual job. You're the one who's freelance."

She forced a cough and then another, but her throat wouldn't clear. "I can't go see Mom until Columbus Day weekend. I'll pay for you to go if you go this month. I don't know how, but I'll pay."

Driving sixty, she said, "I just talked to her."

And then, "No, my going down there does not tell her we think she can't live on her own anymore."

Coughing, she took her foot off the gas and the van too close behind her had to brake hard. The driver honked as she turned on her flashers. She slowed to move right in the heavy traffic, inching her Camry into the far lane, then slid onto the narrow right shoulder. She hit the brake, jerking her whole body forward as she struggled to breathe while cars whizzed by just a foot from her door.

Panting, her chest straining in the dry hot sun, Catherine finally reached the cutout blasted into the rock. It was a trough that slashed along the side of the mountain and curved outward to create an overhang like a tunnel sliced vertically. At the same spot, the trail's cement changed from bleached gray to rose flowerpot. Man-made ridges had been added too, running perpendicular to the canyon wall. At the path's outer edge, square-cut blocks had been brick-laid to mark the rim, but they didn't barricade the lethal drop.

If she stood fully upright, she would stumble backward, the grade had steepened so suddenly out of the last turn. The dangerous pitch was obviously the reason for the new traction lines. She focused on her feet, sure she would lose her balance as her right side baked in the sun that had risen above the soaring opposite, eastern wall of the canyon. The backpack she had been told to buy balled a load that tilted her frighteningly off-center.

She heard them before she saw them, two abreast with their arms swinging, a young couple thumping down the hill toward her in billed caps and special hiking belts that holstered their precious water.

"Mojave, not diamondback," the man was saying. "It was yellower."

"Sounded like a wind-up toy," the woman answered.

"You know it's illegal to kill them here?"

They nodded to her as she shuffled, inching out of their way. She got next to the wall and balanced herself by grabbing It, then slowly raised her head to look ahead, to where the mounting path turned again, left this time and out of sight.

"Don't worry!" the man called back to her, laughing. "I'm sure he's gone by now."

OCTOBER

One bottle, purchased at the Zion Visitor Center only because the high school's principal, who was leading the group, had told her to. Catherine had not understood the fuss. She had never run out of water before doing anything, so she had not seen the need for the insistence. She had bought one. Only one, which she had now finished.

Where was the top of this thing? Breathless, she turned a corner and escaped from the sun into a narrow hanging slot canyon whose chinked red walls thrust upward on both sides of her. Suddenly in deep shadow, hungry pines poled tall and thin trees reached with broad leaves flat as coins to trap the merest sun. Below the tessellated canopy, a dry creek bed ran alongside on the left.

She stopped, gulping the cool, and waited for her gamboling heart to slow to a clip-clop. As she did she began to feel the first physical euphoria of her long climb. She spread her feet, rotated her shoulders back and put her arms akimbo and, eventually, closed her eyes. She felt the slowing clunk of her chest, the cool on her wet neck, and the lump of backpack. She heard no voices but the whispering trees and a bird's song, two syllables with a high climbing swoop followed by a vibrating trill. It was answered from dense dark green far ahead, a cycling alto wah-wah.

The week before, before the last days of frenzied shopping for expensive outdoor items she had never heard of in stores that over-

whelmed her, she had told her son Ryan her latest ideas for his never-ending job search. He had agreed, as he always did, with the logic of her thinking and wondered out loud, as always, where she came up with these things. Ryan had written them on his to-do list, which he patterned on hers, and he had indeed followed up on every one, using even the words she had given him. But he had not once been asked to come in.

"So what should I do now?" he had said as she was packing. "Can you think about it and call me tomorrow from out there?"

Catherine stared up. Suddenly, rising straight up the high, sheer rock face in front of her was some kind of red construction of rough-hewn blocks. Mortared but crude, the chinked stones weren't uniform but a thousand different sizes in a sort of brick wall that mounted hundreds of feet. Nothing but far-off sky cleared the top of it.

Across its face, traversing on sloped paths she couldn't see, a few hikers pin-balled back and forth. A couple moved left out of her sight, then reappeared lower a few seconds later, moving right. She did not know it yet but twenty-one very steep switchbacks had been engineered into the pink sandstone. To get to the top, which all the rest of her school group had already achieved, she would have to climb almost vertically 250 feet. She would have to scale the outside of what in a city would be a twenty-five-story building.

Ryan met with her once a week to "report on my progress," arriving punctually each time with a sharpened pencil in his mouth and his laptop and papers under his arm. It was unconscious, that pencil, a tic from his childhood. She had suggested it to eight-year-old him as a way to stop biting his nails, but the ploy hadn't worked. Nothing

could overcome his need to suck on his hands, but the pencil-in-mouth had stayed.

Each and every Sunday he climbed the stairs from his room to deliver a long-winded exegesis on his job search, which he rehearsed, showing her his notes, his call log, his emails sent, the scoured websites. That past Tuesday he had had a rare interview, but the man had asked odd questions for which she hadn't prepared him. Her son hadn't heard anything further.

"What should I do?" he asked.

"I don't know," she said with frustration. "What do you think? Why don't you tell me?" But he just looked at her and waited.

"Why can't he be more like you?" Catherine said to her mother the next weekend. "You always know what you want. He's a Bassett Hound staring at me. I love him so much, but why can't he run his own life?"

But her mother had fallen asleep. She was doing that more and more now.

Catherine listened to make sure and waited before she whispered to the sleeping old woman, "You always were a total dictator."

She worked up the steep switchbacks that piled like ribbon licorice. As she went, downhill runners passed her. A climbing panting couple yelled after one, asking why he was running, and he shouted back that it was easier on the knees.

She reached the top finally and the sky opened above her. The path became gritty sand and no longer roseate poured pavement. Exhausted beyond any exhausted she had ever been, she strained in a heating day that would ultimately reach 98 degrees. The leeching *sun had found her, soft and parched and exposed as she stamped on, scrub trees dense on both sides.*

The stench of urine hit her. Acrid and piercing, an assault to the nose that squinted the eyes and made her cough. It was everywhere, an invisible cloud of it, an open sewer of pungency. She clenched her nose with a hand and scanned the north slope to her left, where thirty feet up in a clearing two industrial-strength outhouses shocked the hillside with their electric blue. The portable, execrable toilets ambushed the eyes as much as the nostrils.

The smell staggered her. Burning, stale, awful urine poisoned the air and grabbed her, stopping her in the surprising sand.

In the night, Calyce found herself. Overhead the old ceiling fan rushed, tapping the same metal part every two seconds. Next to the other side of the bed, whose throw pillows she had stacked as always on a small velveteen chair near her dresser, the clock glowed 4:20. As usual, the one outside door yawned open.

Calyce lay on top of the bedclothes with her un-manicured feet tilted outward so the outsides felt the rough cotton of her IKEA duvet cover. Earlier she had lain herself carefully, resting her scarfed head gently on the satin pillowcase and pulling down her white nightgown with its eyelet hem ruffle until it spread evenly behind her without a wrinkle and smoothly over her knees. She felt the pleasant air brush her naked shins. The weather at last had sweetened.

She listened for the silence that meant she would not be heard, then with her right hand lifted the nightdress just enough to reach herself. She felt the elastic at the top of her panties cling but she slid her hand past it and down to the cleft in her body, and parted herself, then laid a finger on either side and began rubbing quickly, purposely, between her knuckles. She settled in and closed her eyes and chose a dark man tonight who gleamed with ropey arms and a smile that blinded. He came to her, this full-grown man old enough to have grown children. He gazed at her and told her he loved her. She opened her legs wider to him, but no more than a hand's breath, for that was all she needed.

In her yearning mind, though, he lost his mouth in her, and she saw with her closed eyes the top of his close-cropped head between her legs. She lifted her free hand to caress his hair, holding that hand in the air above the mound of her, holding nothing.

It was he and she in the darkness and her fingers doing lips' work. She whispered that she loved him too and how grateful, deeply grateful she was for his attention.

Quickly and soundlessly she came. She heard the meager slaps within her rise and fall away. There had been no moan, no hitch of breath, no mark at all but the tented nightdress.

Calyce took her hand from her panties and smoothed the white cotton again over her flat belly and the long bones of her thighs. With the tips of her fingers she found the eyelet hem and smoothed it once more to lie evenly across her knees.

She turned her head slowly and heard the slide of silk beside her ear. Through the open door, she searched for but could not find the slivered moon, which had fallen below the house beyond her backyard.

On the far side of her, disregarded as it faced her across the vast deserted continent of her bed, the clock's glowing red numerals changed to 4:23.

The next morning she dressed. Standing damp in her robe at the sliding doors of her one small bedroom closet, she opened the right side first to examine exactly one-half of her carefully ordered work attire. She chose one of her three slightly different black skirts, then, modestly holding her robe closed, bent to retrieve one of her two pairs of identical black pumps. She closed the door with a practiced bare foot and slid the other, where each of her blouses faced left with precisely two inches of air between them. She lifted a white knit three-quarter-sleeve top and a boxy grey wool jacket with sleeves slightly too short for her long arms.

Exactly eight minutes later she descended to her kitchen with her leather bag, which she thumped on the counter.

"Keys." She coughed once as she inventoried. "Glasses."

She took out her phone and checked it, then tucked it back in its designated inside pocket.

She scanned the pristine counter and the empty sink gleaming from her nighttime scouring. She passed through to her living room to brush the corduroy sofa cushions against the nap so the old plush rose. She picked up the four coffee-striped throw pillows and slapped each between her palms, then returned them to their spots, each next to an arm, point down in a diamond.

Leaving, she descended to her tiled entry and discovered what looked like water coming from Damion's room and pooling a foot out from under his closed door. She could tell it was still coming.

"Damion!"

She knocked but no one answered. "Selene!"

She tried the knob, but it was locked. She raised her arm to feel along the top of the doorframe, but the spare key was gone.

"So, setting's fine. You all did fine, particularly Matt with his description of New York, but now your story must be inhabited by your main character and not just stuck on like one of those Colorforms –"

"Like what?" interrupted a boy with black-rimmed glasses.

"Never mind. You'll be graded next on how well your setting reveals character, and then, on how well your character's interacting with that setting further reveals his nature."

"His?" a girl said. "Why 'his'?"

"And third. Are you writing this down? Third, I want to see at least one metonymical object."

She waited. "You know what that is? Anyone? Metonymy is relatedness through direct association. An example is when we say 'the White House' instead of the president's administration. Or 'the crown' when we mean the Queen of England. We bring the whole concept through with just that one related reference."

"So you want metaphors?" asked the same girl.

"No. A metaphor is an alternate way to describe something. She was a fish as she swam. But no part of her is actually a fish. A metonymical object is a small part of the bigger thing it's replacing. If your character is a great swimmer, for example, showing us her trophies will take the place of all that establishing prose. Be efficacious, though. I want you to use just one. The best one. Got it?"

As soon as class was over, she pulled out her phone. A text was there but she couldn't read it, so she fumbled in her purse for her glasses.

Looks like water heater, said her son. He had sent it half an hour before.

"What about it?" she said to herself as she dialed his phone number. She paced but he didn't answer.

Into his voicemail, she had to say, "Damion, call a plumber. Get someone out there right away. It's still early, and you don't have to work until tonight. I have to stay for a meeting. Call me back once you've set that up."

She began to put the phone away but didn't. She squinted at the tiny screen as she texted him too with a single finger.

Call plumber. Stay to meet him. Let me know.

"I had no idea what I was saying." Calyce laughed for the first time that day. "I got that from your lesson plan from last year."

In the bullpen of the English Department faculty office, John DeGroot smiled back. They sat together in the tight space at his desk in the far corner, her chair rolled next to his from her own desk by the door. They flanked each other as they swiveled outward in unison toward the center of the room when the first two of the other English teachers sauntered in.

Her smile wiped suddenly clean, she leaned in to whisper, "Thanks for doing this."

DeGroot's white, fibrous head nearly touched Calyce's. "It made sense when you suggested it."

She watched Amita linger outside until Dan appeared, greeted her warmly, and guided her in.

Calyce registered for the first time that the young woman was stunningly beautiful, her lustrous skin a radiant warm honey brown. Between her eyes and her eyebrows there was a model's acreage, which she had made up perfectly with earth tones, deeper in the crease with highlights at the brow bone. But not too much.

When the rest of the group was assembled, DeGroot brought them all up to speed, giving them details of his brother's confinement and the indefinite prognosis that required his indefinite stay. DeGroot would have to continue to travel to California regularly, as he had been doing since school began. In fact, he had to leave for the next few days, starting tomorrow. He had realized that in his increasing absence and unfortunately increasing mental inattention, he had to seek the help of someone with nearly the same longevity as he, who knew the school and the department and the curricula.

"So I decided on Calyce. She has all the institutional knowledge, and Hank agrees."

Around the cluttered room, all noise stopped and eyeballs

stared. All but Dan looked surprised, but he was nodding. He caught her eye and smiled as he bobbed his head.

DeGroot said, "I'll let Calyce tell you some things she's planned to make things run easier."

She rose to hand out some pages. On them she had outlined that all absences from now on had to go through her. With John out so much, they had to stretch their departmental substitute-teacher budget by covering for one another as often as possible. All absences except for illness ("and don't be sick") ("and don't fake it") had to be pre-approved a week in advance. Also, because of the need for all of them to be fungible, no deviations from the set curriculum for each class would be allowed. That way, anyone could teach anything if necessary.

"So we can't go farther in the lesson plans?" a teacher asked.

"Further," Calyce said.

"I'm sorry?"

"It's 'further.' 'Farther' is used about a physical distance on a map. You can remember because it has "far" in it. And no, no changes to the lesson plans."

"Is this page posted?" another teacher asked. "Did you upload it?"

"Why should I?" Calyce said. "You've got the paper in your hand."

Dan caught up with her as she motored down the deserted hallway. His freckled farm-boy face was pulled into a wide smile that accordioned his cheeks and sent ripples to his throat, so he appeared to have no jaw. His green eyes were sunk deep into the folds.

He said, "Does that Ford commercial make you crazy too, like it does me?"

As she hurried, Calyce looked up from her phone.

"'Go Further,'" she said. "An entire ad campaign for millions of dollars and it's grammatically incorrect. I see you and Amita are getting along."

She blew in late that same afternoon to find Damion's door ajar and the chrome arc light in his living room pouring shine onto the pool of water still on her entryway tile, exactly where it had been early that morning.

"Are you there?"

She stepped over the small flood to look inside. A shallow river flowed between the TV and a small trapdoor behind it on the same wall, opposite the bathroom, which little door too was partly open. The water came from inside.

"Damion?"

No answer. No one was there. There were also no tools, no yellow plumber receipt, no towels anywhere, no mop and no bucket. When she swung her foot to put it on the white furry rug, the rug was soaked.

His car was gone and he didn't answer his phone calls or his texts or his voice messages or his emails from Calyce the rest of that night, even though she contacted him every few minutes.

She had mopped and by 11 p.m., the emergency plumber had finally left after Calyce had paid him.

"Damion," she said in her final voice message. "It's going to cost eighteen hundred to get a new water heater installed. I don't have that kind of money so I couldn't tell him to order it. You need to call me as soon as you can."

"John?" Calyce asked DeGroot the next morning. "Have you got a minute?"

"You're wet."

She wiped her damp neck with a flustered hand. "Uh, I used the weight room, so I decided to shower here."

"You're working out now?"

She pointed to the tiny conference room. "Can we talk?"

Safely inside with the door closed, she said, "John, I was wondering, since I'm Head now, is there any way I could get a raise?"

He took his time. "You're not actually Head, and certainly not officially. That will take the formal vote."

"But you said I was."

"What I said was that I hoped your being Interim Head would make your election a *fait accompli*. Don't look surprised. You remember I was elected all those years ago. All of us in the department here have to vote. Down at the lower school they do the same thing for their own department. But all that won't happen until May. That's when the elections happen school-wide, and that's when the new Heads all get raises."

Roger popped his head into her just-emptied classroom.

"I have it. You want to see it?"

He strode in without waiting for an answer, carrying two books and a paper map. He walked to the long table closest to where she sat at the teacher desk and waved her over as he unfolded the map and spread it out, caressing the edges flat. She had no choice but to lift herself from her chair.

He waited until she stood next to him. "Are you okay?"

"Pre-occupied. But it's nice to look at this. I need a mental vacation."

He put a finger on the Grand Canyon. "You've been here?"

"As a child with my father back in the 1970s. He was from out there."

"That's where this staircase starts. You know the Grand Canyon's a mile deep, with something like forty different rock layers? That's what makes all the stripes you see in the photos. Here."

He opened the coffee-table book he had brought too, and she had to smile.

"Visuals. Always good," he said as he flipped pages. "The Grand Canyon is the result of two forces. You know what they are?"

She played along. "The river cutting into the rock?"

"And the rising of the Colorado Plateau. It's a single tectonic block, and it's stayed together. One hundred and thirty thousand square miles. Bigger than forty-six states."

He winked at her. "I prepared for this. You know what it's made of?"

His eyes were sweatshirt gray. She had never been so close to him before.

She shook her head.

"Layer after layer of sedimentary rock, because it all used to be a sea bed. Over hundreds of millions of years, this sediment was laid in different layers made of different things and hidden until the Colorado Plateau was violently forced up, then eroded."

He put a finger where Arizona, Utah, Colorado and New Mexico came together. "It covers Four Corners and extends over parts of these four states, but it's mostly in Arizona and Utah. It rose in one huge block around the same time the Rockies were formed. You ever driven to Flagstaff from Phoenix on the back roads?"

There was a single black fleck in one of his cloud-colored irises. She could see it.

She said No, she hadn't.

"You're driving north in this hot desert and you hit the Mogollon Rim. This huge barrier cliff that just comes up, and it's two hundred miles long. It's this giant step that takes you up three thousand feet to a higher level. Once you climb it you're in ponderosa pines. In an hour, it's suddenly cool. Chill. That rim is the southern edge of the Colorado Plateau."

He talked as though he were standing at the top of it. Thatched in with the red hair she saw strands of gray. "You've hiked all this?" she asked.

"With this map. This one's mine. I bought you another one just like it. See that jagged line? That's where it starts. Now, imagine a flat table of land that's made up of sediment in stripes, with the oldest on the bottom."

He pointed. "This is where the Grand Canyon is, about three and a half hours north. The bottom of it is Precambrian. That's billions of years old."

The gray ran around his skull at the level of his small ears. The nearest one had a tiny hole in the lob. His mop on top was new penny. Not a Lincoln, but one of the nearly beige modern ones. And thick. Much thicker than a middle-aged man's was supposed to be.

"You really love this," she said.

"I'm teaching here. Pay attention. The thing is, when you're standing at the bottom of the Grand Canyon looking up, those mountains aren't mountains. They're the sides of a cup, like on a golf course, and you're at the bottom looking up to level ground. You get that same sensation at Zion."

She nodded, remembering.

"Your mind says you're high up because you see these high peaks," she said, "but you're actually at the bottom. If you come from the south where the hotels are, the ground comes in and funnels to this tiny slice where the walls shoot up. It's incredible."

Just for a moment she too was standing in the sunlight of Zion.

He nodded. He knew. "I ordered this for you too."

He turned the pages of the smaller book until he found a drawing and showed her.

"This flat table that's the Colorado Plateau runs north from the Grand Canyon's north rim to Zion in Utah, and because of the staircase, the top layer of the Grand Canyon is actually the bottom layer of Zion, which we can see because the Virgin River cuts through Zion just like the Colorado River cuts through the Grand Canyon. The plateau's a block being carved by these rivers. Amazing, right? You went to Bryce?"

She nodded.

He said, "My God the stars there when you're camping. The very top of Zion is a white rock layer that's under the bottom layer of Bryce. Every one of them is a different color. That's how you get that pink at Bryce that looks like salmon, but the Bryce layers are the youngest. The top is only 60 million years old."

"Only?"

"That's yesterday! The whole thing is a series of steps over this huge plateau."

He doffed a make-believe hat, making a show of it. "Which is why we call it The Grand Staircase. The coolest place on earth."

"How old are you?"

"Did you like my presentation?"

"'Coolest'? Really? You sound like one of my kids in here."

"But do they bring you handsome gifts?"

"No it's not fixed," Calyce told Damion over the phone, finally. "Why haven't I heard from you? Did you get my message about how much this is going to cost?"

She had left at lunch to sit in the driver's seat of her car at the far, dark back of the cavernous garage under the high school's indoor pool building.

"No, I don't have eighteen hundred, not with my having paid you that five hundred." She shook her head as she spoke. "I don't want to put it on a credit card. The interest rate is exorbitant.

"Selene's? Until when? But you hate her roommates. That's what you tell me when she comes over every night and uses my shower. All right, *your* shower. But *my* water, which *I'm* paying for. I had to take mine here at school this morning. It was embarrassing.

"What do I want? I want you to contribute. There, I said it. Because you use the water too and you leave your wet towels all over. How much? A few hundred. I can take the rest out of savings but there's only thirteen hundred left. I had to buy plane tickets to see Mom.

"I'm flying down day after tomorrow. I told you. There's something going on and she won't tell me over the phone."

Her mouth fell open.

"But I'm not your landlord. You don't pay rent, so it's not fair to call it my capital expenditure. You're part of a family and you should contribute. It was supposed to last ten years. How many showers does *she* take? No, I'm just saying –"

She sucked in her breath.

"No, I don't want you to move. Please don't say that. Of course she's welcome.

"Yes, I guess it does go into the basis when I sell the house later on. Yes, I'll get the tax benefit. You're right. It does make sense. But I've only got thirteen hundred.

"They would split it? The plumber would do that? I can play the thirteen hundred in cash and put the last five on my credit card?

"That's a good answer. Yes, all right. That's what I'll do."

She had always hated the sea, with its vast empty plate beyond its persistent, melodramatic waves. It was forever the same, endlessly, topographically, and there was such a small change in real color, from steel to grey to that sudden flash of turquoise that lasted only a second under that breaking curve on a sunny day. Sure, she saw it. No need to point again. Yes, she heard the birds keening and saw them diving and running like madmen on stubby legs across the evaporating slick of sand.

Even the clouds, when they happened, puffed above nothing but a straight far line, unless you counted the high-rise condos stitching the long beach, which she didn't. They were man-made. Clearwater was flat, flat, flat, and no amount of toothy marketing or new words for the tiniest increments on the blue color wheel would ever improve the humdrum spectrum.

But her mother loved it, reveled in it, and spent as much of every day as possible walking with her bare toes in the thick sand of Clearwater Beach. She took the bus over the leaping causeway to the wide strip on the other, ocean side of the peninsula she could see from her condo's sliding patio doors. Calyce knew, but her mother didn't, apparently, that she lived in a box facing wet air and a narrow view of the Intracoastal bathtub.

With its mid-rise on the edge of the bay, her mother's building had probably once been a gleaming place to live, a decade before she had bought it. Now it was a latticed has-been stuffed with old people who had stayed, stacked on their tiny cruise-ship balconies, cooking in 1974 fluorescent kitchens whose arched-faced cabinets held crock-pots they still used.

As Calyce turned from Osceola onto the sloping ramp to the basement parking, she saw a pair of crones, as well as three separate ancient women alone, inspecting her from their plastic armchairs, each in a triangle of shade from the tropical sun. Territorial shorebirds, their eyes pierced from just above their allotted ten-foot spans of iron railing.

Her mother wasn't one of them, however. Her narrow sixth floor balcony, the one with a single white plastic chair angled toward the causeway bridge, was empty.

To get the garage gate to slide open, Calyce had to push a button on the squawk box. It took a moment, but her mother's reedy voice finally chirped, "I'm so glad you're here!"

Calyce waited silently for the buzzer.

She parked in a visitor's spot – one of five, with only her rental car in any of them – then turned her head left and right to organize her newly re-stiffed curls on her shoulders, using a newly self-manicured hand to secure her bangs diagonally across her forehead. When she stepped out she smoothed her navy suit skirt and brushed her matching jacket, thoroughly tucking into her waistband the white cotton blouse that stuck to her in the relentless damn humidity.

"Honey are you all right?" her mother exclaimed lovingly as she held both arms out to her towering daughter. "You look exhausted."

Calyce didn't stop but angled around her to go inside. "Just tired. When did you stop coloring your hair?"

"And you're hoarse, too. How long have you had that?"

"Why am I carrying this? Don't you want to walk the beach?" Calyce said with irritation the next morning.

As they had left, the old woman had handed her a folding beach chair with short legs meant for sitting an inch above the sand.

"Is this the new routine?" Calyce asked as she sped ahead of her slow-moving mother.

Effie Guthrie was small and bird-boned, with the face of a woman men didn't whistle at sixty years before but stopped and simply gawked at, in awe, knowing she was something they could never achieve. Even now her cheekbones anchored her skin and her upturned eyes were unhooded by crepe. Time seemed not to have robbed her.

In her standard beach uniform of striped cotton shirt and blue Capri's, Effie spent a full minute devoting all her senses to locking her front door and another to shuffling down the si-sal-carpeted hallway clutching a worn plastic tote the color of molting flamingoes. She was inhaling heavily into her lungs and paying attention to it as she finally arrived next to her daughter waiting impatiently by the elevator.

"Let's take your car. I hate elevators. They take forever."

"Why drive?" Calyce said. "You always take the trolley. And why aren't you telling me to take the stairs, if you hate the elevator so much?"

Effie's pixie cut had been finger-fluffed into place for the day and her signature plum lipstick had been perfectly applied, but she looked off. Drained already, and it was still morning. She watched her mother's mouth gape when she breathed in and her lips purse in puffs with each exhalation. It was a new behavior and it looked affected.

"Are you all right?" Calyce asked again as she had several times already, but Effie just nodded. It annoyed Calyce that she couldn't get a straight answer.

In the basement parking, Calyce slowed to her mother's pace but maintained two yardsticks of air between them. Effie tried to close the gap but with each step Calyce corrected. She opened the passenger-side door for her mother but didn't stay to load her.

"How is Damion?" Effie asked after five minutes of silence, as Calyce drove over the new four-lane causeway toward the ocean. "He tells me he has a girlfriend. A white girl. Do you like her?"

Calyce kept her eyes on the road. "She sure uses a lot of hot water."

"What?" Her mother turned to her.

Calyce evened her voice. "She's fine."

"Pretty?"

Calyce didn't answer.

She steered right on the other side of the Intracoastal, at a new traffic circle napped with palms, and headed north up Mandalay Drive.

Effie asked, "How's his job search going?"

"Ask him. You two seem to talk all the time."

Effie said calmly, "He says he's looking."

"I wouldn't know. He sleeps all day and goes to work until all hours."

They passed the white rectangular Hilton to their left, on the seaside. To Calyce, the low-slung building looked like a wall vent for air-conditioning.

"He's still young," Effie said. "It's taking him time to figure out what he wants to do."

"He's twenty-seven. I had two jobs by then."

"Turn here. There's parking off the street. Very few people are you."

Calyce moved her mouth but kept it closed.

Effie got out, grabbed her pink tote and folding chair, and began walking. As soon as they reached the white sand, her mother took off her shoes. She started trudging in a beeline toward the water.

When Calyce realized it, she said, "We're not walking the beach at all?"

Effie shook her head. She was once again purse-lipped exhaling.

"Mom."

Calyce staked her stork legs in the sand and felt the soft give under her tennis shoes. "What's wrong? Can't you breathe?"

Effie had stopped too. It took her a moment to find her air.

"Not all the time, and it's not the breathing. It's deep, like it doesn't feed me."

"Is it your heart?"

"Heart's fine. But I can't walk the beach anymore. It's because I'm old, that's all. Can you take this?"

Calyce accepted the chair, which weighed nearly nothing, and Effie plodded on, lifting her head every few paces to assess the remaining distance.

It was slow going. The overcast sky glared a harsh light that made Calyce squint, but not her mother.

Effie walked straight into the ocean until it covered her feet. As she looked out to sea with her chest over-working, she didn't speak but soon her body transformed. Her breathing became less labored and she stood taller as she rolled her shoulders back in the stance of a much younger woman.

Effie pointed to her own feet. "Here."

"You'll get your backside wet."

But Calyce dutifully unfolded the chair. Effie fell into it smoothly, with a surprising fluidity, and stretched her bare calves into the lapping water. Every third wave wet the seat and her rear end.

Calyce could either stand next to her or spread one of the towels out ten feet behind. Effie didn't care. She had gone in her mind to the sea.

Calyce set herself up silently directly in back of her mother, where Effie couldn't see her. As she watched her mother's upright head stare unmoving toward the horizon, she registered how utterly white her short hair had become. Calyce counted back to when she had last visited her in Florida.

Effie began absently scooping water with both hands, splashing it onto her knees. She moved both arms in unison, towards herself then out again, but she didn't look down. She kept her eyes on the line of the vast gray ocean. Calyce had seen this before, countless times, and she knew to leave her mother alone. Sitting on her towel with both legs bent uncomfortably on one side of her, she fished out her phone and her reading glasses. She sat silently in the day's glare, trying but mostly failing to read her tiny screen.

"I don't know why you do that," Calyce said as they reached the car later.

Quietly, Effie answered, "I just love the sea. It's as if it's caressing me."

Calyce dumped everything on the hood and heard the metal chair clang.

"He's dead, Mom. He died a long time ago."

"Not when I'm here. It doesn't seem that way to me."

As they waited in silence to make the left onto the down ramp again, Calyce saw the trolley that looped along the shore roads stop in front of Effie's building. It was an open-air bus that looked like a San Francisco trolley car.

"Are you still taking that?" she asked her mother.

"They want you to get on and off too fast. Last time he yelled at me because I was taking so long."

"Mom, it's Florida. He's lucky you're not dead."

Calyce drove into the underground darkness. "You mean you don't go to the beach at all anymore? When was the last time?"

"Today. With you."

Calyce looked over. In the half-light of the garage, Effie was smiling at her.

Early the next Monday morning, which was Columbus Day, Effie approached her in the small kitchen where Calyce was putting water on to boil for instant coffee. Calyce was dressed already in her black skirt and pumps. Her mother wore a thin pink bathrobe and matching slippers, both of which were old but clean.

"You didn't sleep well," Effie told her. "You were coughing."

"No I wasn't."

Effie tilted her head. "Do you not realize it? You were coughing on and off all night. I could hear it through the wall. But not a regular cough. It was higher, like a bark."

Calyce swallowed. Her throat did hurt.

Effie asked, "Hasn't Damion said anything?"

Calyce spent the rest of that morning shopping for her mother, who said she wouldn't go to the store because she would only slow Calyce down. In truth Effie had dressed and already claimed her daily spot on the balcony. In the late morning, before the sun walked over the top of the building, her mother's cheap white armchair and its matching low table still lay in refreshing shadow. On the little table were bulky new black binoculars. Under her chair a small aqua rug softened the rough cement.

"But you always go," Calyce said out the sliding door. "Do you not go to the store now, either?"

"I go, just not all the time."

Effie had already turned toward the sea.

"Mom, where did you get those binoculars?"

"Simon brought them last time when he was here."

Calyce was surprised. "When was that?"

"Last month."

"And he didn't notice that something was wrong with you?"

At the Publix, when Simon didn't answer his phone, Calyce bought as much as Effie's kitchen could hold, focusing on staples that wouldn't go bad and, because she knew her mother wanted them, Effie's favorite hot sauce and bottled salsa, which she put on everything. Calyce bought more instant coffee and light bulbs, bar soap and toilet paper in single paper-wrapped rolls because a cellophaned dozen was too big to be stored. She had so much she had to use the stolen shopping cart the condo owners kept in a storage room in the garage to get it all upstairs.

Her mother kept thanking her all while Calyce unpacked and she wrote a check to reimburse her daughter, which Calyce accepted.

Calyce then fixed lunch as Effie hovered, trying unsuccessfully to help. As they sat outside with their plates in their laps, Calyce asked about the young white woman down the hall who took Effie on errands once a week. Her mother answered that Stephanie ("Oh right, that's her name," Calyce muttered) had been focused on a divorce so she hadn't been around much.

"She's a renter anyway," Effie said, "and living here may be too pricy for her now."

"So you're all alone trying to get places."

"Don't worry about me."

But Calyce said she *was* worried, that her mother didn't look well, that she needed to see a doctor about her fatigue. Effie was dramatically worse than the last time Calyce had seen her.

"But that was ten months ago," her mother said. "I've aged, that's all."

"It's been ten months?"

"Christmas. I came to D.C."

Calyce persisted. "You've always been active, but you don't go anywhere now, and you seem exhausted all the time."

Effie put her fork down. "Alright. But I'll only go if you go. I called Damion while you were out and he says you cough all the time."

"You two were talking about me?"

"Of course we talk. And sometimes we even talk about you. Hand me that Tabasco."

When Calyce left an hour later, she told her mother it wasn't necessary to come down to the car. She should rest. Calyce would see herself out of the building. She didn't tell Effie that her flight was actually much later.

As Calyce made the right at the street, she was already dialing her brother and didn't see Effie waving goodbye from her high balcony. The strong sun shone on Effie's maple syrup skin and her flashing whitecap of hair. A sweet breeze touched Effie's cheek. She lifted her chin toward the ocean to feel it.

In the rental car, Calyce started in on her younger brother.

"She says you told her to see a doctor, so you knew. You should have told me."

Calyce was passing houses and stores as low as the squashed-flat landscape. "All you did was dump those ridiculous binoculars and leave. Simon, she can't breathe. You've left this up to me again. As always."

The next evening Calyce came down to do her weekly cleaning of Damion's room, letting herself in with the spare key he had put back on top of the doorframe. From inside the interior door to the garage, she lifted off the cement an apple green plastic laundry basket filled with cleaning supplies and rolled out her spotless second vacuum. She used her thin rear end to prop open Damion's door as she clattered sideways with a banging Swiffer also crammed under an arm.

She saw immediately that his white rug was gone, replaced by a new one that was velvety slate gray. Two walking pairs of feet had already flattened the short pile to create tracks of powdery dove. One had been wearing socks. The other, smaller, was bare-footed, with only the ball and toes showing, like she hadn't fully touched down.

Calyce switched on the arcing light and something else caught her eye. It was a picture frame. She stepped over to take the photo off the end table.

It had been taken from above, maybe the open staircase to another level of the bar where Damion apparently worked, for he was standing behind a long shiny black counter against rows of bottles and ordered glasses on shelves back-lit by translucent panes. Little globe bulbs hung high and low on single lines like fringe, making a zigzag pattern above his head. Both of his slender hands, graceful as a woman's, touched the bar top. He was smiling his honeyed smile.

Sitting on one of the barstools with a high, latticed back was Selene, her body turned toward Damion but her neck twisted over her shoulder toward the camera. Her long, straight, almost albino hair flowed down the back of her champagne dress, which contrasted with the close-fitting black T-shirt Damion wore. His toffee skin glowed in the V-neck, and the color poured up onto his high cheeks and over his ears.

Her son really was the most gorgeous thing Calyce had ever seen. Selene's extreme lean-in toward him, pressing her small breasts into the bar granite, told Calyce that she felt the same.

Calyce flipped over the frame, which still had its back price tag. HomeGoods. Not anywhere Damion shopped, so this was a gift from Selene. In the photo, Selene was attractive too, in a ghostly, never-been-outside sort of way. The young woman was nearly see-through, and she wore no mascara, ever, but Damion seemed to like it, for in the picture he was leaning toward her as well. What she had going for her, most of all, was youth.

In Damion's bathroom later, as Calyce was brushing the toilet bowl in her rubber gloves, she caught herself in the wall-wide mirror. It had been a long day. Her makeup had disappeared so her small, wide-set eyes had fallen into the deepening folds of her upper lids. Only liner in smoky crayon smudges could make them stand out. Her brows arched naturally high and well, so they never needed to be shaped. They were a good feature. She thought herself lucky not to have any forehead wrinkles yet. And no gray in the eyebrows, Calyce noticed as she leaned in to peer.

Her mouth was what people remembered, with its movie-star bottom lip. When she smiled the same double parentheses appeared for her as for Damion, but to Calyce the fates had also given an additional horizontal tuck just above each corner of her mouth in the valleys below her round cheeks.

She washed her hands and wiped her face with her forearm, dragging it up her forehead and over her stiff hair, which immediately betrayed her. She smoothed it with fat fingers in her yellow glove.

In the artificial light, she saw that her hair was continuing to thin. Still jet black, though, from paying every three weeks to paint her rebellious roots a solid ebony.

She had been beautiful too, but different from her mother.

Calyce feathered the loud vacuum into the bedroom, where there was a new glint of glass from the top of Damion's six-drawer dresser. A bottle, a tall bottle of liquor. She left the machine blaring to inspect it.

The top was on it, a rounded cork stopper. Courvoisier, with an embossed medallion of Napoleon. She held it in her left hand, reading the label. "V.S." Product of France. 40% alcohol.

She had never found booze in her son's room before. She certainly had never found a bottle of it already open.

Belinda was laughing but Calyce was serious. Her friend's curls bounced, which irritated Calyce as she tried to explain again why this mattered.

"But Courvoisier!" Belinda said. "Like *Ladies Man.*"

"You're not listening. My son has alcohol in his room."

"He's nearly thirty. He can drink if he wants."

"Not in my house. We don't drink."

Other teachers had leaned toward them to listen. Belinda noticed, so she said more quietly, "*He* does, and that's the problem. He's still living with you and he shouldn't be."

Calyce too lowered her voice. "There's no way he could afford the same apartment on his own, or his car, or that Courvoisier. Not to mention that girlfriend if he stays a bartender."

"I'm no expert," Belinda said. "I don't have a family, but I don't see where it's written that parents are required to provide their adult children the same standard of living they had as kids. It's easy for me to say, I know, but how long will you be supporting him? When is it finally your turn?"

When lunch was over they collected their things. They threw their garbage into the bin near the door but Calyce lingered, saying, "I put him here. I insisted. He wasn't up to it. The classes here were too hard for him and he never found his place."

"I know," Belinda told her kindly. "You've said that."

Calyce was blocking traffic and didn't realize it. "If I had left him in public school like he wanted, where he had friends, he would have succeeded, and he would have felt good about himself with his academics. He would have done well in college instead of barely graduating. I'm the reason he's been at that bar for the last four years."

Belinda shuffled her out of the way but Calyce continued. "I screwed him up, and it's my job to unscrew him. There's nobody else. Maybe if I were softer with him. You know, a lot less me."

The next morning she began the long climb up the school's wide central staircase whose cinder-block walls had been painted by some long-ago senior into the ascending levels of the earth into the sky into outer space at the top in darkest blue. Calyce started at the bottom, at the curved white core, and she had made it past the yellow outer core and the red mantle when she heard Dan call up to her. She stopped where the teenage artist had painted a wide belt of brown crust and dinosaurs eating banana trees and each other.

Dan caught up with her at a rex with impossibly short arms. Dan was tall too, so she didn't have to look down at him, and he was so thick in the torso that he blocked her view of whatever it was the tyrannosaurus was eating. The noise of jostling young people doubled as it bounced off the cement walls, so he gave up trying to speak until they were both out into the third-floor hallway.

"Did you hear about Janice?" he asked. "She's leaving too, with John, at the end of the year, but she's stepping down as Vice Principal immediately, as soon as they find an Interim."

Suddenly, Calyce was measuring her steps and her breathing to keep them both even. "Yes, I know," she lied. "John already told me."

"I figured, but I wanted to ask you something."

They were at the door to her classroom, a minute before the bell rang. "Don't you think it would be great if it was Belinda?"

"Were," she said reflexively.

He waited until she got it.

"Yes," she said. "She's always wanted to be Vice Principal."

"Wouldn't she be terrific? Can you think of – "

"No. She's absolutely the right choice."

"Everybody respects her," he said as two of her students slid by into the classroom.

"And the children love her," Calyce said. "She's also why we've won *It's Academic* the last two years."

Another girl excused herself on the way in.

"So permanent? Not Interim?" he said.

"I agree completely. Why hire from the outside?"

Their heads were close now, conspiratorial. "So, who should talk to her?"

"I will," she said.

The bell rang, but it wasn't a public-school burr-ring! It was a soft, two-note lilt, repeated twice like a theater's two-minute warning at the end of a play's intermission.

"Umm," she said casually. "How is it that John told you? Were you meeting?"

"No. I was talking with Janice just now. She said they only decided last night. She asked me not to broadcast it but of course I figured you already knew."

She nodded, then turned toward her classroom.

"But Calyce?" he said to her back. "Is that when John told you? Last night? Because right now it's still only eight in the morning."

"Tell us another one," a boy in her class demanded twenty minutes later.

"Gray," Calyce answered. "Why is it spelled two different ways? It's the only color that's spelled with an 'a' or an 'e,' but why do we have two ways to spell such a blah color?"

She was angry so she kept going. "And Playtex. Do they think we're stupid?"

A girl said, "Those gloves my grandma uses to do dishes?"

"You know where the name came from? They're latex. Thick. They wanted women to think they'd have fun scrubbing the toilet if they wore them. So they called them Playtex instead of latex and made them happy yellow. It's nothing but marketing. You have to watch what people tell you. And what they don't, when they should."

⋀⋀

Calyce said, "Mom, I can't talk now. I have to talk to Damion but Selene's been here. She only just left."

Calyce rolled her eyes dramatically to herself in her kitchen. "No, I haven't called a doctor. Have *you*? You did? Really?" She was astonished.

"Alright, alright, I'll do it. Yes, we'll tell each other at the same time what the doctors say. Now, how are you going to get there?"

⋀⋀

It was late that evening when she rapped on Damion's door with her laptop shoved under her armpit. He was half asleep, wiping his eyes with his fist like a little boy.

"We're meeting, remember?" she said as she shouldered past him to set herself up in his living room, flipping open her computer on the coffee table and knocking her knees on the hard edge. She motioned for him to sit.

Damion remained standing, scratching his stomach. "What are you doing?"

She retrieved lines of text indented with bullets. She didn't look up.

"What's wrong with you?" he asked with irritation.

She poised her fingers on her keyboard. "Tell me everything you've done this month so far."

"I just woke up."

"Did you check my list of job websites? You were going to tell me whether to add any."

"It's stupid to do it on a spreadsheet we have to email back and forth. No one does that anymore."

He went into his bedroom, closed the door, and took ten slow minutes to come out again, dressed and perfumed in soft knit that hugged his torso.

He was surprised to see her still there. "I have to go."

"No you don't. You're not working tonight. Here's how it's going to be. Once a month we're going to meet. Tonight we're going to formulate the ten things you're going to do this month and as you do them, you'll check these boxes. By the end of this month I want you to add the ten next things you plan to do in November and we'll go over them. I'll also have things myself, to add to your list."

He was mad now. "Like what? That I have to check the newspaper?"

She calmly consulted her screen. "You also promised to get me your revised resumé, but you haven't and my notes say that's been pending now for two months."

He grabbed his car keys off the Lucite shelf under his giant TV.

"I don't have time for this," he said as he departed.

She was still there, on the same couch and in the same position when they came in together at 11 p.m.

"Hello Selene," she said and startled them.

The young woman saw Calyce's face and politely excused herself to the bathroom, where she began to run the shower water.

While Damion had been gone, Calyce had collected from upstairs that month's bills and a black manual ledger book.

"So, we've got water and gas and electric," she told him. "And groceries. All of those are more now because Selene's here. I won't charge you a share of the mortgage or property taxes or homeowner's insurance, since that would all be the same anyway. And I assume Comcast would be the same too, so you don't have to pay any part of that."

He stood staring. She was talking like he had flunked a class.

She said, "So my math says that in total you need to pay six hundred and fifty dollars a month."

"That's all I make!"

"Is it?"

"What about my student loans?"

"You're paying those too. No more advances from me. And it says here —" She turned the pages of the ledger they'd bought two years before — "that I've fronted you eleven payments. That's four hundred and forty-four dollars and eighty-three cents, times eleven, which is —"

She consulted her screen, where the math was ready. "Four

thousand eight hundred forty-nine dollars and thirteen cents you owe me."

"What is *wrong* with you?" he demanded.

She was mad now too, but she kept her voice low so Selene wouldn't hear them above the shower running. "You've got too much disposable income, obviously."

He smirked. "You mean discretionary. It's discretionary income."

She leaned forward. "It's whatever buys you Courvoisier."

"Is *that* what this is?" Damion said. "I have that for customers. Management – you know, Shawn – he checks the bottles all the time. I give away free drinks. It gets me better tips, so I started giving away Courvoisier. People laughed. It was a big joke, but Shawn said I wasn't charging. So instead of dealing with him I decided to buy my own and take it in. I usually keep it in the back of the car, but this one was open, and I didn't want to spill it. You know I worry about the leather."

"So you weren't drinking it? That wasn't you?"

"And lose all that money? That bottle costs me forty bucks, and there's twenty shots in there. I tell the customers not to pay me, so they always give me a big tip. Sometimes twenty, but usually ten. That's a minimum of two hundred, so I net a hundred and sixty. I also get customers who keep coming back."

His grinned, sure of himself. "See? I *am* using my marketing degree. You say it's business, but my major was marketing. That Courvoisier is why you wanted me to pay those bills all of a sudden?"

It took a moment, but she nodded sheepishly.

"So are we done now with that ridiculousness?"

"How long have you had this?" the young physician asked, listening with his stethoscope to her chest.

Calyce had never seen him before. Her last appointment had been her annual physical, and a different doctor in the teeming HMO had handled it.

"I'm sorry but I'm not hearing what you're describing."

To Calyce, he didn't look old enough to drive. "My mother insisted that I come. I'm a little hoarse in the mornings, but it's gone by noon."

"Every day? Do you have allergies?"

"I get hay fever in the spring."

"Do you snore?"

"I don't know. I didn't use to." She heard the question he wasn't asking. "I sleep alone. I have for decades."

He asked about her weight. She confirmed there had been no changes. Yes, she said, her life was stressful, but whose isn't? He typed into the laptop he held open on one forearm. No, she didn't smoke.

"Exercise?"

"Not enough. Well, not at all. There isn't time."

He was already writing on a prescription pad. "Make time, even if you only walk. And I want you to get some antacids over the counter. See if they help."

He ripped off the sheet. "Here's the name of an allergist. You may be allergic to something new. That happens as we get older."

"Next Tuesday? You can't go earlier?" Calyce said to Effie over the phone from the car. "Today. Just now. It's nothing. He said it was probably allergies."

The next morning, school was bedlam.

Calyce was forced to sit in the vast "forum" auditorium, with its deep risers in stacks on three sides of a square well at the bottom that was outfitted with a standing wooden podium. Parent meetings happened there too, but for the moms and dads they hauled out the folding chairs. For the kids and the teachers – even the older ones – at the weekly Wednesday assemblies, seating was on the hard risers themselves, whose concrete under their thin carpet coverings had already numbed Calyce's bony backside.

She sat as an island on the fourth row, uninterested in the small nearby pod of teachers, who ignored her. Staff and faculty clotted in random clumps as loud, arm-waving teens poured in all around them. Next to Calyce, on her right, four girls stood, dressed as cats. Pretending not to preen, each of them checked the crowd surreptitiously. Calyce had to watch the swinging, wired tail of the closest girl to make sure it didn't put her eye out.

Why was it always cats that allowed nubile taut things to wear stretch black leggings and midriff-baring crop tops? Calyce wondered. Did they really think a headband with cat ears and a caribou tail hid their self-advertising to the ogling boys Calyce saw salivating?

Ten years before, it had been Jingle Bell Rock from *Mean Girls*. She remembered a sequence of Halloweens looking up the backsides of strippers-in-training wearing tiny red Santa skirts and long black gloves. One year, even a set of boys had worn a version, but now it was cats. All cats. Cats for years.

She leaned left and whispered to Belinda, who had just sat

next to her dressed as a fortune-teller complete with turban. "Why cats?"

Belinda raised both her eyebrows at Calyce.

"I don't get it," Calyce insisted.

"Think about it."

"Oh! My God." Calyce said as Belinda nodded. "How could I have been so dumb?"

Calyce was dressed in a black skirt, black hose, black pumps and a white button-down long-sleeved blouse she had steam-ironed that morning. Over top was her twenty-year-old Halloween serape, solid black with white string fringe along the bottom. Sewn onto it and dangling hung a hardware store's collection of clinking, jangling trinkets. On her left breast, just under her clavicle, a large red felt "A" was appliquéd.

On the floor of the forum, in the middle of the flat square well, two nylon camping tents had been set up. One khaki green, the other sky blue, they were both zipped, no doubt for the annual show that was about to start. The entire boisterous student body was already lining up outside in the corridor.

Dan entered the auditorium and looked around, scanning.

Calyce saw that he was blue, literally blue. He wore a stretch white ski cap whose tip drooped forward in an apostrophe. It had been stuffed with something, maybe a small balloon, to make it round. But under the cap, Dan had painted his whole face and neck blue. His T-shirt was blue as well, though his jeans were white. He had covered his shoes with white gym socks.

Calyce turned and found the same flashes of blue and white in pairs, in a trio, and several alone. The entire high school English Department scattered in the audience was blue, she realized, except for her. Even rookie Amita had on a blue dress and blonde wig.

Dan climbed the risers toward Calyce, putting his hand on students' shoulders to steady himself as he praised their costumes. Calyce watched him joke and laugh with the young people, and she saw them high-five him. He made it to her row and waited. When Belinda noticed him, she scooted over a body-width so Dan could sit between them.

Calyce smelled him, bath soap wafting, barely there but different than the air had been without him. His greasepaint was already drying around his eyes at the same time it had begun to run where he was sweating. His apple cheeks were blue glass. Weird.

"Pretty funny," Belinda told him.

After a minute, he asked Calyce, "Any new ones this year?"

"This one." She touched a tiny silk doll's jacket sewn near the front hem of her serape.

"Chinese," he said. "No clue."

"Mulan."

"The movie? But she gets the guy."

"The novel. Seventeen hundreds. She commits suicide."

"Do you ever have *any* fun?"

She granted him a small smile. "I'd rather be blue. No, wait. That's you. But seriously, did you send me an email about this Smurf business? You organized it, I'm assuming."

He shrugged. "Why bother? It's always the shawl. Women Who Stand Up For Themselves Have To Die."

The show began soon after, as the school's Drama Department Head emceed the annual parade of Craziest Costumes around the auditorium, with those on the risers applauding their favorites cycling in from the corridor. One senior had built himself into a replica of the Eiffel Tower, which soared four feet above his head, his eyes peering through the framework. Another was a red-and-white-striped box of popcorn, the cardboard around the boy's waist filled with actual popcorn, which he threw at his friends.

As the parade circled them, the two tents on the floor finally opened. To Calyce's surprise, out popped Roger in a red and black buffalo-checked flannel shirt, shorts, and high-top hiking boots with green wool socks on his muscled blazing-white calves, which Calyce had never seen. When the other tent unzipped too, the school's pretty young brunette biology teacher bounded out in a matching lumberjack outfit. Both wore matching headlamps, which were turned on.

As the kids cheered, Dan asked Calyce, "Are they dating?"

"So here's the deal," Calyce said as she stood jangling before her class of seniors dressed as cats and Avengers and Harry Potter characters. The black girl with the long twists had pinned a hand-drawn paper bee to each of her knees through her jeans.

"Some of you know this because I do this every year. The student who can identify the most heroines from these clues on my serape will receive ten points of extra credit on the next test. That's a difference of a letter grade. And anyone who brings in another thing for me to add here receives five points. You have the rest of the hour to submit your list, and you can come up here and look at this. I don't bite."

"Hester Prynne," one of the boys said from his seat. "*Scarlet Letter.*"

"THE Scarlet Letter," she said, "and now that one doesn't count. You have to do it silently."

She moved her shoulders to set the trinkets tinkling. A tiny train locomotive hung there, as well as a lock of fake hair, a rubber snake attached by the tip of its curving tail, a tiny dollhouse chair, a small loop of green cable, the tiniest bit of white netting, a tiny chainsaw and a miniscule fabric rat swinging by his long gray tail above the silk doll's jacket at the hem. When she turned to show them her back, her students saw a plastic vial, a small dog charm, a white dinner napkin folded to make two peaks, a tiny door, a miniature brick, the letters CO_2, a rubber dagger, the tiniest possible square of cross-stitch embroidery, and a regular-sized pair of rubber navy blue swim goggles that hung by a strap.

As she glimmered and chimed, she said, "Isn't *this* fun?"

She opened her front door a hundred times that night. As dusk switched off the sunlight, the toddlers appeared first, leery as they gripped a parent's hand. Uncertain first-timers, they had to be coaxed through the call and response. Calyce bent low to their eye level and assured them it was okay to plunge both little hands deep into the brand-name candy mounded high above her widest aluminum mixing bowl.

An hour later, suave eight-year-olds began to ring, ring her doorbell and sigh when she demanded that each reveal the "trick" she risked if she didn't offer her candy. These pirates and identically dressed members of some boy band free-ranged without their parents but clustered tightly on her doorstep as the night's bugs veered and spun around her overhead light. And last of all, standing embarrassed but eager with pillowcases so full of loot only they could carry them were the oldest teenagers, the ones never doing it again after tonight unless they were hauling their younger siblings, which they would do in mufti from now on anyway, and not in costumes.

As she waited in her entry for the last stragglers, she sympathized. She thought back to all the years of the costumes her daughter and son had worn. Calyce had made them, initially, but eventually had succumbed to store-bought in seductive boxes from the party store and later to whatever her adolescents had wanted to jerry-rig. And she had always been the parent who had stayed home to answer the bell. Not once during her marriage had she made the rounds with their cavorting children and their ricocheting sugar highs. It was something big she had missed.

At last the stretches between buzzes lengthened and finally stopped, and Calyce returned up the stairs with her paraphernalia. At the top, she suddenly thought about her periods, which five years before had been struggling, then sputtered and ultimately choked to a soundless stop. No matter. But the ensuing desiccation had been a shock.

She couldn't sleep, again. Frustrated, she slung on her robe and went downstairs, heading toward the kitchen through the dark living room. The only light angled in from the fluorescent moon that hung round and high above the rooftops of the townhouses on the street behind.

She startled, though, when the fuzzy moonlight caught a small shape rustling on the loveseat under the window.

"Mrs. Tate." Selene turned from staring outside. "Don't worry. It's me."

Calyce flipped on the light. "Are you all right?"

Selene tugged on the fake-chinchilla Afghan from Damion's room. "I'm sorry. I know it's your space."

"It's the middle of the night. Where's Damion?"

"Working. Lots of drunks so lots of tips on Halloween."

Calyce looked at her. The child was lonely. "You want some tea?"

"Can I help?"

She followed Calyce and together they found something sweet, too. Calyce saw that the young woman wore one of her son's black shirts and a pair of his gym shorts, whose waistband was much larger than her bud-vase waist. She tugged on them to keep them up.

"I'm sorry I'm here all the time." Selene cupped the warm mug with her translucent fingers. "I try to keep to myself down there, but it's so cold. It's so much warmer up here."

They spoke at length about Damion, these two women who shared Calyce's son, and the older woman saw that Selene seemed to be in love with him. She knew him, knew his weaknesses, and yet she glowed when she spoke of him and rubbed her arms slowly with her hands as she did it, as if he were there holding her. What Selene displayed wasn't the infatuation of first sex and first "we" but something calm and steadfast, certain of itself and its strength maybe to last. Calyce remembered it.

"You love him," she said.

"I do," Selene said without hesitation or embarrassment.

"Does he know?"

Selene nodded.

A moment later Selene said, "He feels the same way."

Another fact, simply stated. Calyce believed her.

Calyce felt about that then, giving herself a beat to be with the fact of this mutual love, and she found it to be good and this woman worthy and her Adonis son to be the beneficiary of someone solid, though Calyce could not explain how she knew. So she asked, and Selene shared her story.

"I got my associate degree from Montgomery College. I

thought I wanted to do landscape design, but I don't. I really don't care about what plants are there. I just want to light them, so I'm an apprentice electrician."

"But you're a girl."

Selene said she craved the outdoors and hated sitting at a desk. The work was hard. Ladders can be dangerous and muddy crawl spaces filled with spiders and sometimes snakes. But the money was good and so were the benefits.

"They're paying me to be an apprentice. And best of all, I won't have to work at nights usually. I can be home in the evenings with Damion."

She leaned both her elbows on the dining table as she said, "That's why I don't want him working at the bar either. I've been telling him that what you're saying is right. I don't think bartending is good for us in the long run. I want him to look for a new job just like you do. I want him to have a daytime career."

November

It was noon before her mother answered, after Calyce had waited through nine burring rings. Effie claimed the noise had startled her awake and she had had to run from the couch, but she could barely deliver words, her breathing was so labored.

Yes, she said finally. Not her regular doctor, but a new one in the group general practice. A woman. Young.

"Why didn't you tell me?"

"I've been waiting on the results of the EKG."

"What EKG?"

"Some special kind. I'm having it on Thursday."

"Are you all right?" a boy asked as she returned her phone to her bottomless bag and tossed it under the desk, which wasn't hers but standard-issue, identical in all the classes.

Calyce ignored him. "First, our grammar lesson for the day. The difference between 'lie' and 'lay.'"

All of her students, every one of them, moaned like cattle. They did it at the start of every grammar lesson she taught now at the beginning of every class.

"You all need this," she said with annoyance. "What's our motto?"

It was a joke for them. They chanted in unison.

"Technique before creativity."

"Throughout literature, women are punished for self-actualizing. Anna Karenina is just one example." Calyce fingered the tiny toy locomotive sewn above her right breast.

"And so is Juliet. She's the one who comes up with the plan with the priest about the poison so she can be with Romeo. The play could be said to stand for the proposition that when a woman dares to run things she has to die.

"Middle-aged women don't even exist in literature except in relation to men or their families. When they don't do what they're told? Exile." Calyce touched the Eiffel Tower charm by her shoulder.

"Or suicide." She turned to point at the laboratory vial on her back. "For Madame Bovary, it was rat poison. See my rat?"

A boy said, "But what about *Pride & Prejudice*? She wins."

"She does get the man but she gets him by being herself, so I count that as an exception. But Elizabeth Bennet's not middle-aged. Everything about her mother, Mrs. Bennet, is her trying to get her daughters married."

"But who wants to read about middle-aged people?"

"Not people. Women. There are plenty of middle-aged men in literature, doing what they want, living lives outside their families. But there aren't books about me. I'm cast as Penelope. There's no book where I'm the female Odysseus."

"Look at Harry Potter." Calyce ticked on her fingers. "There's Sirius Black and Snape and Dumbledore, and that werewolf. All middle-aged or older men. And there's Ron's mother, with all these same powers, and she spends her time in the kitchen or knitting bad sweaters."

"She fights!" Her students were outraged.

"Not until the end, when she's the archetypal protective mother. My point is that we're all looking for role models of how to be. It's a key task of literature, and it's failed middle-aged women like me. Libraries are filled with boys becoming men by *not* doing what they're told and being rewarded for it, but where are the books for me, to teach me that I can choose myself and I won't be punished?"

"But that sounds so selfish," a girl said.

"Exactly. When a woman says it, it does."

Still dressed, Calyce sat awkwardly on the examining table very early the next Thursday, her long legs dangling like a child's. She had found an allergist in her network who offered 7 a.m. appointments, and the thirty-five-year-old was now checking her nose and mouth. But then he frowned. Four small lines cut into his skin between eyebrows she swore were plucked.

"I do see a lot of post-nasal drip," he said under his cliff of hair that was stiff with product. "And I heard your cough a minute ago. You're definitely hoarse, though that's clearing. But your nose isn't inflamed and your eyes are fine, though what you're describing is consistent with fall allergies. You say you have spring hay fever, so let's get you tested. Most people with spring allergies are also allergic to ragweed. It's airborne too."

He left the tiny room and sent in his chatty nurse, who scratched the lighter skin of Calyce's under-forearm with a tray full of allergens. She bustled out, saying she would be back in fifteen minutes, so Calyce was alone on the crackling white paper when the first of the two bumps appeared.

The nurse explained when she returned that the one nearest

Calyce's wrist was histamine, used as a control, but the second was oak trees. The ragweed spot was bump-free.

The allergist blew in again, his white coat flapping. His frown arrived too as he examined her unhelpful arm. He sat for the first time, on a little rolling stool. "So it's not allergies, at least not to anything that's standard for fall. Oaks pollinate in spring. That's why your eyes and your nose are clear. You need to see an ENT."

"It's just a cough."

"That I can't explain. He'll have a laryngoscope. I don't."

"My doctor just called," Effie said in a stream of words over the phone that same night. "She got the EKG back, and she wants me to see a cardiologist. 'Do it now,' she said. 'Don't wait.' She had her office call, before she called me, and they got me in for an appointment tomorrow."

An hour later, Calyce was downstairs cleaning again, but churning this time. She worked the vacuum like she was scraping ice in winter, shoving it hard under Damion's sectional, then bulldozed the bathroom countertop, scooping everything including Selene's plastic hairbrush into the bowl of the sink with a crash so she could rub Clorox over the entire counter. Into the cabinet underneath she threw Selene's hairdryer, which had been on the floor by the toilet, still plugged in.

She carried in Damion's clean clothes and hung them carefully in his closet, sliding her hands down each side of each T-shirt and each pair of jeans so they hung independently. She put his clean underwear in one drawer and Selene's in another, then grabbed a clean white towel from her delivery basket and folded it in thirds lengthwise under her chin. She hung up two of them, leaving precisely one inch of shiny silver bar between them.

She retrieved his socks from the living room and his work-out sweatshirt that still smelled like him. With two fingers she plucked a pair of boxer briefs from the floor on his side of the bed and from the other a red lace thong with blood that made them brittle in the crotch, together with a nude camisole.

"'Nude' for her," she said out loud. "Not for me."

She had them draped over an arm when Selene walked in and surprised them both.

Calyce said, "I thought you had class tonight."

Selene eyed the dirty underwear. "It was canceled. I can do all that."

"I was down here anyway. You know, if you put things away as you use them, it's not so much work."

Calyce pointed to a bag of groceries on the entryway floor she had used to prop Damion's door open. "I thought you'd want those in the little fridge down here."

Selene spoke slowly. "We've already got too much in there. I was going to cook us dinner tonight. Damion and me, upstairs."

"So you want me to take it all back up?"

When Effie spoke to Calyce next, her mother was intentionally calm.

"I have a narrowing of one of my heart valves," she said like she was reading a newspaper. "It's age, they say. It's stiff and that's why I've been getting so tired."

Calyce closed her eyes.

"It's irreversible," Effie continued. "But I can have surgery. That's the option."

"Or what?"

A space arrived and grew and drained empty. "Well. It's irreversible."

"And with surgery?"

"Years, apparently. Simon's coming. I already talked to him. He and I are meeting with the surgeon Tuesday. And before you say it, there's no reason for you to come down."

Calyce was walking outside, bundled up and cold without her gloves, hiking up the block on the sidewalk north of the school with her one free arm pumping.

"I can't believe you didn't tell me," she was saying into her phone as her heels struck the pavement hard as horses' hooves.

"Move the appointment," she instructed Simon. "I need to be there and I can't do it until the Friday after Thanksgiving … Then get another surgeon."

She marched up the road and left the school behind. "It's not Mom's job to call me. It's yours."

It was much colder outside than she anticipated. Her phone hand was freezing.

"Move it," she interrupted.

She interrupted again. "Because I said so."

In her cold hand the line went dead.

Damion had asked to meet with her that next Sunday. When she came to his room at the appointed hour, he and Selene were ready, sitting together at the sectional's corner farthest from the door, with Selene cuddled close under his arm. A sheet of paper lay face-down next to Damion. Calyce had no idea what it was, nor did she know what was on the page that Selene was holding.

Damion thanked Calyce for coming, then once she was settled leaned forward grandly to slip his hand behind himself and pull out a hidden, folded, fat wad of cash. He handed it over to his mother, who sat confused while he and Selene Cheshire-cat smiled.

"What's this?"

"There's more," he said. "Hold on."

He cupped his hand and Selene opened her palm to drop coins in it that she had been hiding. He gave them to Calyce also, counting them out, one dime and three pennies.

"Eight hundred dollars and thirteen cents," he said. "That's six hundred and fifty for my share of the utilities and groceries for this month and another hundred and fifty and thirteen cents toward the student-loan payments you've already made."

Damion turned over the paper next to him and consulted it. "That leaves exactly four thousand six hundred and ninety-eight dollars – "

"Ninety-nine," Selene corrected as she looked at Calyce.

"Ninety-nine, even, that I still owe you. I – we – plan on giving you that same amount every month." He looked at Selene. "Don't we?"

"We do," Selene said to Calyce.

"But where did you get this?" Calyce asked her son.

"You want me to show initiative, so I showed it," he said.

Damion was enjoying this. Selene nudged him with an elbow.

"Oh," he said, "and there's this."

Selene handed Calyce the sheet she had been holding – an

updated copy of Damion's resumé, which Selene said she had already uploaded.

Calyce went outside as soon as they finished and walked her neighborhood for an hour, turning corners, reaching asphalt bulbs at street ends as she rose and fell for the first time on the slopes of her tightly packed neighborhood. She stopped at a little story-land footbridge that had been built for display by the developer over a tiny rivulet, which she had never noticed before. But now she saw the wink of the water and heard it sing over the decorative rocks. The tall stalks of specially planted reeds rubbed each other and whispered. They calmed her.

The late-fall afternoon brought low-angle sunlight that fired the houses, making them golden. The air was brisk and clean and smelled of changing weather. She took one deep breath and another and then stopped entirely to open her lungs, spreading her legs wide at parade rest as her father had taught her, clasping her long fingers behind her thin back. She raised her chin in the middle of the street to look at the scrim of uninteresting clouds.

She finally said out loud, "This is what I wanted. He's self-sufficient, making his own money. And why shouldn't she help him with his resumé? I don't have to do everything anymore. He's a grown man."

She walked herself into accepting this new chapter as she passed roads she had never seen, until she received a beeping text. She pulled her phone from her jacket pocket. It was an automated message from the ENT, confirming her upcoming appointment.

It could be anything, Google said, basically. From a sore throat to cancer. Esophageal cancer. Survival rate poor. Most dead within a year.

As she internet-searched in her bedroom, a text popped up on her screen, this one from Simon.

Mom wants this guy. No times Thksgvg Fri. Appt still day after tomorrow. I WILL HANDLE.

By midnight Simon still had not returned her voice message demanding to talk to him live, and Calyce was hungry from the waiting. Halfway down the stairs, though, she saw that Selene was already there, burrowed again into a corner of Calyce's couch, watching television in the dark. Jimmy Fallon.

Absorbed, Selene was laughing and didn't see that Calyce had stopped high above her.

I don't want to talk to her, Calyce thought to herself as she backed up silently to return to her room. Fortunately, Selene didn't notice.

Once Calyce had closed her bedroom door, she murmured out loud, "This girl has taken over my house. She's everywhere. And I'm still hungry."

"John, I'm sorry, but you're going to have to find someone to cover for me. I'm at the airport. I'm on stand-by and they just called my name. I have to go down and see my mother."

Calyce handed the gate agent her ticket and hurriedly rolled her bag past her. Everyone else had already boarded. "She has a doctor's appointment I can't miss, in Florida, but I should be back at school the day after tomorrow. I'm sorry for the short notice but I'm sure you can relate to this, given your history with your brother."

I want to take this opportunity as Interim Head to encourage everyone in the English Department to advocate for Belinda Rhoades with school administration. As you know, she is very interested in becoming our new Interim Vice Principal now that Janice DeGroot has had to leave to tend to John's brother, who has been institutionalized.

Calyce took a sip of the bubbly water in the clear plastic cup in the round drink indentation on her tray table, then continued typing.

I have known and worked with Belinda since she began at the school as part of the first wave of teachers of color the school specifically recruited. (Before that, we were hired individually.) She is beloved by everyone, teacher and student; she exemplifies our values; she promotes our mission; she pursues our goals. We could not have a finer Interim Vice Principal, who frankly should be promoted to permanent VP immediately.

Each of you please let me know what you have done to promote Belinda's promotion to the latter position. Time is of the essence. I will be back at school on Wednesday. Calyce.

As soon as she got inside the terminal in Florida, she hit SEND.

Calyce and Simon flanked Effie at the conference room table at the cardiologist's Clearwater practice. They sat with their backs to the Zen water feature surrounded by bonsai trees that Calyce could hear gurgling incongruently against the wall behind her. Across the table, in the chair directly facing her handsome mother in her white-bowed georgette blouse, a serene black man Calyce's age had been doing his best to put Effie at ease while at the same time explaining that the open-heart bypass procedure could kill her.

Graying Simon gripped his hands so tightly that his knuckles showed through his skin. He was shaking his head at the doctor.

"Yes?" the dignified surgeon asked.

Simon said, "Why can't we do a stent along with the valve replacement, so she doesn't have to be cracked open?"

Calyce shot him a look.

"That's the term," he shot back. "They put a balloon up to push back the blockage and they can replace the valve at the same time without having to cut her open."

"Just because you look things up on the internet, it doesn't make you a doctor," Calyce said.

The cardiologist allowed a moment for the energy to dissipate, then continued in the same reasonable tone.

"As you know, Effie, you've got a calcified aortic valve. We thought that's what was causing all this fatigue, but it's not. The cardiac CT you had after our initial meeting unfortunately showed that you also have a couple of severe blockages in your left main artery."

He handed what looked like an x-ray to Effie across the table. Someone had gotten an entire x-ray onto an 8 ½ by 11-inch piece of white paper.

"Let's start with a normal artery," he said, referring to his own copy, which he held up as he traced it with his slender hands. "It's not yours, Mrs. Guthrie. See that big artery coming down from the upper left? See those branches? Go up to before it splits, to that big main trunk."

Huddled, the three of them followed along on their own copy as the water burbled. Against her arm, Calyce felt her mother's shoulder.

"That one artery there supplies seventy percent of the blood to your heart muscle. We call it the left main. The two arteries that branch off it – see those? – supply blood to the front wall of the heart and to one side. Now imagine what happens if the blood flow is cut off. It's catastrophic, very different than if there's a blockage farther down one of the branches. A blockage farther down means that only what's south of it is affected, so a smaller part of the heart is harmed. It can be survived, unlike a complete blockage in the left main, which cuts off everything. Does that make sense?"

Calyce and Simon both looked at their mother, who nodded calmly. Calyce could feel her own heart hammering in her ears, but Effie wasn't even breathing fast, at least not so Calyce could see it.

The doctor handed another x-ray sheet of paper across the table.

"Now that's your left main artery, Mrs. Guthrie. If you look, you can see it's got two depressions in it, both on the top edge. They look like divots." He turned his copy of the page toward them, touching the spots one after another. "Can you see how the blood flow's constricted? Twice, with one in the middle and the other down by where the artery branches? This was that test where we put that dye into your elbow. Your left main artery is long, too. Longer than most.

"Now, fortunately, and oddly, we don't see blockages anywhere else. For some reason yours are all in this one area. But they are calcified like your aortic valve is. You can see it here."

He gave them a third sheet that showed webbing with two lightning streaks. "Two of your arteries are a bit calcified, including the left main. See that white?

"And Mrs. Guthrie, let me assure you, it's age, not anything you ate or did or didn't do. Some people just collect calcium. It's like bone, and it hardens the arteries."

Effie said suddenly and nonsensically, "I've always hated rocks."

The doctor went on. "In situations like these, open-heart bypass is really the gold standard. Though interventional cardiologists have been having increasing success with cardiac stents, it's not the preferred standard of care for complicated multiple lesions in the left main. So Simon, you make a good point but a stent's not recommended in this situation."

The doctor then said only to Effie, quite pointedly, "Ultimately it's your decision, but it's not recommended for patients who are not at high-risk for bypass surgery, and you're not. You seem fine other than your heart. All those years of walking the beach."

He smiled. It was genuine.

"Your only disadvantage is you're female. For whatever reason, older women don't do as well as older men. But you should have the same survival rate as any other woman your age."

"She's eighty-three," Simon said. "And she's exhausted."

"Which is most likely attributable to the cardiac issues. Frankly, I'm surprised she's as well as she is. With this degree of blockage, and two of them, and her aortic valve, she should have angina at least. Which leads me to this. The combination of these two conditions and their severity, each of them, means that you need to make an immediate decision, Mrs. Guthrie. Today, if possible. Because you could have a cardiac event, and if you do, it would be devastating."

Effie regarded the doctor. "Am I right that open-heart bypass lasts longer?"

He nodded.

"With less chance of having to do it again?"

"You've done some research of your own."

"But you could die on the table," Simon told her.

Behind them the water gargled.

"Is he right?" Effie asked the doctor.

"Yes. It's possible you wouldn't survive surgery. There could also be complications afterward, both here in the hospital and after we discharge you. It's a six- to twelve-week recovery."

Effie turned to Calyce and away from Simon on the other side of her. She put her bird's-foot hand on her daughter's arm.

She said, "I plan to live to be a hundred. We still have lots to do together, don't we?"

Then Effie looked at the doctor. "I've decided. It will be open-heart bypass."

Calyce and Simon sat outside on their mother's small balcony, Calyce on the cheap white armchair and Simon on one of the kitchen's dinette chairs, which he had dragged through the sliding door. The meeting at the doctor's had been long and Effie had exhausted herself. She had made it to her bedroom but still wore her shoes as she lay curled on top of the bedspread like a baby. Calyce had checked on her once and debated removing them, but she had decided not to risk waking her up, so her swollen feet remained encased in her low, chunky heels and stacked neatly on top of each other.

"We need to talk about how we're going to do this," Calyce said to Simon, who was checking his watch, which was big and bulky with multiple faces showing different time zones, in inexpensive metal.

The afternoon was beautiful, with clear blue sky and powerboats buzzing the Intracoastal. At home, late autumn had leeched the green but here, Calyce saw again, the tropical lushness never changed. A deep-sea fishing boat headed to open water past palm trees that never lost their leaves.

"God, I hate the ocean," said her brother when he saw it.

"We all do, because of Mom."

"I always hated it."

"No you didn't. Remember how we used to slam the waves at Ocean City? I'd hold your hand and we'd run in. We just never went after Mom left, and then once we knew where she was."

Seagulls rose shrieking as Simon said quietly so his voice wouldn't carry through the open door behind them, "I will never understand why he took her back."

But then, "My flight's soon."

"You can't leave until we figure this out," Calyce told him. "It's at least six weeks, assuming it all goes well. And she's got doctor visits, and that social worker woman told us she needs a support network. She can't be alone."

"Do it next month," he said as the red and orange trolley pulled up on the street below. "Don't you get a long break in December? Come down and do it then."

"But what about after that? It's at least two months of recovery."

He shrugged. "Maybe Nina will come."

"She's in Patagonia."

"Isn't she too old for that?"

"So this is about Nina now? What about you?"

In the open doorway, Effie appeared bleary-eyed with her short hair flattened completely on one side. Calyce and Simon fluttered when they saw her and Simon stood as soon as Effie said, "Isn't your flight at six? Or did they get another pilot?"

"No," Simon said. "You're right. I have to go."

Calyce said, "I'll walk you downstairs."

"I heard you two," Effie said.

"We'll talk when I get back up,"

"I'm not having it done next month," Effie said. "It's Christmas. I'm going to wait until January."

They protested, but she was immovable. She wanted Christmas with her family.

"Then that's what we'll do," Simon said too quickly. "I love you, but I have to get going."

Effie gazed adoringly at her only son. "I love you too. Give my love to Sandra and the girls."

In the building garage, an irate Calyce demanded that he explain how in hell they were going to do this in January, but he didn't slow his stride to his rental car.

"It's what she wants," he said. "I can maybe come down some weekends, but I have to work."

"What about Sandra?"

"Clearwater's a long way from Dallas."

Calyce raised her voice. "It's a lot closer than D.C."

"Is it?"

He thought. "I don't think so, actually, not as the crow flies."

He opened his door. "You'll figure this out. You always do. Isn't that what you always tell us? You're the big sister."

But before he pulled out he rolled down his window. She felt the blast of air-conditioning. "I know. Why don't you do it in D.C.? Her insurance would cover it and you wouldn't have to take much time off from school."

Calyce arrived home late that night tired and still angry. It was well after midnight when she clomped up the stairs to the main floor banging her rolling suitcase on every stair and cursing it.

At the top, she switched on the light.

She saw Damion on her couch under the window with his head between Selene's naked legs.

He didn't stop.

Selene was moaning and holding the top of his head.

But Selene had heard her. She turned to Calyce and looked straight at her as he kept going.

"Stop!" Calyce said.

Damion looked up.

He jumped, pulling back and up and off the couch. Moving quickly, fully dressed, he wiped his mouth as he stood, lost his balance and fell against the coffee table with a loud bang. He moved to the center of the room, where he stood barefoot with a stiff erection ridging his pants.

Selene pulled down her black dress to cover herself.

Surprisingly, though, she stretched her legs in the space Damion had fled and rolled, catlike, toward Calyce.

Selene's eyes were unlike anything she had ever seen.

"Mom, um…" Damion was saying.

"Go downstairs and do that," Calyce said. "This is *my* home. *My* living room. Go downstairs right now. *Both of you.*"

Damion turned to the stairs immediately but realized Selene hadn't moved yet. He waited, ashamed, not looking at his mother as the young woman sat up languidly, without hurrying, then stood and placidly smoothed her dress before slowly following him.

It was strange that John DeGroot wanted to see her again. They had already talked early that morning, her first dragging day back from Florida, when they had happened to be alone in the department office. She had told him already with irritation about her mother, that she had refused to have surgery until January.

"I don't know what I'm going to do," she had told DeGroot before the school day had started.

"Why is it solely your responsibility?"

Much later he had ducked his head into her classroom and asked to see her at the end of the day. Now, he was closing the door of the department's tiny conference room.

"I know this isn't the best time, but a couple of teachers have come to me during the course of today."

She was in no mood. "About what?"

"I have to say I agree with them. I know this is a hard time for you, but you left us with no coverage."

"I called."

"From the airport, and you called me. We had to juggle at the last minute. You announced this strict substitute system, but you didn't follow it for your own absence. You even missed your Advisory, and you've got seniors dealing with college applications."

His tone was dead, flat. "And what was that email you sent about Belinda?"

"She'd be a perfect Vice Principal."

"I agree, but what you did was dictate to the entire department that they had to lobby for her, and you told them to report back to you about the specific steps they took. Apparently, you didn't clear it with her, either. I talked to her today. Belinda says she knew nothing about it."

Calyce was astonished. "She's upset?"

He sighed. "And the kids are coming to me. Who cares about the difference between 'lie' and 'lay'?"

Calyce was making little head shakes. "It's important."

"You remember at the middle school when you had your class count all the instances of 'fig lang'? You wanted the teachers all to call it that, figurative language. We had this same discussion back then. You can't quantify literature, Calyce. Grade them on the force of their words, not whether they split infinitives."

Not three minutes later, one of her seniors accosted her in the hallway and asked her to write a recommendation letter for him for colleges.

"No," she answered firmly.

Open-mouthed, he asked, "Why not?"

She chose her words. "I don't think I can do you justice."

"But I'm getting an A in your class!"

She inhaled. "You're disruptive. You challenge everything I say and think you know better. Your work is good. I can't fault it, but you lack structure and proper mechanics. Your spelling is poor and you turn in your work late."

He made a face. "Is that all?"

"I don't like your tone, but it's a good example of what I'm describing. It's better that you ask someone else."

"I am so sorry," Calyce said to Belinda in the school's parking lot a few moments later. "I didn't mean to embarrass you. That was the farthest thing from my mind."

Her friend, at first wooden, softened immediately when Calyce shared her genuine remorse. She bear-hugged Calyce, pulling her in tight, breast-to-breast.

They talked for an hour in the underground shadows as Calyce told her everything about Florida.

"He's right," Belinda said when she finished. "Simon's an asshole but he's right. You have to do it up here."

Calyce then told her what happened on her couch.

"Last night? Holy shit. What did they say?"

"Nothing. Not this morning either and I saw both of them. He's not even embarrassed now."

"Why aren't they in his room? It's downstairs, right? They're in your whole house like you're not there. Did they know you were coming home last night?"

Calyce nodded. "I even called him once I landed. He said they were still up."

Belinda laughed. "Were they ever!"

That night Selene was out at class, so she confronted Damion in the kitchen. Calyce demanded to know what he was thinking, doing that in her living room where *she* lives. He knew she was on her way home from the airport.

She said, "Sometimes I eat dinner on that couch."

He was defensive, protesting that it was his house too, but Calyce knew him.

"Was it her idea?" she asked her son.

He hesitated, embarrassed, stumbling over the graphicness.

"Yeah, uh … she wanted to, uh … do it there. I kept telling her 'let's go downstairs,' but she wouldn't."

That Saturday Calyce went to an appointment with her family's old ENT. He was well past retirement age, so she hadn't been sure he was still practicing, and he was out of her network, so the cost to her would be much higher, but she had had enough of young people.

She hadn't seen the gracious man in ten years, since Damion had last had an inner-ear infection, but he came into the examining room with his hand outstretched in a cloud of shaving cream smell and an authentic, recognizing grin that brought his shimmering eyes with it. She felt the dry folds of his papery fingers as he said Damion's name and asked how "our boy" was doing.

"Any more balance problems?"

She chose not to mention the stair incident. "Not really."

"Married? Any grandchildren?"

She shook her head.

As she explained why she had come, he jotted notes in longhand. She had repeated the same story so many times she used a cadence.

"Any heartburn?" He scribbled. "Chest pain?"

"No."

"Trouble swallowing?"

"No, but sometimes it feels like I've got something in my throat."

"Nausea? Regurgitation?"

"Not that I know of."

"No asthma."

"No."

"Huh." He thought for a moment. "Let's numb up your nose and the back of your throat."

Soon, he had shoved a long, lighted, flexible white tube up one of her nostrils and down her esophagus. She felt odd pressure between her eyes, and her natural gag reflex, though suppressed with spray, wanted to eject it. She concentrated on not throwing up as the doctor talked out loud, his eyes on a color monitor he had angled away from her.

"Mucus in the throat, but not in the nose. There's no swelling, though, and your larynx looks fine. No esophagitis."

As he pulled it out she watched a long white plastic worm exit her body through her nose.

"You don't have gastroesophageal reflux. I thought maybe you had GERD, but you don't. So maybe it's allergies. I don't know."

The next week, Indian summer hit and the temperature rose so the shy sun was warm at lunchtime and everyone, teachers and students, ventured outside as they hadn't in weeks. Calyce, too, decided at the last minute that she had time at mid-day, and she left the cacophony of lunch plastic to walk for half an hour in the nearby neighborhood. She breathed in the surprisingly tepid air as she watched swirls of waltzing leaves cleave then spin from the peeling, showy birches that didn't know they were supposed to just shut up and do their prescribed job of merely dotting the gridded streets at designated intervals.

As she returned, passing the parking meters along the curb, she saw Roger and Dan making their way back too, each with a brown Chipotle bag. When they saw her they waved and slowed.

"We were just talking about you," Dan said. "Roger was telling me about this thing you have for Zion. He says it occupies your every waking moment."

Roger said playfully, "She also thinks about me."

They were laughing and kind to her, so Calyce confirmed it. She mentioned her deep love for the place, its beauty and its eternal existence. "Until I went last year on this Quest trip, I had never seen anything like it."

Dan lowered his voice as students walked near them. "We've been talking about Belinda. I think the best way to get this done is to talk to people one-on-one rather than doing texts or emails."

Roger said, "Dan knows her really well."

Calyce said, "You do?"

"She's the one who was so welcoming when I first came, remember?" Dan said. "I wasn't sure how I would go over. Do you mind if I talk to the rest of the English teachers and maybe the people I'm closest to outside the department?"

"I think it's a great idea," Calyce assured him.

"I'm just keying off you."

As they reached the school's front doors she said, "Just don't tell anyone you got it from me."

"Mom, I need to talk to you," Damion said to her later that night. He had approached her at the dining table, where she was grading writing pieces in hard copy with her laptop open.

She looked up to see him holding his own hands. She pointed and he sat. He exhaled but he didn't start talking.

She took off her glasses. "So what is it?"

He shifted in his seat. "Uh, well, she doesn't want you downstairs anymore. She says she'll do the cleaning, and she wants to do her own laundry. She doesn't want you to do it anymore. And she'll put my dirty clothes outside the door."

Calyce put down her pen.

Damion continued. "And she wants to leave the dirty dishes outside the door too, so you don't have to come in and get them. I told her you don't mind, that you like cleaning, but she wants to do it herself from now on."

"And you agree with this?"

Damion shrugged. "It's what she wants. It's my room. Ours, now, and she wants privacy."

That Tuesday was the first of two days of parent-teacher conferences. Scores of neurotically ambitious, narrow-eyed parents barreled down the hallways and sprinted up the stairs at an oddly child-less school, for on conference days, two in November and two in May, their overly indulged, overly scheduled and overly monitored children were banished to sleep in late happily at home.

Calyce hated those days, for she was lousy at small talk. She also had little to say about any particular child. The good ones had parents who already knew it. The poor performers were constantly justified, explained, defended, and over the decades she had heard it all so often she had no more patience.

Parents sat in chairs arrayed against the walls of the corridors outside the various classrooms, waiting for their fifteen-minute allotments in random order. First come, first served, so it was potluck for the teachers, who didn't know who they were shaking hands with until they read the nametags, at which point they had to re-arrange their faces, depending. Right then, Calyce was barely listening to an expensively blonded mother extol

the supposedly misunderstood academic virtues of her (inatten-
tive, hair-twirling) ninth-grade daughter, who Calyce watched at
lunchtimes climb into her junior boyfriend's Range Rover. There
hadn't yet been a question the child could answer in class discussion. Or rather, had bothered to. Her kohl-rimmed eyes gazed
toward the window most of every hour. The girl had derided the
entire first quarter, the written proof of which her intense, horse-
faced mother now angrily brandished in her starving hand, for
paper grade reports for the quarter had been distributed to the
parents at a long table just inside the main entrance.

The perched woman was behaving like her daughter, inter-
rupting, sighing when Calyce was only three words into a sentence. This crow dressed in all-black then looked up at the clock
on the wall behind Calyce and hotly demanded to know why she
spent so much time on grammar the kids could just Google. Calyce instead should be drilling "the children" (her princess) in advance on every review point to be covered on every coming test.

"I disagree," Calyce replied. "Grammar is a necessary part of
a proper education."

The woman laughed out loud. "Where did they find you?"

Calyce closed her spiral notebook with grades in it. "I've
been here twenty-six years."

"Maybe that's why. You don't understand modern writing."

Calyce ceremoniously looked at her watch again, which she
had worn today as she did on every parent-teacher day, expressly
for moments like these.

"I'm afraid our time's up. Thank you for coming." Calyce
rose, holding her pen with both hands so she didn't have to shake
hands again.

"But I've got four minutes left."

Calyce loomed silently above her until the woman finally stood.

"I'm sorry but others are waiting."

That night, in the middle of the night, she piston-coughed as she stomped down the stairs toward the throbbing music that banged through the closed door of Damion's room. She nearly pounded, but she withheld herself. Instead she bent to take his dirty laundry off the floor. She thrust her son's soiled underwear under one arm so she could also lift the two spaghetti-stained dishes and the two stacked coffee mugs making rings on the entryway tile.

John DeGroot was empurpled. Calyce had never seen him so mad.

"Do you have any idea who she was?" he demanded early the next morning. "She's one of our biggest donors. Tens of thousands a year. Her book's on the bestseller list right now."

It rained in torrents that evening as Calyce sat in the dark, alone in the house with no company but the frenetic TV screen from the couch in her living room. Not the one where she had come upon Selene being serviced, but the other, the one facing the kitchen she had just cleaned after a late solo dinner of microwaved baked potato slathered in butter and sour cream along with a paperback Junot Diaz at the dining room table.

Now she watched the half-hour sit-com with only the corner table light on. It was a fat-bottomed, faux-ceramic Southwestern lamp she had purchased years before that had horizontal ridges meant to convey handmade pottery, but it in truth it was only heavy plastic.

The show had a laugh track, Calyce noticed. The main character's every smirk was screamingly funny. It was a riotous party she heard but wasn't actually attending. She picked up the remote and turned it off, then heard only the harsh rain and the infrequent thunder that punctuated it. She listened to the water hitting the windowpane to her right. Otherwise, there was utterly no sound. Not even the icemaker hummed.

She turned the TV back on. Again the colors flashed, hammered by the aggressive laugh track.

She flicked it off and once more plunged into silence. She listened for a step, a thump, a rub, a squeak of floorboards. Nothing. No dishwasher sound. No fan whirring. No living sound but her own breathing.

She reached for the lamp and switched it off. She sat in total darkness.

She turned on the screen again. The laugh-trackers howled. The male lead had just tripped on an ottoman.

She flicked it off and heard the emptiness.

She turned it on.

She switched it off and sat in blackness.

She had invited Belinda to take a hike with her and to her surprise she had said yes, so they met the next Saturday morning in the parking lot at Great Falls, on the Maryland side, where the Potomac River hurtled violently as it tumbled and crashed through a shredding rocky gorge. Kayakers loved the place, and it killed them.

It was so cold that last weekend before Thanksgiving that Calyce wore two layers under her fleece. Belinda arrived in sapphire blue, diamond-sewn goose down, the new kind of jacket that hugged the body rather than upholstering it. They began a walk that roundtrip would take an hour, starting at the old white-painted brick tavern building that served as the Visitor Center. It had been built in the 1800s next to the then-new C&O Canal, which had for almost a century flowed barge traffic more than one hundred and eighty miles from nearly the Pennsylvania border to Georgetown in D.C. The narrow dirt towpath that ran on one side of it provided a bucolic interlude at the western edge of the manic city. Calyce hadn't been there but once before, which she now couldn't understand.

As they walked, Calyce was saying, "Ever notice how short the shows are now? I was watching *Big Bang Theory* and it seemed like it was all commercials, so I looked it up. *Cheers*—remember *Cheers*?—used to be twenty-seven minutes. This new show is just over nineteen. The rest is ads. That's an entire subplot, lost."

Belinda had her hands in her pockets as they crunched in their tennis shoes in the overcast morning. "You still deconstructing everything?"

"I can't write it, but I can rip it apart. Seems like that's all I'm doing."

The day smelled crisp-edged like winter was coming.

"Ever notice how many stories there are now?" Calyce asked her. "They're everywhere, all the time. The news is all stories, and endless shows on cable and Buzzfeed and all those movies now on iTunes and Netflix and Amazon. And the movie-movies. It's twenty-four hours. I don't think we've ever had so many stories at one time in history."

"So where's yours?" Belinda said suddenly, her brass earrings swinging. She hadn't worn a hat and her hood was down, so her soft hair blew like grass in a wind-wave.

"What do you mean?"

"You keep saying there are no stories about us, middle-aged women. Men don't fight over us anymore. We aren't beautiful. We live our lives, go to the grocery store. You talk about it all the time, so why don't you write about us? For example." Belinda smiled. "Why not write about some lumberjack going down on you and your son walking in?"

She laughed a fat guffaw that got even louder when she saw how embarrassed Calyce was. "Seriously. I've never heard of anything so outrageous."

Calyce said that it had been Selene's idea. Damion was blameless, really, just giving into what she wanted in the heat of the moment.

"On *your* couch, in *your* living room? Where's the reaction you had the other day? You always do this. You get angry then bury it. He should have told her no."

Calyce remembered then that they had kept on, with Selene staring at her. Calyce remembered the smell, too. In her shock that night she hadn't registered it.

Above them the pudding clouds began to slice icy drizzle. Soft glitter turned to freezing shards then jagged pellets within seconds on their shoulders, driving with such force that the two bundled women turned together without speaking and rushed back toward the distant parking lot. The grey cusp of winter had charged in to overtake them.

Again that night, when her barking cough had once more jerked her awake, Calyce gave up and groggily descended to her kitchen. She put water on to boil for tea with honey, but she couldn't find her mug. She searched for it in the cabinet, in the dishwasher, and again on the countertop. Large enough to cup in both hands and with an extravagant looping handle, it was her favorite, but she couldn't see it anywhere.

"Did she take it? I can't believe she took it again."

Calyce found the mug with one other outside Damion's door. It hadn't been stacked there when she had come in but it was there now, dirty, with a smeared spoon in it, needing to be washed before she could use it.

She picked up the mugs, holding the spoon, and she scooped up the wrinkled shirt Damion had wadded and tossed by the baseboard. She got two steps before she stopped, then turned as she thought.

She dropped the shirt back onto the tile and banged down the extra mug. It clanged but she didn't care. Into it she let fall from two feet up the spoon, which she aimed perfectly. It rang.

Upstairs a half-hour later, Calyce pulled toward herself at the dining table a few sheets of white copy paper. She clicked her pen. Her mug steamed contentedly beside her.

"Today we're going to work with surprise endings," Calyce said to her class. "The assignment is *Hard Times* by Ron Rash."

Catherine's son Ryan was still at home despite being in his late twenties. He was still in his downstairs childhood room, and it looked like he would remain there forever. He had tried, and he kept trying, but there seemed to be some one thing missing in him that employers wanted, some ineffable quality. Or maybe it was his almost palpable lack of oomph.

Catherine had made it to Scout Lookout, though she did not know the name. All she knew as she walked the gentle new incline was that she had finally gotten upwind of the outhouses.

She saw the sign.

On a large color picture of the precipitous fin of rock that presumably rose somewhere beyond her, a universal, international, no-language black and white picture of a stick-figure hiker falling into mid-air with tumbling rocks accompanied these frightening words:

Since 2004, 6 people have died falling from cliffs on this route.

The 1.1 mile (1.8 km) round-trip route from Scout Lookout to Angels Landing is a strenuous climb on a narrow ridge over 1,400 feet above the canyon floor. This route is not recommended during high winds, storms, or if snow or ice is present.

Past the sign, sandstone layers stepped in soft, gritty, flat layers dusted with sandy powder that slid hikers to their deaths. That was why it was called slickrock.

To her right, low bushes clung to the eroding cliff-top whose sheer wall plunged hundreds of feet to the bottom of Refrigerator Canyon, *where she had just walked. To her left the burnt-orange rock simply stopped at a naked ledge. As she inched forward she saw the east rim of the canyon far away, unreachable on the other side of a mile-wide gap that only birds could cross. There was no railing, no banister. One step and she would be airborne.*

She realized she was seeing a bird, a huge one, hanging just above her in the wind that blew. She noticed the air then too, and the dust it brought to her face. The bird was a broad-winged black and white one with long black-tipped feathers like fingers groping. It had no feathers on its head but skin instead like a plucked chicken, only reddened as if sunburned.

A woman in sneakers was pointing and jabbing her companions to look up at it and away from their feet as the massive creature dipped in soundless concentration, self-correcting with a flick in the updraft, a white boomerang zigzagged on the underside of its vast wingspan.

"It's a condor," she heard the woman say. "They eat carcasses. Biggest flying bird in North America."

Catherine had never been so close to something so deadly. She was in its world now, full of currents a thousand feet up, and it was hunting. She watched it cock its head.

She arrived finally where Scout Lookout ended at a rock hill of hardened eddies that eons ago pooled and glopped when they were fluid sand, each now-hardened rosy lip just a bit higher and inward from the curving lip below It, making swaying stripes. Only the narrowest of resulting ledges allowed for a foot jammed sideways to maintain a body's balance.

To her right a heavy chain led upward as it hugged the sandstone. Someone had sunk thick metal posts into the eroding slickrock and attached them with thick weighty links through needle eyes. From where she was standing the chain seemed to continue all the way to the top, but she would have had to bend in half to hold it. She wondered how long the fat chain had been there. How many hands had tugged on it? How many at a time, and how hard? If she bet her life on it, would it hold?

To her left was a thousand-foot plunge without a railing. One step and she would fall eight long screaming seconds to the bottom. She was standing on solid rock but in open air three-quarters of the height of the old World Trade Center, three-quarters of the way up the Willis Tower in Chicago, entirely above the pointed top of the Eiffel Tower, a full 250 feet above one of the orange towers of the Golden Gate Bridge, and a hundred feet above two London Eye Ferris wheels stacked on each other.

She had never been so high before without being safely inside, surrounded by metal.

She was thirsty and hot and the sun blazed on her bare arms, which were red from their cooking. She knew that once she stepped over there, to her right, and committed to that first life-or-death chain, she would be without shade until she stopped, and again until she returned to this place.

She checked her water. She didn't have any.

Her companions were far, far away. They had long ago forgotten her.

She shifted her backpack and felt its weight again. She could not go on without it, for it contained all her belongings – her wallet, her keys, her expensive Sony camera with zoom that added a constantly shifting three pounds in the fat wide bottom of the large second compartment. The straps connected with a cross-strap that pressed into her sternum, and she suddenly felt like she was strangling.

She began. She stepped right and carefully lodged her foot to buy herself as much width as possible, but almost immediately the little space disappeared and she was trying to move over sloped and sanded *rock. She bent, clinging to the chain but not trusting it to hold her. Afraid, she couldn't keep herself moving. The bulk on her back slid, knocking her balance off.*

She looked ahead and up, then to her right to see the curve that fell away, down into Refrigerator Canyon. She looked up the rock face, where she saw now that the chains stopped. One of the posts was even uprooted on its side, and chainless. To get to the next short run of links, she had to somehow just arrive there, in the air, with nothing to brace her. She reached for a stone, a ledge, a piece of earth to hold on to, but there was nothing.

Panic set in. Her breathing shallowed. Heart racing, she couldn't figure out where to put her hands and people were coming now, both ways, and all of them were waiting. There was only one trail up or down, and she was the blockage, hunched in terror.

She sat and tried to push her way forward on her butt, only that didn't help either. She was stuck, turtle-like, her backpack wedged behind her against the rock. She was taking up as little space as possible on the mountain, but they couldn't move by her and she couldn't move on her own.

DECEMBER

At lunch that day Catherine made sure to sit by the door, where Mike would see her, as she took the seat at the round table that faced the entry. She knew exactly when he would arrive in the faculty lounge, if he came alone, and as the minute approached she lowered her eyes so he wouldn't catch her yearning.

Act casual, she told herself. Aloof, all while she prayed that no one else would join her, for she knew that Mike would weave past her to his friends if she weren't a stray needing company.

And there he was, towering in the doorway, so tall she knew without looking up that she would see the deeply shadowed bottom of his square jaw. He would be wearing the beige tattersall, she knew too. Yesterday had been the Black Watch and tomorrow would be the red MacPherson. This last was her favorite because it made him a flame from his narrow waist to the top of his rumpled red head, which he couldn't keep his fingers out of. Sit here, sit, please sit with me today, she mouthed to her sandwich.

He stopped. She thanked God. "You by yourself again?"

Then, as Mike ate complacently, scanning the room, she struggled for topics to bring him back to her. She offered the conversation she had had the day before with their boss Frank, the school's Head of Academics. She reminded the handsome biology teacher of her hunt for new literature as English Department Head, and she told him, putting on a bright smile, that she had spoken up rebelliously for once at the last faculty meeting. She had mustered herself – "You know how I am" – *to question the high school's single-minded focus on Jewish and black oppression. Even the History Department did* Himmler's Jewish Tailor *every year.*

"You know what Frank said? That it's our demographic. The parents expect it. But what about the Asian experience? David's right. You know David in my department?"

Mike nodded.

"He said the only thing we do is The Year Of the Boar and Jackie Robinson, *and that's in fifth grade. We've got more and more Asians. David gave me* Everything I Never Told You *and I told Frank I want to do it next year. Aren't you proud of me?"*

With her hands she shifted on the steep slope and twisted full around to face it, her backpack cantilevered into thin air. She found a tight spot for her right foot and jammed it in, but there was nowhere to move her left and only smooth round rock above her. There was nothing to grasp but she reached anyway. She strained in the bright sun but the new length of fat chain started ten feet above her on the eroded sandstone.

She twisted around again and tried to push herself up the incline on her butt, but the pack jammed against the rock and trapped her.

"What do I do?" she kept saying to herself. "How are they doing this?"

People waited. They piled up now beneath her on the slant to Scout Lookout, wanting impatiently to climb up. Above her too, they waited with growing irritation, holding onto the high, far end of the chain she could not reach, watching from a spot that was more horizontal. No one was helping her, or even offering to, as the hot day scorched them all.

She was stuck and without a clue and no one else could move until she made a choice.

Catherine had roused her gumption to ask Frank for a private appointment. It was the first one she had ever requested of her direct supervisor, in a diffident email she had revised five times and hesitated three days to send. Frank had then taken 36 hours to respond with a sentence fragment allowing her fifteen minutes at 7:30 a.m. on a school day four days later.

At the appointed time she rapped lightly on the closed door of his office, which was hidden on an upper floor where students, parents and new teachers could not find it. Frank liked his aerie, she had overheard him say once.

Why?

"Scarcity principle."

She was there very briefly, she hastened to say when he did not invite her to sit, because she knew he was very busy. She "just" needed his approval to endorse Alice to succeed her as English Department Head starting the next year. The woman was clearly the heir to the position, though she did not say this to Frank explicitly. She assumed he knew it, for he had known hard-working and good-hearted Alice as long as she.

But Frank balked. He then deflected, after which he finally had to tell her outright when she did not get the message, which annoyed him, for he operated in a thin-aired world of microscopic eyebrow twitches. He began with a general observation that "we need more diversity," to which she naïvely responded with a paean to Alice's blackness. He had to then refer expressly to the new black Vice Principal, whom the faculty had driven upward nearly in a coup, but still she did not understand. He said "diversity" again, and a third time before she finally asked, confused —

"So who do you want?"

"Whom. It's whom."

He waited until she understood that she had to re-say the sentence, and he waited until she did it, after which he mentioned David. Frank rebuffed her subsequent protest, explaining that the young teacher was impressive. He knew this because David had been "popping in for chats."

"Chats?"

David was the future, Frank said. Knowledgeable, published, and he made a real contribution, which was "sorely needed in your department. Didn't he just recommend a novel to you that you've already decided to use next year?"

Just as important, Frank said, David clearly met a demographic that was growing at the school, yet was underrepresented. Several wealthy Asian parents had told him plainly at the last parent meet-and-greet that they were disappointed not to see any Asians in management.

"We've got everything else," he said. "Blacks and gays and trans but no Asians. How could we have missed that?"

She asked, "But what do I tell Alice?"

He shrugged. "Tell her she doesn't fit the bill."

"But there's nothing wrong with her."

"She's not entitled to the job. We never promised her."

"But I've never criticized her in any performance review and neither have you."

"So it's subtle. Make it something vague that impacts her leadership style. I don't care, but make it her. If it's her, she can't fight you."

"But without my endorsement she'll lose. You know how this works."

"And don't ever tell her we've talked. This has to come from you, so it's strictly internal within your department."

Calyce said to her students, "But first I want to redefine this class. I think I've been doing it wrong. Creative writing is subjective, though I think we can all identify what's good. What I want to do this hour is create a rubric I'll use for grading for the rest of the year. I want us to formulate this together because I'm throwing out the way I've been doing it."

That first Saturday of the month, Calyce took the large fake-pine wreath off its high hook on the pegboard nailed to the far wall of her garage, the wall shared with Damion's room. That was where she kept through all the years every bit of the old seasonal paraphernalia of a family of growing children: the wooden painted hanging Valentine hearts connected with red ribbon, the two Easter baskets with their residue of crystalline green cellophane, the Halloween black bat with slippery wings and plastic skin so soft it felt feral, and the two plastic orange buckets with jack-o-lantern eyes that Damion and Maria had used as toddlers. Through the pegboard holes two bouquets of glittered balls on thin stalks massed in firework bunches of fuchsia and royal blue. These she would poke into the two small planters by her front door the morning after Christmas to herald the week-long run-up to New Year's.

The children had made the tacky wreath so long before that she had still been married. Alone together one weekend when the kids had been in elementary school, she and they had trooped to the craft store to buy the circle of plastic bottlebrush pine with silvered tips but no pinecones, no ribbon, and none of that red cheap stiff velveteen. They had clamored and she had allowed them to buy whatever small trinkets they wished from the fifty-cent bin, and in this way the artificial store-bought thing became a joy festooned with sienna chili peppers and feathered Styrofoam white birds and branches tucked with gold balls, from which a sequined star dangled and swung whenever they opened the front door. It was a Christmas wreath to dazzle Las Vegas and so unlike her, yet she cherished the garish relic of childhood.

Every January before, when the holidays had ended, she had climbed the six-foot ladder again to display her trophy exactly in its spot, centered above where her car stopped when it pulled into the garage. As she took the wreath down this time, she wondered if Damion noticed it when he drove inside.

Calyce spent the solitary rest of that Saturday afternoon researching the specifics of open-heart bypass, including surgeons in the D.C. area, Medicare coverage, and referral requirements. She made a handwritten list of what they had to do once Winter Break started and Simon brought their mother up from Florida.

"What are those?" Selene asked her that same evening.

"Advent candles," Calyce said.

"They could start a fire if you forget them. I'll get you those electric ones like restaurants have. They're safer."

Selene dumped the grocery bags on the counter and unloaded leeks, a box of chicken broth, a five-pound bag of Yukon Gold potatoes, and a pint of half-and-half. "Do we still have butter? I saw it this morning."

"You're making a cold soup in December?"

Damion walked in and hugged Selene, wrapping his arms from back to front around her. He was smiling, deeply contented. Calyce felt second-hand warmth.

"Mom, I've got something for you." He dug in a back pocket to tug out a folded square.

She opened it to see that it was a check repaying everything he owed her for the month, and he was paying it early.

He said, "It's not just Christmas that pays well. Tips are good the whole month of December."

Calyce frowned. "Were they this good last year?"

"You just don't remember."

He asked Selene, "What are you making?"

Calyce said, "Vichyssoise."

"No," Selene corrected. "Potage parmentier. It's a warm leek and potato soup. And I got bread too. The rosemary kind you like."

She looked at Calyce. "I'm sorry, but I only bought enough for two."

At dinner Damion and Selene sat touching on one side of the dining room table. Calyce sat opposite, picking at a small plate of red seedless grapes. Selene had set the table with only two placemats, so Calyce had had to fish hers out of the drawer in the sideboard.

"I'm sorry," Selene said. "I didn't think you were eating."

A few minutes later, Calyce said to Damion across from her, "When your grandmother comes later this month, you're going to have to move up to the guestroom."

The two lovers lifted their heads in unison as their right hands rhythmically worked their spoons.

Calyce said, "From your room down there it's only one flight up and down to this main floor. To get to the guestroom from the front door it's two, and that's more than she'll be able to do while she recovers."

"How long will *that* take?" Damion asked.

"It could be as long as three months, depending. I've already told you this. Twice."

He flopped back in his chair. "I have to be in the guestroom for three months? You're kidding. You know what she did?" he said to Selene. "She left them, the whole family, and she didn't come back for a year."

"This isn't the time for that story," Calyce told him.

"She ran off with some boat guy," he said. "She made my mom take care of the whole family. What were you then? Fifteen?"

"Damion."

"My aunt and uncle were little and my granddad travelled all the time, so my mom had to do it."

Selene asked Calyce, "Where did she go?"

"Florida," Damion answered. "So she could be with this guy. Right, Mom? A sailor?"

They looked at Calyce like they were watching TV, slurping soup and waiting for her answer.

"Fishing boat captain," Calyce finally said to be done with it. "One of those charters that goes out to deep sea."

That night a text hit her phone but Calyce couldn't read it until she found her glasses.

Not coming Xmas. Still in Chile. Mom says to come just for Jan surgery.

Calyce punched the buttons. **What about surgeons? I emailed you several possibilities. I can't do this alone.**

Two hours later, words snapped back to her from the far Southern Hemisphere. **You'll do your usual fine job organizing. Really don't have service here.**

⋏⋀⋏

"So what do you have to do?" Calyce asked a junior girl in her Advisory. She wanted to know what Abby, the girl's chemistry teacher, had told her.

"She says I have to take the test on Tuesday, in the morning, right before I leave for the hospital. They're rebuilding my ankle."

"She wants you to take a test the morning of surgery? When?"

"Eight."

"When's surgery?"

"One, but they want me there at ten."

"And you can't eat anything the night before. No water even?"

Agreeing, the child shook her head.

"And you can't take your ADHD meds," Calyce said.

"I can't have any drugs at all in my system. But she said she has to have the grade next week, that having me take the test after Winter Break would give me an unfair advantage."

"That's ridiculous. Are you in town the first week of Break? Could you take it then?"

"Yeah. I'll be at home recovering."

Calyce patted her arm. "You go to class now. Let me see about this."

⋏⋀⋏

As she walked the corridor a moment later, Calyce began coughing and couldn't stop. It started as a searing high in her throat, just below where she swallowed. She wheeze-coughed and coughed again, and then it suddenly became a gag reflex and she had to pray she didn't bring her lunch up and out onto the carpet.

She knocked on the doorframe as she entered the laboratory classroom that was empty except for a thirty-something teacher writing on the whiteboard with a dark red marker.

"Abby?" Calyce said hoarsely. "Have you got a minute?"

"I simply don't understand why you won't yield on this," Calyce said five minutes later. "The child needs surgery. She won't be able to focus Tuesday morning. It's unfair."

Abby crossed her arms, the marker tip now pointed out like a weapon. Her furious eyes were the only things alive on her shut-tight face. "It's not going to matter, Calyce. She's not one of the brightest anyway."

"How would you like it if a teacher required you to take a test an hour before you had surgery?"

Abby said stubbornly, "Her surgery's not until the afternoon."

Just as stubbornly, Calyce said, "You're insensitive and heartless, you know that?"

Alone in the house, Calyce sat at her dining table that night talking to Simon, who had just informed her that he was not in fact travelling from Dallas to Florida the next weekend to retrieve their mother and bring her to D.C. as planned, for what everyone understood could be her last Christmas. Instead, he and Sandra and their two teenage daughters would be staying home. Simon's elder girl, a high school senior, had finals right after the first of the year, he said, and the family had decided that studying was the top priority.

He would, however, be arriving the night before Effie's surgery in January, once it was scheduled. He planned to stay in a hotel for two nights "to make sure she's all right." He had discussed it with his wife. He wouldn't leave to return home until early the morning of the second day after the bypass.

"You're leaving before she's discharged?" Calyce was incredulous.

Yes, because he had a job and routes to fly and pilots were only wage-slaves now. "That two days is already going to be tough, what with my taking Christmas. Not to mention, what message does it send her if we all flock to D.C.? We're telling her she won't have another one."

"But who's going to bring her?"

He was done with the conversation. "You're on Christmas break soon. Why don't you go down and get her? Don't you have two weeks?"

⋀⋀⋀

An hour later Selene and Damion pulled in to find Calyce in the garage, on the stepladder, digging passionately in one of her CHRISTMAS-marked wall cabinets, her head so far inside she didn't notice Damion's car inching alongside her.

Selene said a moment later to the legs on the ladder, "I bought you lights for the lamppost out front. I thought it could use some."

"I don't put lights on that," Calyce answered from deep inside the cabinet. "It's a candy cane if I can find the ribbon in here somewhere."

She was moving things, brushing against the bottom.

"Then maybe on the door wreath," Selene said.

"Nowhere to plug them in. Damion, can you take this?"

Calyce pulled out a box without a lid.

"The crèche?" he said. "You don't put that out."

"I am this year. And everything else Simon doesn't like. Time to put Jesus back in Christmas. It's his wife, your Aunt Sandra. They're not coming."

Calyce walked toward the department office the next morning with her mind on everything but school, so she didn't see Roger hurrying to catch up. He didn't call out to her so she didn't slow, and when he spoke it surprised her.

"Are you going to the faculty Christmas party this Sunday?"

"Winter party," she corrected as she motored. "No Christianity. School policy."

"So are you going?"

Ten minutes later she was staring open-mouthed at John De-Groot just before the weekly departmental meeting started in the big bullpen of their collective office.

"You're not serious," she whispered to him.

"They're complaining that you're constantly monitoring them. You keep track. But I want you to announce it, not me. You tell them you're moving your desk. Put Amita there and make points with the young ones."

"But I've had my desk by that door for eighteen years. I like it there."

"It's time for a change."

"But I don't want to sit there," Amita told Calyce quietly as soon as the meeting ended. "With all the traffic in and out, I won't be able to concentrate."

"It'll be good for you. You'll see. I always liked it there."

"But then why are you moving?"

Calyce had to think of something.

"I'm Interim Head now. If I sit there, I'll look like a receptionist."

"And I won't?" Amita said.

That night Calyce was checking roundtrip flights to Clearwater when Damion climbed up the stairs to the dining room. She waited but didn't hear the softer footfalls of his diaphanous girlfriend. She caught herself wondering if Selene ever touched down.

She reminded him again that he had to move upstairs by that coming Friday.

"Already?"

She ignored him. "Do you know how much these tickets cost? It's a fortune to go down and back the same weekend."

"Isn't Simon paying?"

"Why should he?"

"At least the difference. He's the one who bailed at the last minute."

The teenager was alone and crying in the classroom when Calyce opened the door and flipped on the lights, which set the girl to wiping her face sloppily. She was a senior with long blonde hair and eyes that looked like a summer day. Calyce had taught the girl the prior year, so she knew her to be devoted and studious, with good parents.

Through sniffles, the girl described the previous afternoon's email from Yale, in which the college had rejected her outright. Early admission decisions had been issued the day before, and Yale hadn't bothered to defer or even waitlist this straight-A student, who knew already that three other classmates had been accepted. Good students, but not all great, none obvious future leaders of the civilized world, and none better than this child sobbing alone in a remote classroom.

"Yale was all I ever wanted since I was little," she said with her face streaking. "My mom and I were Rory and Lorelei from *Gilmore Girls*."

Calyce sat next to her. "You used to say that."

"What do I do now?"

Calyce thought for a long moment.

"You feel as bad as you want for as long as you want, but you don't let it stop your applying over Break to everywhere else."

"But I don't care about the others."

"You don't right now. Just get on mechanically to the next schools on your list. Call me if you want over Break and let me know if you need a recommendation letter. I'm happy to do one. And Zoë?"

"Yeah?"

"Yale made a colossal mistake. You and I both know that. And I'm happy to say that to your parents."

They were alone in the department office at the end of the next day, she and Dan, for the first time she could remember. The room was always bustling when he arrived in the mornings just minutes before classes began, and he ate with all the other eager young teachers in the lunchroom every day. Dan was a crowder, she had seen, and not a loner. He came and went with noise and electricity.

To Calyce, at her new desk in the middle of the bullpen, he said, "Did you hear about the consolidation? Of course you did. What do you think?"

She froze for an instant but quickly covered. "You tell me. I want to hear your reaction first."

"I think it's good," he said. "It makes it seamless from Pre-K to the high school if we have one unified department. That way we know how it all fits together."

She nodded, then said, "I need to spend some time here on my lesson plan. Do you know when John's getting in?"

⋀⋀

When DeGroot didn't appear, she went to search for him. When she didn't find him in the school, she hugged her blazer to herself and went outside into the icy wind to look for him in the underground garage. She was heading down the ramp, ducking under the white semaphore arm, when she finally spotted him striding up. He too was clutching his jacket.

She accosted him. "You didn't tell me they're consolidating the English Department school-wide."

"I just found out," he answered. "How did you know?"

"Dan told me."

"Oh yeah. He and I exchanged emails this morning."

In the cutting wind the trees in the traffic circle in front of the school waved their barren branches.

"It's a good thing," she said. "The middle school doesn't prepare them well enough. We constantly have problems with the basics.

We can tell them what to cover now. I'm tired of having to re-teach things the kids should already know by the time they get here."

He stopped short in the flinching cold.

"You've got it exactly wrong," he said brusquely. "The parents think the high school's English is largely redundant, not the middle school's. They told Administration the kids are being re-taught things at the high school that they've already learned."

"Well, that's ridiculous."

Four boxes blocked her front door that evening. The stack reached past the doorknob, all addressed to her mother. Calyce saw that one was from Harry & David, her mother's perennial gift to her. If this were like every other year, the most expensive present would be for Damion.

Calyce shifted the packages. Here it was. Nordstrom's. The other two were probably for Maria, her husband Greg, and little Jimmy.

This doctor was young too, like nearly all of them, and he was already a specialist. It had been a transition for Calyce when a doctor became her age, rather than some older man, but this was something new, this toddler in his white coat with his full name embroidered over his left breast pocket.

She had found him at the last minute after yet another disorienting spasm. Barely competent, she thought, because he had time available on a Saturday when she couldn't take any more weekdays off, not in the days before Effie's surgery. But at least he was in her HMO.

She slouched once more on a sterile examining table. This ENT too felt her throat, neck, and lymph nodes. He had wanted to shove that long white thing down her nose too, but she told him it wasn't necessary.

"There's no swelling," she said. "And the larynx looks fine."

He smiled. "You a doctor? Let me ask you, when do you eat dinner?"

He was standing very close and had a smell of masculine she wasn't used to. He asked, "Do you eat late in the evening?"

She nodded. "I got into the habit with my son because of his work schedule. He doesn't eat with me anymore, but I still do it."

"When?"

She shrugged. "Nine?"

"And when do you go to sleep?"

"Ten. Eleven."

"And you feel this high in the back of your throat, it says here. Today too?"

She nodded.

"When did you eat last?"

"Two hours ago, maybe."

He thought, then said, "Mrs. Tate, I think you may have laryngeal pharyngeal reflux."

"No reflux," she answered. "My regular ENT says I don't."

"This is a different kind. He probably told you about GERD. See, the esophagus has two sphincters."

He made a fist and tightened and untightened it as he spoke. "They keep the contents of your stomach in your stomach where all the acid is and prevent that acid from rising into your throat. There's one sphincter at the bottom where the esophagus meets the stomach and another behind your trachea, where your Ad-am's apple would be if you were a man." He put two fingers on his own.

"With this kind of reflux, the stomach contents come up through that upper sphincter too, all the way up your throat. It's called LPR. Silent reflux, because there's often no heartburn. You know, that burning feeling in the lower chest. I want to do a twenty-four-hour pH probe. It's a device that measures the fluctuating pH levels in your throat so we can see how much reflux you're getting. It's a tube about the size of a strand of spaghetti that goes down your throat and comes out your nose and connects to a monitor you have to wear. Do you work? Unfortunately the lab's not open on the weekends. You can take it out by yourself. The only thing is inserting it, which they have to do at the lab on a weekday."

"I'll be on Winter Break starting next week. I teach at a high school."

"Then that's when we'll do it. LPR sounds small but it isn't. It can scar the throat and voice box, and if not treated it can cause worse things."

He didn't say it but his face did.

"Cancer?"

"Rarely, but yes. The reflux alters the lining of the throat. That's why I want to know if I'm right and if I am, how bad this is already. We're about to start the holidays with all that food. I want you to take care of yourself. Can you get this done before Christmas?"

The annual faculty winter party was held, as always, at Sharon Epstein's house, one of a hundred square, brick, center-hall Colonials on Sharon's three-syllable-alphabet street in Upper

Northwest, D.C. One of the high school's longtime art teachers, she had lived in it for thirty years, raising her three accomplished children with her non-profit-executive husband in a too-small house that today they could not possibly afford to buy. The furniture was eighties lacquered wood. The main-floor powder room that they all used more and more as the yearly Sunday fête wore on was still painted Wedgwood blue and sickly mauve in wide stripes. Calyce hated it so much she drank as little sangria as possible.

The party always started not at night but 5 p.m. so people could get home and to work the next morning, which was always the Monday of the last week before Winter Break began and everyone had two weeks of vacation. The festivities were as rigidly scheduled as April taxes.

Also ritualized were the "heavy appetizers," paid for by the school, which meant dinner for some if the attendees were greedy, and the same ones were greedy every year. All the newbies came and about half the veterans, each group cramped into its own diminutive room. Calyce found it laughable that the room never changed though the rosters did, with each new generation of young, fervent teachers knowing apparently instinctively that the dirtying kitchen was for them. As the years passed, they each moved out to join the grown-ups in the living room, where Calyce was now standing, having barely been able to close the front door the crush was so dense.

She had come late and planned to leave instantly once she had just as ritualistically thanked Sharon, who would say she was glad Calyce came, exchange a few words about their respective grandchildren, and wait politely for Calyce to move on.

Calyce had dressed in a black suit with a tri-string of artificial pearls she too had had since the eighties, when Barbara Bush had made them popular and the look had enjoyed a brief rage among new professional women. The clip-on earrings were also pearls, though the tiny clusters were real. She wore no coat, for she didn't want to lose it as she once had in a mountain on a bed upstairs.

Her dark hair, which she had just had done, was all soft waves and shoulder-length curves away from her face. Her bag for a change was black and small with a handle that looped over her forearm. The length of her unremarkable skirt was conservative 1960s middle school: if she knelt on the floor, it would have touched the ground. She was out of place and out of look, for everyone else had dressed in what Sharon called "elegant casual," which Calyce didn't own and couldn't pull off, except for those few men who wore the ugly Christmas sweaters that had become another sacrament of the annual bacchanal. As the evening progressed they would drunkenly tug them off and hand them around for "aw, come on, try it" photo opportunities – yet another reason Calyce was already craning her neck above the fortifying crowd, peering over the tops of heads, searching for Sharon and her quick exit.

But then she saw through the archway to the dining room John and Janice DeGroot laughing with arms around each other in the center of an adoring circle. Calyce considered waiting until the worshippers thinned but realized she would just be standing alone where she was even more awkwardly, so she unmoored to make her way through the clear patches, speaking to no one but making her face smiley.

As she maneuvered she spied Belinda, who had approached them as well but from a different angle. Calyce watched the sudden hugging, and not just from the DeGroots. The entire herd was now congratulating her old friend on being named the high school's new permanent Vice Principal.

When it was Calyce's turn, she told Janice DeGroot sincerely how much she would miss her.

Janice said into her ear that it was time. "I'm too old now." Then she pulled back to announce to the group that it had been a tsunami for Belinda, whose new job would begin after the New Year.

"I've never seen anything so well-orchestrated," Janice said with a grin.

John leaned into Calyce to whisper, "I'm sorry I was so hard on you about the desk. I've got a job lead for your son. The guy's hiring, and I told him everything I knew about Damion. I'll email you the information."

Calyce passed through the kitchen to complete her one circuit and saw Dan, who was in a tight pod with two of the other high school English teachers, wearing a bulky dark green sweater with teddy bears wearing mufflers. The pod greeted her but the pause she had caused in the conversation was palpable.

Calyce looked from one to the other before Dan said finally, "We were talking about the consolidation."

Another teacher said, "What does it mean for who'll run the department? Don't they all get to vote too?"

A third asked, "What if everything's run out of the middle school?"

"It won't be," Calyce answered. "The high school's the top of the pyramid. The only way to consolidate the curriculum is from the top down."

But then he was there at her left elbow, Roger Bosch in a tweed jacket and plaid tie and perfectly pressed caramel gabardines. His face was shiny smooth and his fouetté hair tamed into a stiff meringue.

"Hi," he said to the group, beer in hand.

Her colleagues all fidgeted and peeled off. Roger asked if she had seen the deck, pointing to the back door behind them.

The winter crepuscule had already fled during the half-hour she had been inside, and stars now pierced a velvet-cloak indigo. Roger looked up as they stepped onto the wood. "It's not up yet, the winter circle. You can find it from the Belt of Orion. See those three stars in a row?"

In the quiet, he moved behind her to point and she felt his hand on her right shoulder. They were alone, she realized.

Calyce side-stepped away from him.

He said to her in the yellow porch light, "I'm glad you were here tonight because I have a Christmas gift for you."

Somewhere, someone had lit a fire in a hearth. Calyce smelled smoke and burning wood.

He reached into his inside coat pocket to pull out a drawstring pouch, which he gave to her. It was heavy with small hard things that shifted, and she heard the slide of glass. She tugged on the string, then put her fingers in to draw out a polished stone cut into five points, black with white spots all through it. A star.

She held it in her palm, where it was warming already to her touch. Gold light bounced on its smooth tumbled surface.

"It's beautiful."

"I got them online from a rock shop in Springdale. I got all ten. They're each different. I thought you'd like a memory of that place because you love it so, something tactile to hold, to remind you that you can always go back there."

She didn't know what to say. She kept holding the stone, feeling its cool, carved, soft-sharp edges.

He said, "You know, Angels Landing used to be called the Temple of Aeolus. The first East Coast visitors were classics-educated, so of course they saw Aeolus up there at the top of it. You know who he was? The god of the winds in Greek mythology, the one who gave all four winds to Odysseus."

Calyce said, "No. He gave Odysseus just one, the West Wind, to sail him home, and he put the other three in a bag. You read the Odyssey?"

Roger smiled as he faced her, his eyes dropping to her movie-star lips.

"You think all I know is AP Biology? Odysseus takes that bag back to his ship, but his men are so mad that Aeolus didn't give them anything that they open it, and all the winds spill out and drive them off course and when Odysseus finally comes back to ask for the winds again, Aeolus says no. He says you had them once, you don't get them again."

He was close, too close.

"I should go," Calyce said. "I have to get home."

She put the stone in its bag and the bag in her purse, snapping the flap carefully so as not to lose them.

"Thank you for these," she said. "Thank you and Merry Christmas."

Saw you at the party but didn't get to talk before you left. I'm having a New Year's Eve party and would love for you to come. Let me know and I'll send you the particulars.

The text was from Amita. It buzzed Calyce's phone as she climbed into her car.

That night, alone, her lover was a tall outdoorsman who loved the rocks and dry cliffs and touched her with cool hands whose flat palms slid over her stomach and down around the soft-sharp mound of her.

"Did you call John's job lead yet?" Calyce asked Damion the next evening. "He's waiting to hear from you."

"Relax. I'll call him."

"Tomorrow morning?"

"Mom, stop it. I told you I would."

She said, "I sure wish I could still get you to do what I wanted. Life would be so much easier. Don't forget to buy a tree. And untie it so the branches fall down. I gave you money. You know where the lot is."

In class that Friday morning, during one of the two periods shoved in before school assembly and early dismissal for Winter Break, Calyce told her seniors about extra-credit work they could do over vacation.

"Anyone who recommends five interesting short stories to me for class gets an A as an extra quiz grade, but don't send me *The Cask of Amontillado*. You can't Google – she made air bunnies – '*best short stories for high school writing class*.' I found all those lists already."

"You want flash fiction?" a boy asked.

"I'll consider anything. I've read hundreds of books but few short stories, really, and no flash fiction."

"Hundreds?" a girl said. "Why? That's a huge amount of reading."

It was Christmas and nearly vacation and the shroud between teacher and student lifted for the briefest moment.

"When I was little I used to read three books a week. It got to the point that, when I would ask the librarian in our town, everything she'd recommend I had already read. Books took me to somewhere else, particularly in high school, but you kids have your Smartphones. You all have a wonderful holiday and be sure to email those stories."

Effie was noticeably worse when Calyce arrived in Florida. In just a few weeks, her mother's skin had gone grey and concave as though life had been sucked from her. She was manifestly exhausted too, in part from her finally ceasing the charade that she was fine.

"It's alright that Simon couldn't come get me," she told Calyce. "He's got a job and a wife and two girls at home. You and I will have fun."

"It's not a party, Mom, it's open-heart surgery. And I have a job too."

Calyce hadn't told her yet that Simon and his family were staying in Dallas for Christmas.

She surveyed the two large open suitcases on Effie's bed, which the old woman had overstuffed. "A bathing suit? You don't need all this."

"You never know."

"Where did you get these bags?"

"I bought them. Or rather, Stephanie bought them for me."

"She's finally done with her divorce? You have to pay for that second bag, you know. And what about your mail?"

"It's being forwarded," Effie said. "I gave Stephanie a key and

I'll close the blinds. I think that's it. I'll turn down the AC when we leave."

The drink cart bumped by on its maiden trip up the aisle. Effie commented that Calyce should be in her element on a plane since she loved height and air, to which Calyce replied in a *non sequitur* that she really, truly hated the sea.

"Simon feels the same way," Effie said. "It's not the ocean's fault."

With his name now in the conversation, Calyce had no choice but to inform her mother that he wasn't coming to D.C. for Christmas. "His excuse was that Asha has to study for mid-terms."

"That's understandable." But then Effie brightened. "So it'll be just us girls and Damion."

"Nina's not coming either. She says you talked."

"She said she wasn't sure. But that's okay too." Effie stroked Calyce's arm on the armrest. "We're a team, you and me. You're my Samwise."

Calyce moved her arm.

"You're too hard on them. You always are," Effie said. "They'll come for the surgery."

"Samwise was in Simon's books, Mom. Not mine. I never read them. You know 'Samwise' means half-wit?"

Later, Calyce clambered over her mother to the aisle. Inside the bathroom she spoke to herself in the mirror as she washed her hands. "They leave this all to me every time and she doesn't notice. No wonder I'm exhausted."

Back at her seat Calyce told her drowsy mother that she would have Damion's room downstairs, to be closer to the front door. Effie replied that it wasn't necessary, that she would be fine upstairs next to Calyce. There was no reason to force him out.

Effie said, "He thinks you're mad at him about something. Are you?"

From her mother's defense of him, it was clear that Damion hadn't told her about the couch episode, and Calyce certainly wasn't going to tell her. Rather, she said, "He earned a degree from Bowie State that cost a small fortune. He had all these plans for a career but he's been a bartender for four years."

"He's got time. Why are you always wound so tight? You didn't use to be. You'd take that skateboard twenty-five miles an hour down that hill, remember? What happened to you?"

When they banged in with one of Effie's two heavy suitcases, Damion hugged his grandmother for so long she had to tell him she couldn't breathe. He pulled away, but just a little, after which there was much mutual back-rubbing and loving gazing.

He said, "Let me go get the other one."

"You're in here," Calyce said to her mother. "Damion, open your door."

"No, that's okay," Effie told her. "I'll go upstairs. I said I'd use the guestroom." She patted Damion. "I wouldn't think of depriving you."

"Open your door," Calyce repeated to Damion, but he was looking at his grandmother, who said, "We talked it over yesterday, didn't we, Damion, and we decided I'd take the guestroom."

"You talked to him in Florida and you didn't tell me? Not even on the plane?"

"He has to come and go at all hours. I'll be fine in the guestroom. Damion, if you'll take the bags up."

To his back, Calyce snapped, "Did you call John's job lead like I told you?"

"It's the holidays, Mom," he said as he went up with the first one. "Nobody's hiring right now. Isn't that right, Grandma?"

At 10 p.m. the next night, Calyce was sitting in her room in her two-piece drawstring pajamas. She had one foot dangling over the side of her bed and the other tucked beneath her knee. She had just installed herself there, facing the open Juliet-balcony door after a long day at the lab having a thin white pH monitor tube laced through her nose and down her throat, then pulled up an inch to measure the acid in the top of her gullet, rather than lower, as was usually done, the technician had explained. The tube exited her right nostril and snaked down her face to her neck to her collarbone, taped every two inches and connected to a red monitor she had to haul around with her for the next twenty-four hours. The medical tape was white, as it always was, against her tree-bark skin.

When Calyce swallowed she could feel it. Her soft palate and her throat felt strangely irritated. For much of the afternoon she had been gagging, not from nausea but from weirdness, though that reflex at last had subsided.

They had told her to eat normal foods so they could get a normal reading, so she had dutifully cooked for dinner something she thought she should be ashamed of: spaghetti with meatballs, which she had made from scratch. Effie too had savored the meal, saying how nice it was not to have to eat alone anymore.

There was a knock on her bedroom door, which opened to Effie thrusting in her smiling face. "You busy? How nice to be at the top of the house. My gosh it's cold in here. Did you tell the doctor you're sleeping with that door open? But I'm like you. I can't stand it when it's stuffy."

She sat without asking in a velveteen slipper chair. "What are you reading? What are those pages?"

With the tube down her throat, Calyce answered hoarsely, "*The Siege of Berlin.*"

Five minutes later even Damion had arrived, saying he'd been searching for them both. He came in as he hadn't in months and climbed on Calyce's bed as he hadn't since middle school, happy to tell his grandmother about his girl, his "serious girlfriend." Effie would meet Selene soon, he promised, but she was out at class tonight.

He said, "I don't know what I did, but somehow I caught the eye of a goddess."

As they talked a text hit Calyce's phone. **Ayt?**

She left them to hide in her bathroom. **Yes.**

Belinda texted back instantly: **You need to get DeGroot's endorsement.**

Why?

We just had a meeting before he left. You can't take the job for granted. Sorry.

Why?

With the department consolidated from Pre-K up, you have to prove you're the best choice.

Why?

Javier wants it too.

Calyce pulled the thin tube from her nose herself, the sensation one of something sliding upward like a snake from the inside. She then tried once again to reach DeGroot. He didn't pick up so she had to leave messages, three of them by two o'clock, when she decided that any more would annoy him, but still she dialed only to hang up before it went to voicemail.

As she held her phone again that evening, her new ENT called personally. She didn't know it when she saw the caller ID, assuming it was his office, but his voice came over the line.

"It's what I thought," he said. "The pH levels confirm you have LPR. You're going to need to change your diet, and I want you to stop eating so late at night starting right now. We'll see if those changes plus the antacids make a difference for you over the holidays. And continue with your exercise. It helps."

"I have to start right away?"

"It may sound like nothing, but you risk serious complications if this is left untreated. I've got a pdf of the foods to avoid, and I'm going to send it to you. Let me confirm your email."

"But they look so lifelike now and they're much less work," Effie was saying to Calyce in the kitchen. "You know the fake trees these days even come with lights on them?"

"I like them real. Damion, why didn't you get one while I was in Florida? I told you to."

"I didn't know what kind you wanted."

He pointed to the grocery list Calyce was writing. "For Christmas Eve, chili like always, and cornbread."

"With hot salsa," Effie put in.

"But we're eating early," Calyce said. "No more late dinners. I'll use the leftover cornbread in the stuffing."

"Are you making green bean casserole?" Effie asked.

"Steamed. And no candied yams this year. It's going to be pineapple sweet potatoes."

Damion whined, "But we always have yams."

"They're too much sugar, but I'll make your egg-custard pie. Mom, we need to leave for the doctor early tomorrow morning."

"But it's going to be Christmas," he said. "We have to do all the usual for Grandma, including candied yams. And Mom, I want Selene to help with the tree lights. You don't go that high with the ladder. And she's bought new ornaments."

Effie asked him, "Are you going to any more parties?"

Damion nodded. "There's one tonight."

"I thought you were working," Calyce told him. "And I like doing the tree with just the family."

But he was talking over her. "Selene wants to make pearl onions for dinner. She says not to worry about buying them. She'll bring everything she needs."

At Georgetown Hospital's medical office wing the next morning, Calyce held Effie's right elbow as they slowly walked from the parking lot. Her mother was breathing in airbursts by the time they got to the elevator.

"I'm nervous," Effie admitted.

Calyce had poked the button but did it again. Then she poked it again, and again.

The appointment was so the surgeon could meet her, go

over the procedure and review any troublesome results of the additional tests he had ordered after her information had arrived from Florida. Calyce assumed the pompadoured man also wanted to personally assess her mother as a physical body. Calyce gave the surgeon credit, though. He met with them in his small office rather than in an examining room, and he stood when they entered, came around from behind his desk, and shook Effie's hand as well as her own. He was formal. No first-name business.

But he had something of concern to report after they had sat in the two guest chairs. Her mother's A1C results were not good, at 7.1, which meant, unfortunately, that she had diabetes. Maybe not for long, so maybe not chronically, not yet, and the number wasn't as high as it might be, but still. Effie was speechless.

"Any trouble with your kidneys?" he asked. "How about your eyes? Any loss of feeling in your feet?"

Effie could only shake her head in answer.

"I see you're slender. Not a smoker. Do you exercise?"

Calyce spoke. "She walks the beach every day in Florida. For miles, even in the rain. She has for years."

"I want you to keep that up as much as possible before surgery, and get a glucose meter. Try to limit carbohydrates and sugar. I know it's Christmas but that's how you can help me."

He went on to explain the post-operative complications that diabetes can cause. Her mother was at increased risk for infection of the wound, which risk if it happened could be substantial. For the surgery, he would have to break her sternum and hinge her ribs. With the diabetes, she might heal more slowly and have to remain hospitalized longer.

"Let me ask you," he said to Calyce. "Your mother seems to be completely on the ball, but since this has started, have you noticed any mental deficits? Say, over the last year?"

Calyce hesitated. "No, but I haven't seen her much. Just twice, and both in the last two months."

To Effie he said, "Is there someone else I can ask? It's important because the older we get, the more disoriented anesthesia can make us. You're going to be under for as long as five hours, barring complications. It could be longer."

"You could ask my son Simon," Effie said. "He comes to visit more often, but other than him, no. I'm sorry to say that I've lived alone, with no family."

Mom has diabetes, Calyce wrote in a group text she had set up for her, Simon, and Nina. **It could make this much worse. Should we go forward?**

No answer from the other two came over the next two hours.

Has either of you seen any change in her mental state over the last year? The doctor wants to know.

Still silence. The night passed and dawn bloomed.

Does Mom have a will? A DNR? I don't want to worry her if you know.

Simon replied then, probably on his way to work. **Yes. I will send.**

Calyce replied. **Send what? Which?**

He answered in all caps. **SHE WANTS SURGERY.**

And then, five minutes later, **Don't screw this up for her.**

Calyce kept calling DeGroot once a day until it was at last Christmas Eve morning when she reached him at home on his landline. He said purposely that he was having waffles with his wife and grown children, who had just arrived for the holiday.

"But hold on," he said resignedly. "Let me go somewhere private."

When he spoke again, after clearing his throat through her Happy Christmas Eve, he told her flat out for the first time that he could not endorse her candidacy. He had to consider everyone in all three schools on two campuses now, not just the English teachers at the high school.

"I've known Javier almost as long as I've known you," he said. "Decades. He's a good man and a good person. A tremendous teacher and the kids all love him. I won't choose between you and quite frankly I'm surprised you would ask. It puts me in an extremely awkward position. You should have realized that, Calyce."

That same Christmas Eve afternoon, Effie and Damion braved the local mall with her driving an electric sit-on cart and Damion playing traffic cop through the waves of last-minute shoppers. They came home giddy but beyond fatigued, though delighted to have spent hours in each other's company, which they seemed unable to get enough of. They whispered together and chortled like drunkards the five minutes it took him to get Effie slowly up the stairs.

Calyce then heard Damion haul up something big and drag it into the powder room. Both he and Effie laughed as they poked their heads into the kitchen to instruct her "not to go in there."

The four of them that night sprawled in her dirt-brown living room, the two young people reclined on the floor as Effie claimed a loveseat. Their ramekins of chili had been scraped clean and forgotten on the corner table. With Effie's prodding, Damion had dragged out his childhood favorite, The Game of Life, and everyone but Calyce had been playing it for a half-hour with Damion moving for his grandmother.

"I can't believe you still like that game," Calyce said from the kitchen. "Whoever dies with the most money wins? That's the measure of success in life?"

"It's a game, Mom." Damion was winning. He had stacked his fake bills in front of him on the carpet like a cash drawer.

"Why not the one who lives the longest?" she called to them. "Or gives the most away?"

Effie piped up. "You're saying this? Miss Do-It-By-The-Rules?"

Calyce opened the dishwasher.

"I'll help," Selene called out when she heard it.

"That's okay," Calyce answered briskly.

"She doesn't want help," Calyce heard Damion tell Selene. "She never does."

"That's not true," Calyce whispered.

When his turn was over, Damion walked in to sidle close.

"Do we have presents for Grandma?" he whispered, "And for Maria and Greg? I got something for Jimmy."

She was slicing the remaining cornbread. "Of course."

"Did you see the lights outside? Selene wanted to surprise you. We've never lit up the candy cane before."

She cubed a few slices. "I saw."

She scraped the knife-edge along the board to slide them into a storage bag she had propped open. "I'm going to mix up the oats. Will you go down and get the glitter out of the Christmas cabinet?"

An hour later they came, her daughter Maria and Greg and darling Jimmy, who yelled "Gammy!" as he ran to Calyce and hopped in front of her with his arms out until she scooped him up and held him. He nuzzled her with his cheek as they became one single, connected mass of giggling love.

"Merry Christmas Eve!" Calyce said to him. "Are you going to feed the reindeer with me?"

They walked holding hands as Calyce balanced the big metal bowl of shimmering oats against her coat with her free arm. The other five had all stayed inside, where Greg and Maria were getting to know Selene, whom they had just met, so Calyce and Jimmy had the spangled night to themselves. The stars shone so bright and clear they looked faceted.

The little boy was overwhelmed by his oversized black puffer jacket, which was brand new but had brown stains already at the sleeve hems where they had met chocolate, the vestiges of which she saw on his wrists too when she pulled on his mittens. Jimmy looked like he was trapped inside an inflated balloon with only his face showing as he smiled and bounced happily alongside her.

She had him dig his mittens into the aluminum bowl and sprinkle the "reindeer food" over her few front square feet of grass, then do so again in her backyard after taking the boy down and out the sliding door in Damion's bedroom. There, in the small, patchy rectangle that was hers, the child lifted his cupped hands and blew on the grain to make it fly. Bits and dust and taupe oat flakes wafted in the light she had turned on at the back of the house, as the gold glitter she had mixed in glinted. She told him, as she always did, that the shine helped the reindeer find it.

She only spread a little herself, to make sure the fun was mostly his.

She took him down the street too, after clearing it with his parents. They arrived shortly after eight at the little footbridge she had found over the stream that in warmer months grew rushes and cattails. She made sure he didn't stumble into the frigid water but stood safely on the thatched slope to scatter what remained. She had him scour the bowl to get the last flakes, then made a show of handing it to the child to up-end and shake, moving her hips with his as she sang "Jingle Bells" at full voice like a happy madwoman, rolling her backside and laughing with him in the dark.

Inside again, she made Jimmy hot chocolate, some of which he missed getting into his mouth. He put the cup down and wiped west of his lips with his jacket sleeve as he balanced on one leg, then leaned forward to spread his arms in airplane wings.

"Gammy, see what I can do?"

Calyce countered with her one-foot stork stance, the ball of her right foot on her left instep, and he mimicked it, which is how Maria found them. She started doing it too and the three of them maintained it, hopping to retain their balance. Greg came in and tried but soon fell out of it, which made Jimmy ecstatic that he could best his father.

When Damion appeared, wondering what they were all doing, he wouldn't even try.

"You all look stupid. Except you," he said to his little nephew.

She hugged her sleeping grandson as she lifted him gently into the car.

Alone in her room, she slid open her top right dresser drawer to lift out the drawstring pouch, then found a random stone star that looked as though it had been dunked in watercolors. It had swirls of gray, white, cinnamon and peach along with a warm red-brown. She caressed it with her thumb, turning it on one of its points, back to front and back again between her fingers.

From her bedside table, she picked up one in jadeite, a solid celadon cut thicker than the new one so smooth in her other hand. She put the light green star back in the bag and lay the watercolor in its stead on the table's upper right corner nearest her head when she was in bed.

They had to wait until afternoon Christmas Day for Maria and her family to arrive because Jimmy now celebrated the morning at home. Selene had stayed over so there were four adults wandering the house aimlessly in their pajamas, then in their clothes, waiting, unsettled, for the focusing joy of a child.

Calyce kept busy preparing dinner and still demurring Selene's help, which Selene reported privately to Damion, who then made his own circuit into the kitchen to press his mother to let her "do something, anything. She's driving me insane."

"Why not call your parents, dear?" Calyce suggested to her. "Where do they live?"

"Minnesota."

Effie remained stationed in the living room near the tree, which sparkled with a thousand lights, or so it seemed to Calyce, who had never before loaded so many on her fresh pine. So many strings had been used that Selene had had to buy a power strip. Funny, Calyce thought, she's not worried about overload.

Selene had bought new ornaments too, which hung from the branch tips like brightly painted fingernails. Her "thing," she had said, was the solar system, so she had purchased glittered crescent moons in gaudy colors, but Calyce liked them. They reminded her of nighttime outside.

As they waited, and waited, Effie told Selene about the wise men figures posed near the barnlike crèche, which Calyce had set up at the base of the tree because she had no fireplace or mantel.

Effie told Selene to pick up the kneeling wise man. "See the beard? See where it's been chewed off at the bottom? That was Calyce. She used to like the taste of the plaster. That means more to me than all of it, and that's why I gave the whole crèche to her when her father died, rather than to Simon or Nina."

Calyce stole away to check her email. In her room, inhaling alone for a moment, she saw there was nothing from Belinda or anyone in the English Department. No one anywhere for that matter wishing her a Merry Christmas.

Nina called long-distance but wanted Calyce to pass the phone to their mother, telling Calyce that she still didn't have much service. Or battery.

Simon too phoned for a minute, promising his mother he would see her "very soon." He had nothing but stiff courtesies for Calyce.

As Christmas day dragged and they exhausted conversation, Calyce announced after calling Maria that they were going to open presents anyway, since Jimmy had been delayed by a nap. They gathered awkwardly in the small living room to assess who was the younger of Damion and Selene. When it turned out to be Damion by four months, he was assigned present duty.

One of Calyce's wrapped gifts to her mother sat on the floor next to the tree rather than under it. When Damion slid it to Effie and she noisily opened it, Effie didn't look at Calyce but at Damion as soon as she realized it was a TV.

"I thought you'd put it in the guestroom, then take it home with you," Calyce told her. "This way, you won't have to spend all your time with me here in the living room."

To Damion, Calyce gave an envelope with a note in it that said she was forgiving $250 of his debt to her.

To her, Damion gave not one but two envelopes. In the first he had slid two one-hundred-dollar bills, which he explained wasn't payment but extra money for her to spend any way she wanted. The second he said to open when she was alone.

"Now it's my turn," Selene said from her spot on the carpet near Damion. Her gift to him, she said with a smile, they had already shared privately that morning.

"It's not what you're thinking," Damion said to Calyce.

Selene handed a little gift bag to Calyce with white tissue paper sticking above the top edge, where the young woman had failed to remove the clear plastic drugstore hang-hook. In the bag was the printout of an order for three established plants of Showy Evening Primrose, which Selene then enthusiastically explained were for Calyce's front yard, where she had "no flowers yet." They would arrive in the spring.

Calyce thanked her, then gave her in turn a sterling silver bracelet with manufactured opals glinting blue and green like the earth seen from space.

"But you've already given me Damion," Selene said as she hugged her, which Calyce found awkward.

The two boxes for Effie from Simon and Nina jointly were a white terrycloth bathrobe and matching white slippers. "They're thinking ahead," Effie observed before giving Calyce her Harry & David and Damion his gifts from Nordstrom's.

To Selene Effie gave a bottle of Night Jasmine perfume, telling her, "Damion says you like this."

All the gifts were opened except the last one kept out of sight from Calyce in the powder room. Damion and Effie together made a big show of telling her to close her eyes, getting up to drag it out together.

"It's from me," Effie said. "Look!"

It was a large thin brown cardboard box, unwrapped, with black lettering below a picture of a large flat-screen TV.

"It's for your bedroom!" Her mother clapped like a child. "It'll fit on the whole wall so we can watch up there together on your bed. We won't have to come down. I know you gave me that little TV to take back with me, but I'd have to watch it alone in the guestroom. This is so much more sociable, don't you think?"

A well-dressed, beautifully spoken young man from Charleston with equatorial skin, Greg had fallen hard for high-cheekboned Maria, who had received in the gene pool the most beautiful parts of Calyce and Dorothy-Dandridge Effie.

Maria in turn had been so intrigued by the unfamiliarity of him and his sophisticated background that she was soon willing to give the urbane man a hand in her future. She had volunteered so enthusiastically in fact that Calyce had had difficulty persuading her to wait until after she graduated to marry.

Jimmy had followed a year after the small ceremony they both had wanted and Calyce had insisted on paying for. They had been married for nearly four years, long enough for them to know that the Georgetown School of Foreign Service master's program was the first step in Greg's professional calling.

His family had some money, enough so he didn't have to work while going to school, which to Calyce made him wealthy. She had met his people briefly before the wedding. They had been besotted with her "lovely Maria," who was swooningly happy. Her daughter had been right – Greg was a good husband and a doting father.

Jimmy's parents released him to play after Christmas dinner as the adults remained at the table. Calyce refilled their coffee cups before telling them that her becoming English Department Head was no longer a certainty.

Damion shrugged. "Why do you care so much?"

"But Mom, it's your turn," Maria protested.

Calyce took Damion's question seriously, sipping before she answered. "I care because I've earned it, and we've never had a person of color run the department in the forty years of the school. You can't just talk about equality. You have to do it. The school's finally got a black Vice Principal. It's time for that to happen in English too, particularly given the extraordinary black presence in literature. It's one thing to read about it. It's another to take action and promote deserving blacks into positions of power."

Effie said, "Over whites?"

"Over everybody. Otherwise, it's just an abstraction."

At the table still, Damion expounded with one arm over the back of Selene's chair. He explained expansively to the group that things were different now, far different for his generation than for his mother's.

"It's much more difficult to find a job," he told Effie. "Greg here has even had to go back to school."

Greg started to speak but Damion held up a hand. "We were born in the AIDS epidemic and became aware on Nine-Eleven. I was thirteen, in middle school. And then I graduated from college in the middle of the worst recession our country has seen since the Great Depression. No wonder we can't find jobs."

Greg said, "But I –"

"You've been out of college for years," Maria interrupted.

"We're only just now making a recovery," Damion continued as if she had not spoken. "But I have some good news. Yesterday I had a phone interview and I've got a follow-up face-to-face after the first of the year with this guy who's opening a new club in downtown D.C."

Calyce jumped in. "Is that who John DeGroot told you to call?"

"Mom, this is *good* news. He's a big deal. Not some contact of some teacher at your high school."

In the bathroom upstairs Calyce opened the second envelope Damion had given her. It contained a handwritten note saying that he was paying not only all his December bills but a double payment toward his loan balance. In the envelope was a thousand dollars.

He had given her twelve hundred in a single day.

At the bottom of the note, he had written –

The Courvoisier works. Merry Christmas.

She and Maria cleaned up while Effie and her "three men"

talked in the living room. Damion and Greg had ferried in all the dishes. Greg had also loaded the tablecloth into Calyce's washing machine along with the soiled damask napkins.

As they tidied, Maria suddenly hugged her mother.

After a moment, when she didn't let go, Calyce patted her arm awkwardly. "What's this?"

Her daughter whispered, "You must be so worried about Grandma. Please, please don't ever have this happen to you."

Calyce was half-awake still in the middle of that night. When she finally gave up and got up, she slammed her toe into the huge TV box Damion had hauled upstairs and slid between her bed and her bathroom.

The pages of the short stories on her nightstand required too much brainwork, so she absent-mindedly checked her email, which she hadn't since early afternoon. Four new ones had appeared in her school inbox, two from seniors proposing even more stories and a third from Amita reminding her of Amita's upcoming New Year's Eve party.

The fourth had come in at nearly midnight from Lee, the high school's principal, who had apparently found herself alone too as Christmas night had turned into the 26th.

I'm scheduling the family orientation meeting for our Quest trip to Zion in May. Are you coming to Utah this year? Please let me know so I can include you on the email list and get you the meeting date.

In Calyce's personal inbox was an automated email from Effie's surgeon's office reminding them of Effie's appointment the Tuesday after the New Year.

Two days later Calyce stood with Effie, Damion, and Selene in her kitchen before an array on her counter of open containers that held the leftovers of leftovers they had already attacked for lunch.

"I can make turkey tetrazzini," Calyce offered. "I bought linguine and mushrooms."

"Let's go out," Effie said. "Damion wants sushi. And there's a movie he wants to see that starts at 7:20."

But when Effie told them which movie, Selene reacted. She was suddenly irate.

"You just *decided* that?" she snapped at Damion.

"I thought you'd want to see it," he answered.

"He obviously thought you'd like it," Effie said at the same time. The two of them were a chorus.

"You can't just do that," Selene told him. "You have to consider me."

"I did."

He was mad now too.

"What you did was decide that *you* wanted to see it. You've been talking about that movie non-stop since we got here, and you know I don't like car movies."

As Calyce and Effie stared, Selene went on. "You keep doing this and I keep telling you, that to find out what *I* want you have to actually ask me. And then you have to actually listen."

Calyce had never heard anything like this. Certainly, no such statement had ever been directed at her son.

On the way to the car, Calyce said to Damion quietly, "Now

that Christmas is over, I want you to follow up with John's friend about that interview."

He was suddenly as angry as Selene had just been. "I thought you'd be happy about this club thing, but no, there's no pleasing you, is there, Mom?"

January

The powers that be always scheduled the school's Empowerment Assembly for the first week after Winter Break, since Administration knew that no new teaching happened during the short interval before school-wide midterms the next week. Only review days occurred as teachers recapped the entire first semester's material, so two hours of devoted LGBT celebration were always calendared for the morning of the third day back at school. Not the first or the second, but the day by which Administration figured everyone would have reliably returned.

Calyce stuck her head into the high school office on the first floor near the front entrance. The small offices inside were arrayed along an outside wall with windows looking out to the plastic green playing field and the pool building. She searched for Belinda's new space and found it, but her friend wasn't there.

Calyce recognized a few things Belinda had moved in from her desk in the History faculty office upstairs, but they were a tiny portion of what Calyce was now seeing. Over Break, Belinda had covered every wall and surface with personal items that didn't look new but likely brought from home, a home Calyce had never visited.

Three large black-framed original charcoal drawings of young women's faces and headpieces made a triptych on the door wall. In a far corner, by the glass, a herd of tall painted wooden giraffes clustered with their thin heads looming over the nearest of the two guest chairs. One of the animals was six feet tall. On both chairs were brown, white, black, and tan geometric mud cloth lumbar pillows. They looked new, and they had been carefully placed, exactly centered against the school-issued beige chairs' woven back cushions.

On the way out, Calyce was nearly run over by Lee, who had shot out distractedly from her corner office next to Belinda's. The high school principal stopped, though, when she registered it was Calyce, as Calyce realized she hadn't yet replied to Lee's email.

Calyce told her quickly, "I don't think I can come to Utah this year. I've got a freshman English class and there's no one to substitute. It's all we can do to cover for John."

Lee's face flashed irritation. "I've already scheduled the orientation dinner for next week. I had to when I didn't hear from you. Can you at least come talk to the parents about the trip?"

"Yes," Calyce said. "Yes of course."

Across the hall a loud crowd had already gathered in the auditorium. Other kids and teachers, both newly coming out and long-timers, had lined up already in a long queue that stretched the length of the short hall outside and nearly completely up the stairs to the first level of classrooms. Calyce spotted Dan midway up, talking with the AP Statistics teacher.

Calyce stopped walking. Thinking, she cocked her head at Dan but recovered an instant before he saw her and waved, having fun.

She smiled a quick smile and hurried into the auditorium, where she found a seat on the stair-step of the second row. A minute later, a sixty-ish white male Latin teacher sat near her but at arm's-length, being careful to keep a space vacant between them.

When neither spoke, he finally said, "You'd think we wouldn't need these assemblies anymore, what with gay marriage having been decided. We're all kumbaya."

Calyce waited a beat, then had to say to him, "Have you ever heard of *Loving v. Virginia*?"

"No." The man was wary, knowing her.

"It was the Supreme Court case that struck down the miscegenation laws that forbad blacks and whites to intermarry. 1967. You think that eliminated race discrimination?"

She turned to see Lee enter with Belinda, who took a seat at the front. At the last moment, just as Lee was leaning in to speak into the podium's microphone, John DeGroot sneaked in sideways, spied Calyce in her solitary vortex, and hopped the two steps to where she was. The Latin teacher scooted even farther away.

"Damion never called," DeGroot whispered. "My sister's brother-in-law called me last night."

"He's family? You didn't say that."

"Distant, but yeah. It's embarrassing. What happened?"

"How's your mother?"

Roger had slipped in beside Calyce as they all exited the auditorium. Calyce was scanning for Belinda, hoping to catch her.

He asked, "When's her surgery?"

"It's on MLK Day, the Monday of the long weekend. Belinda!"

"Can I do anything to help?"

"Darn, she got away."

She said to her students, "You've really never heard of Rock Hudson?"

She then told them about the midterm, though only a couple of them took notes. They were seniors, they had just submitted their regular-decision college applications by the January 1 deadline, and they no longer cared about high school. All they had to do was maintain a second-semester transcript sufficient not to get their offer retracted at year-end from whatever university they accepted by spring. And it would be a short term, too, because all the seniors vacated the high school in May for a month for their senior "quests," which someone in Administration had dreamed up years before to eliminate the problem of lingering, insouciant, rowdy near-graduates causing chaos, or property damage.

Calyce had only four months more with her senior creative writing class.

"For the midterm I'm going to give you three short stories," she told them. "You'll have to read them, then write your own, on the same theme, in the time allotted."

"What theme?" a boy asked. He was the only student paying attention. The others were talking and she couldn't get them to stop.

"It'll be obvious from the titles but you can prepare if you want by reading every short story Bessie Head has written, and Ray Bradbury, and Katherine Mansfield."

"Aw, come on," he said.

"And this time I'm writing one too. I'll distribute it later in the month and we'll critique it together. It'll be your chance to get even with me."

That night before she went to bed, Calyce in her nightgown and robe walked a clothes basket full of clean wash down to Damion's door, in front of which sat one of her big ceramic serving bowls with remains of lettuce and creamy salad dressing, along with a fork and a soiled paper napkin.

She knocked. "Damion?"

"He's not here," Selene called from within. "He won't be back until after closing."

"I'll leave these things here," Calyce said to the door. "And I've got mail for him."

She retrieved a handful of bills from under the clean laundry and slid them beneath the door along with a note she had written.

Calyce, Belinda's email said, **I'm sorry but you can't leave notes on my chair anymore.**

They might get lost. I'm also sorry that I'm so busy when you've come by, but I have a crazy tight schedule now. My first 15 minutes free is next Tuesday at 9:15. Let me know if that works.

Belinda, Calyce wrote back, **let's do dinner instead. You've never seen my house. Friday the 12th?**

Calyce entered the lunchroom and stood, her insulated fabric lunchbox in her hand. The room was noisy and banging with movement and color, the crash of voices, the screech of chairs and the clinking, popping, scratching of plastic containers, elbows, and opening soda cans. She also heard the crinkling of potato chip bags and the ringing of some real silverware somewhere above the scraping sound of plastic knives and forks. She smelled microwaved, cheesy food.

The room was full, which meant to Calyce not that every chair was taken but that every table had at least one occupant, and no one, not a single person, had raised their chins in greeting or flapped their hands to invite her over.

She registered a set of five English teachers with just one empty chair at their table. They were all looking at her mid-bite in that first moment of recognition before politesse kicks in.

Calyce turned and took herself and her lunch out of the room, passing Dan coming in from the hallway. He invited her to sit with them, pointing to that same table, but she declined. He did it again, saying "Seriously," but once more she said no, this time adding that she had decided to take a walk, the weather was so nice.

"It's forty degrees outside," he said.

"But better than yesterday. I've been getting a lot of exercise lately, and now I want to do it during the school day too."

He said to her back, "I had no idea you were such an avid walker."

"What the hell is this?" Damion demanded as he waved the note she had written.

Selene spotted the fat grocery bags Calyce had just parked on the kitchen counter. "What did you get?" she asked.

Calyce told Damion, "You never called him."

"You think I need a note from Mommy slipped under my door to remind me?"

Selene slid behind Calyce to inspect the bags.

"Don't you embarrass me like that again," Damion told her.

Calyce hesitated because of Selene, but then said, "You embarrassed *me*. John was only trying to do you a favor. You promised me repeatedly and you didn't do it."

They had all left him, his angry sons and daughters, circling and spinning around him and away. He was alone now, abandoned on the pointed mountaintop with its ice-blue sky above and no air, no breeze, no kissing of his face anymore by his loving children. Aeolus, immortal, the keeper of the Four Winds, had no usefulness now that they had swirled themselves out beyond his realm, his grasp and embrace. If they returned, if they ever did, they would no longer be controlled.

Love to! Belinda texted as Calyce was writing her piece for the class. **But promise, no work discussion. Purely social.**

"And here's the money for the bills. You don't have to slip those under my door, either."

Damion had stomped back up loudly an hour later, past an astonished Effie in the living room with Selene right behind him so closely it looked like he was hauling a trailer.

Furious, he flung the cash at Calyce where she sat at the dining table. They were all small bills, ones and fives, a flock of them that took flight as he jerked his hand, all shooting into the air between them, then riffling to the polished tabletop. They reflected as multiples in the sheen.

"Fuck her!" Calyce heard Damion say to Selene downstairs a moment later as he slammed the door to his room and left Calyce with cash littered on her. Ones had landed even in her lap and on her arm. A five had swung as it descended, alighting on her keyboard. She stared, stunned, at the money.

She plucked bills from her arm, from her lap and her computer, laying them beside her. She replaced her fingers reflexively on the home row of her keyboard ready for the next staccato in her story about Aeolus, but nothing came. She stared at the screen but didn't see it, nor did she hear her mother glide toward her.

Effie began picking up the money with her talon fingers. She piled the bills neatly in her palm as she bobbed quietly around the table, making as little noise as she could, then went into the kitchen to put the stack somewhere Calyce wouldn't see it.

She returned and stood near her daughter but didn't touch her. When Calyce didn't move, Effie went to the other side of the table and pulled out a chair, then sat and waited.

After a moment, Effie finally spoke, her voice soft and loving. "I'm proud of you."

Calyce didn't answer.

"I had no idea," Effie said. "Does he do that a lot?"

Calyce nodded.

Effie tried to make a joke of it. "At least he's got the money." But then, "He's always nice to me. Do you think it's her?"

Calyce looked up then, suddenly dependent on every word. "It's not me? I'm not the cause of this?"

Effie laid her arm on the table, stretching it across but not quite reaching Calyce, then said kindly, so kindly, "Sometimes our children get mad at us and they don't give a reason. Some-times they even hate us and won't say why."

One of the mothers had offered her mullioned home for the meeting, and three other parents had brought food, so by the time Lee stood to speak at the top of the inexact circle of chairs arranged against the walls of the red-lacquered Georgetown din-ing room, the picked-clean Crate & Barrel platters bore nothing but large ornate service forks, which, Calyce noticed, were ster-ling silver and a hundred years old. The meal had been good, that usual private-school combination of some light protein with out-of-season fresh vegetables sprinkled with herbs and two dif-ferent salads of leafy greens followed by chocolate chip cookies for the teenagers, who eyed each other as they each sat tethered to their assigned parent(s) and tried to act as though mom/dad hadn't come.

One of the girls was in Calyce's writing class, and they smiled fleetingly at each other. The girl's father even made small talk at Calyce across the expanse of room, as Calyce sat tightly between two other families, all of them balancing their plates on their laps with their elbows pinned.

Lee spoke at length about the logistics and paperwork in-volved in the upcoming senior Quest trip to Zion and Bryce she led every year in May. An avid outdoorswoman, she was in her mid-thirties, fit and taut in a menswear-tailored white dress shirt she had tucked into her black trousers. Beautiful in a sun-kissed California way, Lee had tamed her long, thick blonde hair into a low ponytail. As the evening wore on, though, and she played with it near her ears as she always did, wisps escaped and the horsetail loosened.

Lee began to describe the long, difficult climb up Angels Landing, a very high rocky promontory connected by the thinnest edge to the west side of a narrowing canyon formed by the often-flash-flooded Virgin River. The exposed precipitous scramble to the top risked death, for a fall would be straight down 1,500 feet.

"People die," Lee said. "One woman was an experienced hiker there with her family and she just stumbled and fell. You don't fall and live unless you happen to fall into a chink, but that's just luck, and even then, you'd have to be rescued, probably by helicopter. That's why the school requires each family to sign a complete release in order to do this. We can't be liable."

"The woman who died, how old was she?" a father asked. His son had his arms crossed and was sunk down so low that his toes couldn't be seen under the dining table.

"Mid-fifties, I think," Lee told him.

"That's too old," he said. "You're not fit anymore and you can't recover if you lose your balance."

Lee turned to Calyce. "Do you think it's too hard?"

Cornered, Calyce answered quietly. "I didn't make it. I tried, but I couldn't get up that first hill. I think there's some magic to it, but the kids didn't have any trouble."

The same father turned to his sprawling son, "See? What did I tell you? Twenty years younger and she would have made it, no problem."

Calyce walked with Lee to Lee's car. It didn't snow much in the city because of the dense population, which threw off heat, and because of its location on a tidal plain, but D.C. could be knife-cold. It was one of those frozen nights.

"So I have to get someone else to go," Lee was saying to Calyce. "I wish you'd said something earlier than a few days ago. If you'd told me over Break I could have had your replacement lined up to come tonight instead of you."

For this midterm, three short stories follow: *The Wind and a Boy* by Bessie Head, *The Wind* by Ray Bradbury, and *The Wind Blows* by Katherine Mansfield. 1) Write a short essay about what each of these stories reveals about its writer, so that none could have been written by either of the others; and 2) write a piece of original flash fiction, totaling no more than 300 words, about the wind, without using the wind as that tired metaphor for change.

Effie was watching the big new TV upstairs in Calyce's room when Damion came into the kitchen alone searching for his mother, who stood chopping at the counter with her back to him. She recognized his footstep of course but didn't turn, so what he saw was her profile, a willowy, handsome woman with a long neck curved over green peppers. Her hair was still perfectly in place even at the end of the workday, and she still wore her black skirt and purple silky long-sleeved top, but her large feet for the first time stood bare on the linoleum. The nails had no polish, and the toes were knuckled and bent like bare roots.

"Your feet aren't cold?" he said. "It's January."

She didn't respond.

He said, "I'm sorry about the other night. I'm just so worried about this job stuff. I've been out of school so long with nothing to show for it. This interview today with DeGroot's guy didn't go well and I think it was my fault. I didn't have enough on my resumé and the guy was an asshole, frankly. I'm sorry, but he was. He gave me five minutes then told me to leave."

Calyce took that next Friday off to ferry her mother to and from Georgetown Hospital. The surgeon had ordered blood tests and a chest x-ray, as well as cardiac catheterization, which frightened Calyce, who was suddenly sharply aware of Effie's imminent life-or-death surgery. A tube threaded up Effie's artery to her heart from her leg seemed monumental to Calyce, and yet it was termed a "routine" pre-op procedure. The idea of cutting into a heart was impossible to entertain.

The appointment that day with the surgeon had driven it home, for he had mentioned the need for Effie's end-of-life wishes, in writing, so if anything happened, though it was statistically unlikely, the "care team" would have her instructions.

"Let me go," her mother told them. "Just let me go. Give my organs to whoever needs them."

Belinda came for dinner right on time, bringing a bottle of white wine to accompany the baked flounder Calyce had already told her they were having.

"You know I don't drink," Calyce said at the front door when she saw the bottle.

"But I do." Belinda smiled. "I thought you hated seafood."

"My mother loves it, but I don't know if she'll eat. She's nearly asleep."

Damion's door opened and Selene came out on her way to class. She nodded courteously when Calyce introduced her.

"She's pretty," Belinda said when she was gone. "Is that Damion's room?"

"Do you want to see it?"

Calyce felt for the extra key above the doorframe.

As soon as they entered, Belinda said, "You always say *room*. I thought it was a kid's room but this is an entire apartment except a kitchen. He's even got a fridge."

In his bedroom she looked out his sliding glass door. "Is that a gas grill with that table and chairs?"

Calyce flipped on the outside light. She had never seen any of the setup before, and it was expensive. "He must have just bought all that."

∧∧∧

At dinner Calyce couldn't avoid the topic of the English Department's school-wide consolidation. She couldn't help herself. Yes, Belinda admitted reluctantly, she had known it was happening, and yes, she had known before John DeGroot.

Calyce asked casually then for Belinda's endorsement, assuming it was a given. Her friend, though, repositioned the orb of the wine glass between her fingers. She cupped it and swirled. The conversation became still.

"I can't," Belinda said.

"Why not? A black woman in management who endorses me will help."

"That's exactly the problem. It'll look like collusion, and politically it's a bad idea, especially as my first official act. I can't play favorites."

Calyce put her fork down. "He's at the middle school. He has nothing to do with your being the high school Vice Principal."

"But I can't cause friction between the two campuses."

"I campaigned for you!"

"It was Dan who went all over the school. He talked to everyone."

"I told him to."

"But he's the one who did it. He's campaigning for you too. Do you know that?"

The rest of the meal was so uncomfortable that neither woman could find a topic on which to light. Belinda was back at Calyce's front door less than an hour later, when she asked suddenly, "Have you been to the middle and lower school campus to talk to the English teachers there?"

"It would look like begging," Calyce said stiffly.

"Well, you need to do something. You know there are more of them there than at the high school?"

The next Monday morning Calyce was coughing again. The sharp bite in her throat had returned. She fought it, blast-coughing repeatedly as she walked to her classroom but even the air she inhaled seemed to have an acrid taste.

"Calyce!" Roger called after her.

She had to turn, hand to mouth. "What?" she said weakly.

"Lee talked to me about my doing Zion. Are you alright?"

"I'm fine … You're the right choice … It should have been you all along."

She turned but he persisted. "How's your mom?"

She whirled around angrily. "She's *fine*, now may I please go teach my class?"

To: **All** English teachers HS MS LS
From: Calyce Tate, Interim Head H.S.

I thought it would be helpful if we all met to discuss where the department is as a whole, what challenges it faces, and how best to work as one to create an experience for our students that moves seamlessly from the necessary rudiments of the lower and middle schools to the advanced curriculum of the high school. I am particularly concerned that we eliminate overlap. I've arranged for us all to use the second-floor conference room at the high school next Friday afternoon, starting at 4 p.m. Come with ideas! Your presence is expected, so no need to RSVP.

She looked for Roger at lunch so she could apologize, but he wasn't in the faculty lunch room.

She began a systematic search that eventually led her to a far stairwell that mounted one whole wall of the tall building. Through the punched windows that rose diagonally with the stairs, she located him at the distant end of the playing field, walking alone bundled up, so she retrieved her coat to head outside.

She approached him with her cold hands deep in her pockets. He had seen her coming across the plastic turf and had stopped, waiting, but he hadn't taken a step toward her.

"What are you doing out here?" she asked.

"Why do you care?"

This was going to be an honest conversation.

"I'm sorry," she said. "I'm sorry I was so rude."

He said nothing.

"You were just being kind," she said. "I can be so difficult sometimes. I know that."

"And obtuse," he said.

"What?"

"Do you know how long I've been interested in you?"

"*Me?*"

He snorted and his breath leapt in white puffs. "I thought I was obvious. Everyone else saw it but not you. Will you go out to dinner with me?"

She looked at him. He was well-built and kind and smart, with astonishing dove gray eyes and a natural glow that was for that minute because of her.

"No," she said softly. "I won't."

"Your mother? Too soon? Too much on your mind?"

Yes, this was going to be an honest conversation.

"No, it's not my mom."

But though she tried, that was all she could bring herself to say to him.

Later that day, Calyce and DeGroot sat at their respective desks in the faculty office, alone together in a rare suspension of the flux of English-teacher traffic. She had been speaking to him about Damion's interview. He had swung toward her on his swivel chair when she had asked uncomfortably whether he had any other leads.

"Maybe something less … advanced," she said. "More entry-level."

DeGroot crossed one leg over the other. He scanned the doorway and the corridor beyond. Knowing him, Calyce tensed.

He said, "I wasn't going to say anything, but it sounds like you don't know what happened. Bill says your son showed up an hour late and had nothing to say. He hadn't done any research, so he had no idea what the company did or what Bill's job was. He also came right out and said he didn't know what position he was interviewing for, even though the job was posted on the website. Bill had to get him a job description, but even then, Damion couldn't match any of it to his resumé, so Bill had to do it for him line by line. He wasn't prepared and it seemed to Bill that he had no interest. Bill says he was wasting his time. It didn't last long. Bill ended it."

Her chest was pounding so hard the adrenaline rush reached her voice and her hands, a clashing of drums that made her fingers shake so much she had to clasp them.

"I'm sorry. John, I'm so sorry. I didn't know."

That Friday at 4 p.m., the high school's second-floor conference room was deserted except for herself, DeGroot and Dan, who all sat at the same table and waited as Calyce faced the doorway, ready to greet everyone else who entered, planning to welcome them as if she had invited them to her home.

But by 4:15 no one else had walked in.

At 4:30, DeGroot said he had to leave.

"Maybe it's the weekend," Dan said compassionately as the two men packed up. "Maybe you should reschedule your meeting for an afternoon that's not a Friday."

Simon had finally come two days later, late the Sunday night before Effie's surgery on Monday. Still in his airline jacket with sleeve stripes like he was in the Navy, he had blown through the door into his mother's arms without saying a word first to Calyce. Trim, large-handed Simon also hugged his nephew, who held him while they exchanged the man-thumping and seal-barking of males who adore each other but interact only occasionally.

"The bed's made downstairs," Damion told him. "I'm sleeping at Selene's."

Calyce said, "But you're still coming to the hospital in the morning, aren't you?"

Simon and Damion exchanged a look, then Simon smirked as he said, "You can't stop yourself, can you? We're both fully capable of being where we need to be when we need to be there. Aren't we, Damion?"

Damion said, "We sure are."

"I'll be fine," Effie said to her granddaughter Maria on the phone. "You've got a long day tomorrow too. You need to take care of your mother."

"I'm fine!" Calyce called from the kitchen so Maria could hear her. "I'll see you tomorrow at the hospital."

Late that night Effie had a long, private conversation with Simon that didn't include Calyce. She knew because, when Simon helped their mother up the stairs, he closed the guestroom door firmly behind them.

When they were all finally tucked in, lights out and dishes put away, the house was silent. Two stories above Simon downstairs in Damion's room, Calyce stood facing herself in her bathroom mirror. Still fully dressed, she spoke softly to her own image.

"I *am* scared, Maria. I'm so scared she won't wake up."

Effie, Calyce, Simon, Damion, and Maria all waited very early the next morning in a spare hospital room. In just a few minutes an orderly would come in to wheel Effie in her truncated bed down the hall into surgery in the adjacent wing through double steel doors that opened on a breathless piston. Calyce could hear them working loudly from her post at the foot of her mother's pulled-taut linens.

They were all making ridiculous small talk as Simon ignored his buzzing phone and Damion failed to resist his, which he checked twice in three minutes. The texts were from Selene, who was training at her new job and couldn't get away.

Around them, nurses hummed with unexplained but meaningful activity. One thing Calyce recognized, because the surgeon had warned them, was the monitoring of Effie's blood sugar.

The nurses' tolerant "ma'am's" had elongated with their frustration at Calyce's relentless questioning. A single word at 7 a.m., "ma'am" had become a two-syllable diphthong by 7:20.

But then it was time. One of the family's repeating topics of conversation had been Nina's imminent arrival, but she still wasn't there despite having texted Simon that her taxi was nearing. The orderly had stuck his head in to say he'd be "right back" to roll Effie away. They gathered around her, both men with their hands clasped as both women nosed their hands around the perimeter of the old woman uselessly, nervously shoving in her covers. Effie assured them all, joining eyes with each one in turn, that she was excellent. Positive and hopeful. This was the right thing to do.

Nina burst in, breathless and trailing a gauze scarf she had wrapped over the top of her head and x'd in front of her throat to throw over the back of her shoulders. She was tall like Calyce but alive with a vital energy that spun in her wake and startled Damion and Maria, who hadn't seen her in years and didn't remember her explosive impact. She was a diva who didn't know it, a Hollywood star who had never spoken to a camera, whose presence commanded all the air in a room without being aware of it.

She elbowed her way to the bedside. No one minded; they simply moved over. She kissed her mother and held her hands, but like Calyce, she maintained a certain distance from Effie, a reserve unshattered even by the circumstances, although Nina was warm enough. Effie was overwhelmed at seeing her "girl," and at them all being there with her in that room in that moment, whatever the reason.

The orderly returned and began packing Effie up. Calyce directed him, demanding that he be gentle.

Nina said to her, "Let the man do his job."

He strained to turn the bed toward the doorway, making one of the wheels squeak.

Effie looked at Calyce and said, "I want you to promise –"

The bed banged around the narrow corner as the orderly swung it like a line of shopping carts.

"What Mom?"

" – that if I die you'll stop relaxing your hair. That stuff will give you cancer."

Calyce followed them out, watching the top of Effie's head and her veined hand waving goodbye above it as she was wheeled away from them.

"But I like my hair!" Calyce called after her.

Damion had to leave immediately for something, he said, so he peeled off, saying that he and Selene would see them later at home when it was over. Calyce was to text him if anything happened.

Simon, Nina, Calyce, and Maria settled in for the long wait, which the surgeon had warned would be at least five hours. The surgical waiting room for families was a very large perfect square with chairs arranged as in a church, in rows all facing the same direction with a wide aisle running between them from the entrance to an unadorned wall bathed in a yellow spotlight illuminating nothing. The stackable chairs had shiny chrome legs and curved seats with thin fabric cushions in an odd ochre color that looked to Calyce like old vomit. They also had no arms, so for the next many hours, they could all either sit or stand, but there would be no leaning.

Two other families were also there that morning, but the room was so cavernous they sat far away and could barely be heard despite their many generations and large numbers. Calyce's group had merely four.

When Calyce led her daughter and her two siblings in and chose all their seats for them, she retained for herself a sightline to the nurses' station, angling a chair so she could watch it head-on. She put her things at her feet and smoothed her skirt as Nina kept talking about the trip she had just taken.

The two nurses wore bleached mint. They had similarly bobbed hair, curled under, stiff as helmets under the pin lights of the low ceiling.

While Nina told her story, Calyce opened her laptop and opened her document.

They had all left him, his angry sons and daughters, circling in their rage and spinning away from him. He was alone, abandoned with his empty sack on his lush pinnacle with no air, no breeze, no kissing of his face anymore by his sweeping progeny. Aeolus, immortal, the keeper of the Four Winds, had no usefulness now that they had swirled themselves beyond his realm and grasp and embrace. If they returned, but they wouldn't, but if they ever did, they would no longer be controlled.

What does a man do when he has just one definition, and he no longer keeps, and he has chased away the flock for which he was shepherd? He was nothing now but husband, but she too had left him for a man from the sea who drank her on a far shore.

Aeolus reached to the mossy stone to take the empty leather in his huge hands. He opened it and bent his sumptuously curled head to stare deep into the dark inside but heard nothing, not the moan of the slightest wind.

Because of his own disregard, he had simply given them away without ever once inquiring of them what their wishes were. Docile children, they had done what he had directed, but as they had twisted in that fetid space they had grown into adult gales fueled by his betrayal, so their return had been only to taunt him before they hurricaned away, taking all the water in the sky along with them.

And so it was that, because of him, the deserts of the Southwest came. The hot sun unshielded baked the green from the rocks and the spongy grass from the earth, leaving a father forever on a high gritty stone so dry it couldn't cry either.

"Will you stop bothering them?" Nina said to Calyce two hours later when she returned yet again from pressing the nurses. "They'll let us know when they hear."

Simon was once again idling on his phone. Maria was paging through a magazine. Calyce got up and grabbed her own coat. "I've seen everything there is to see in here. I'll be right outside, through those doors there."

Nina said, "I'll go with you. Simon, come get us if there's news."

They exited near the ambulance bay in front of the emergency entrance. Heavy snow had begun to fall in flat, floating dish flakes, the kind that announce they won't be sticking. In the cold the two sisters stood under the ER's overhang. It was the first time they had been alone in ten years. Calyce had seen the gray threading in her sister's coiled braid, mercury silver at the base but dark at the ends. She knew Nina, who noticed everything too, had seen the bootblack uniformity of her own.

They heard an ambulance blare on its approach.

Nina said, her shoulders hunched and freezing near her earlobes, "A lot different from Angels Landing, I bet."

Calyce turned. "We can talk about it now? In there you told me you'd had enough of Zion."

"I'm just trying to make conversation."

"Why couldn't you have taken care of Mom in Florida so she didn't have to come up here for this?"

"Oh come on. You like it this way. You get to be in charge."

Flashing red, the ambulance pulled in. The back doors opened to a shiver of activity the two sisters watched silently.

Nina said after a minute, "You need to go earlier in the year. May's too hot already."

"You've been there?"

They watched the rolling gurney being propelled by two paramedics toward the entrance. "No, it's just obvious. It's the desert."

"It doesn't matter," Calyce said. "I'm too old now anyway. I'd never get up to the top."

A pause, a beat. The falling snow crinkled like cellophane on the sidewalk beyond the overhang as they watched the automatic ER doors close again.

Calyce said, "One of the teachers asked me out last week but I said no."

Nina turned to her. "Why?"

Calyce took a deep breath. "He's white."

Just then Maria hurried out the same side door they had used. She had left her coat inside so her bare fingers were wedged into her armpits.

Maria said the nurses had called Simon over to say the operating room had called to report that surgery was "progressing."

"That's all?" Nina asked.

Maria refused to return to the warm. Calyce put an arm around her as another ambulance arrived with its klaxon blasting. The boxy red truck pulled up behind the still-open rear doors of the ambulance in front of it.

Maria said as she bounced, trying to keep herself from freezing, "I hate those things. Remember Dad? He was never the same after that fall off that ladder. I don't know why he didn't hire someone. It doesn't cost that much to have someone clean your gutters."

Maria turned to her Aunt Nina. "You didn't see him again after the divorce, but Dad never fully recovered. His balance was so bad he had to sit down to take off his shoes."

Inside again, Calyce sent an email to the high school English teachers only.

I'm sorry that most of you could not attend the recent departmental meeting, but I have prepared a paper questionnaire soliciting your views on how you think the Lower/Middle School could work more seamlessly and successfully with us. In order to maintain confidentiality, I will distribute the questionnaire to each of you by hand later this week. So this process is as effective as possible, please be entirely candid. Return them directly to me, please, by no later than Monday.

They had been told to wait there, at the nurses' station. The surgeon wanted to speak to them.

When he appeared he had removed his mask, which hung around his corded neck, but his small cadet blue beanie remained.

"She was more frail bone-wise than we'd hoped, so we had to use sternal plates to pull the breastbone together."

He explained that they weren't plates despite the name but X shapes like bicycle chain sunk into the bone on either side of the sternum after surgery, to pull the sides of the breastbone and the ribs together. Usually wire was used, and that is what they had planned, but once they had gotten in there, he said, put her on bypass, and performed what became an unexpectedly protracted coronary graft surgery and valve replacement, they had opted to take every possible precaution to minimize the chance of post-op infection of the long wound. They had had to consider her age, too, and her recently diagnosed diabetes.

"Unfortunately, and as you and I have discussed," he told Calyce, "she may also have some fuzziness mentally, and that could last several months. It happens with the elderly. But I want you to get her moving as soon as I authorize it. Get her back walking, especially once she gets home."

Maria called her husband and Calyce phoned Damion but had to leave a message. Simon punched the number for his wife. He was still on with Sandra when Calyce finished, so Calyce heard him confirm that he was indeed departing from Dulles airport at 10 a.m. the next morning for Denver, where his next flight assignment would begin.

"You're leaving Mom in less than twenty-four hours?" Calyce interrupted, but Simon ignored her until he had said goodbye lovingly and hung up.

"I was talking," he said.

"You're leaving?"

"So's Nina," Maria said. "She just told me."

"You are?" Calyce said to Nina.

"We're driving to the airport together," Nina said. "I'm leaving from Dulles too, so he's taking me."

When Nina walked into Calyce's kitchen that night, she saw

that Calyce was alone. Simon sat in the living room with Damion and Selene, all three of them with glasses of red wine. Damion was regaling his uncle as Selene sat tucked contentedly under her lover's arm.

"There's white too if you want it," Calyce said with her head down, working. She had rolled up her long sleeves rather than changing, to save time.

"Does Damion ever help you?" Nina asked.

Calyce didn't respond.

"You're not taking care of yourself. Your hands are ashy."

"No time." Calyce kept moving. "But at least I'm walking. I did three miles on Saturday. And my throat's better."

Nina poured herself a glass, then leaned against the counter. "So this is it. This is your life now. How's the job?"

Calyce shrugged. Nina lowered her voice. "Anyone besides this white guy?"

"No. Can you get the roaster pan out of the oven?"

A minute later Nina leaned out to confirm that the rest of the family was still happily planted in the living room as her older sister once again, as always, made them all dinner.

Nina took another swallow. She thought, then finally said, "I think we ought to do Angels Landing together. I can get you to the top. I've had years of hiking."

Calyce's hands stopped.

She fixed grateful eyes on her sister, who said, "Don't you get a spring vacation in April?"

Calyce didn't want her released but after ten days the hospital's "astounding patient" Effie met every one of the discharge criteria, including having climbed a full flight of stairs.

"She's chomping at the bit to get outside. And I'm confident she has excellent at-home support," the cardiologist said as he patted Calyce on the shoulder the next Thursday. "The plating should allow her to heal more quickly and with less pain. She's already breathing more easily. The mental cotton should pass once she's home and into a routine. Stay with her as much as possible so she regains her mental acuity. Try not to leave her alone."

Calyce slipped out of bed, into the short hall, and over to her mother's door, which was mostly closed but not entirely. A diffuse bluish glow outlined its edges. Calyce had asked Maria to bring one of the nightlights they used for little Jimmy, and Calyce had made sure it was reassuringly burning.

She felt the soft carpet under her bare toes as she pushed the door open, then sneaked in to see Effie sleeping and stood silently to listen. She heard the hiccupping snoring of her childhood and breathed in the sharp smell of medicaments. She said without realizing it a prayer of thanksgiving, which she sent to heaven with each of her mother's shallow exhalations.

Calyce stepped to the bed and carefully brought up the covers, moving Effie's feet inside the sheets with a mother's practiced hand. She waited once more, to see if she had awakened her, but, satisfied, soon moved to the doorway.

She had not left yet when her mother said groggily in the weak light, "Thank you."

"For what?" Calyce was whispering too for no reason.

And then, "I told them to go."

"Who?"

"Simon and Nina. They wanted to. I just gave them permission."

Rookie Amita sheepishly returned her completed questionnaire by the end of the very school day Calyce had distributed it. She lingered too, to talk, even apologizing for not being able "to make the meeting. I had something last-minute." She also answered eagerly Calyce's small-talk question about what had been going on while Calyce had been out for Effie's surgery. That was how Calyce learned that her cohorts had been streaming down to the lower and middle school campus across town, in upper Georgetown.

"He's so nice," Amita said. "I had never really spoken to Javier before, but Dan wanted to go, and Ashley too."

Amita's face darkened. "I think I should tell you the teachers down there aren't happy with how this questionnaire is worded. They've been exchanging emails. That's what Dan said. They've been copying him. I thought you'd want to know."

Calyce heard her mother calling as soon as she closed the front door. From the guestroom at the top of the house, Effie's fragile voice was keening for "Da-mi-on!"

Calyce raced up and rounded the corner of the kitchen, where she saw her son with his ear buds in, gazing mesmerized into the open refrigerator.

"Don't you hear that?" Calyce said, loud as a traffic cop.

"What?" He pulled one of them out, but Calyce had already left to run up the stairs.

That night, long after Damion had departed for the bar, Selene found Calyce in her bedroom reading the flash fiction pieces her class had submitted. Selene knocked softly, then entered the third-floor room for the first time. "I was wondering if you were going to the grocery store tomorrow."

"Probably. Why?"

Selene had a Vera Bradley cash wallet in her hand, the fabric white magnolias with yellow leaves on a black background. Selene flipped it open.

"Could you get us some more of that red curry paste we like? And Nutella?"

She pulled out a ten-dollar bill and handed it to Calyce. "This should cover it, along with the gas."

"Flash fiction, huh?" Dan said as he handed her own piece back to her. "This is good, very good. You wrote a myth, but do you think the class will remember the underlying story?"

Calyce speared a chunk of melon from her Tupperware. "They did the Odyssey in ninth grade. That was only three years ago."

He bit his sandwich. "Your writing isn't what I thought it would be. You're so, um, definitive that I would have thought you'd be more Ernest Hemingway."

"Declarative, you mean." But she smiled back.

As they cleaned up later, he said, "I've enjoyed this. We should do it again."

"I've enjoyed it too," she surprised herself by saying.

"Let me ask you," he said quietly. "Why did you do that questionnaire?"

"We're the leaders, aren't we, the teachers at the high school? The other campus is just a funnel."

Her mother had been post-discharge for six days. She professed to be "fine" but her mind wasn't clear all the time. She thought her charter boat captain was still alive, and she sometimes thought Simon was still young and single despite his having been married for twenty years. But she was getting better.

When Calyce got home that late afternoon, Effie was propped up in the living room on one of the loveseats with her bed pillow behind her back and her feet on one of the small ottomans. The little TV on the square corner table was on next to a glass half-filled with water but there was no food plate near her and none in the kitchen sink.

"Where's Damion?" Calyce asked.

"He went to the store but he hasn't come back yet. I think the visiting nurse came but I couldn't get downstairs fast enough. I tried, but she was gone when I finally got to the door."

"When did he leave?"

Effie didn't remember. Yes, he had given her her pills that morning, but no, she hadn't taken her noontime set yet. He had said he would give them to her when he got back.

Once Calyce had ministered to her mother, Calyce went upstairs to her bathroom. She shook with rage, her fingers electrified and her heart tocking as she tried to think.

She grabbed her leather satchel from her bed and returned to the bathroom, closed the door and locked it, then rummaged until she found her phone. She dialed his number, but he didn't answer until the third ring.

"Listen, Damion," she said, still shaking. "I'm sorry but I have to work late. Something came up here at school. Are you at home?"

He lied, and when he did it, she took in her breath as she sat on the closed toilet.

She said, "You are? ... Good. You're not working tonight are you? I ask because a group of us are going to have dinner afterwards ... Not until midnight, for sure. It's a long meeting ... Thanks for staying in and watching her until I get home. I really appreciate it."

After she hung up, she sat staring at her toes for a long time.

At precisely 11:50 p.m., Damion and Selene came charging through the front door. Calyce heard them laughing as he unlocked his own door and they bumped inside.

At 11:55 p.m., Damion alone climbed the stairs to the darkened main level, where Calyce was sitting silently in the corner of the dining area, waiting. He didn't see her as he walked into the kitchen and turned on the light. A moment later, he was moving through again, carrying a plate and a bottle of wine toward the landing.

Calyce flipped on the wall switch.

He turned to the sudden blast of light.

She gave him a chance. She looked at him, waiting, but he said nothing. From his eyes, she could see his mind whirring but he hadn't gotten there yet when she said flatly, "You lied to me."

"We were downstairs," he said quickly. "When did you get home?"

She spoke with a voice he had never heard before.

"Here's what we're going to do. You're moving out. Don't argue. It's more convenient for Mom to be down in your room. She won't have to walk as far or negotiate the stairs to let in the nurse if no one's home, like you weren't today."

Catherine had plopped herself on a ledge of rock at Scout Lookout with her backpack still on, forlorn and hunkered in the cooking sun. She was not drinking water because she had none. Sweat poured down her back and under her breasts where her bra cups pooled the water against her skin. Her hands were trembling from the adrenaline.

Over the next twenty minutes, until her school group giddily returned to her, she silently watched the two streams of hikers coming and going from the slope face she could not climb, and had given up on finally, and had retreated from. An old couple holding hands and a group of four middle-aged women with fanny packs could do it. She saw them start and not turn around. A laughing family clamored down and high-fived each other, followed by some sports team of young men all in matching red tank shirts. One of them was even wearing flip-flops.

And then the kids, the very young ones, hopping ahead of their clucking young parents. Billy goats, young lambs, they charged beyond her, these reckless children who did not notice for a moment her sitting there.

"They are all better, just simply better at it than I am," she said out loud to no one.

FEBRUARY

Mike had come to sit with Catherine finally after a lonely hiatus when he had chosen for weeks to eat with his Science Department buddies. But she had caught his eye this time as he had entered. She told herself it was accidental, that she only happened to be looking at the clock above the doorway at the very moment he appeared, but her doing so meant that his moving around her this time would have been affirmatively rude. She was gazing now into his linen-gray irises and searching for things to say as he chewed his food with one forearm on the surface of the table.

As he scanned the room beyond her, her mind offered up Alice's request the day before for a private meeting, which because of their schedules had to wait until after school dismissal that coming Thursday. Surely, she then told Mike, Alice wanted to confirm her endorsement to be new English Department Head. She told him she had been avoiding Alice for weeks (the same weeks he had not sat with her, but she didn't say that) because the news wasn't good. She couldn't endorse her.

"Because there are, uh, political issues."

She made herself stop. She made herself wait this time and not tumble on.

There. He was interested. He turned his head to look at her. "What issues?"

"Diversity," she said, repeating Frank's word.

"But she's black."

180

"We already have a new black Vice Principal. Frank says we don't need Alice too."

"That's crazy."

She told him what Frank had said about electing Asian David.

"That's illegal," he replied angrily. "It's discrimination. Used to be that whites got screwed but now it's every group that came before whatever's next. Alice earned that position."

A vein thunder-cracked across his right temple. As he gulped air she felt the power of him. He was lightning in a jar all of a sudden about this and it excited her. She wanted more.

She leaned forward. "Frank told me to lie to her."

"For real?"

"He wants me to say there's something wrong with her, something I've never told Alice in any performance review, but there isn't. She's great. I can't do that." So she had made up her mind.

"What will you tell her?"

He was close, looking into her eyes.

"I don't know," she said. "The one thing I can't do is say that Frank's involved. He told me not to."

"Damn weasel. He wouldn't last a minute out where I'm from."

So there they were, touching forearms as her heart pounded.

She realized she was mouth-breathing. She looked at his arm in his plaid shirt du jour and felt the strength of the sinews she saw when he rolled up his sleeves every spring. Thankfully he had put his left hand on his leg under the table. The gold stripe had dipped out of view.

"You know how to hike," she said suddenly. "Can you teach me? I want to go back to Zion this year and I want to make it to the top this time. I need your help to learn how to do it."

When she finally met with Alice, it was an awful thirty minutes. There was not a single "why?" Catherine could freely answer. She had both to dodge the kind woman's ensuing desperate wondering out loud about everything, including Frank, and simultaneously to avoid the thorny path to Frank's hidden agenda.

Eventually Alice demanded to know whether there was anything fatal in her performance, because no one had ever said so. To that at least she received a definitive no.

Alice's deep voice rose. "You know I'll lose without your endorsement?"

"Yes, but maybe it's time to ... I don't know ... do something different. Maybe pursue your hobbies. You like to paint, don't you?"

"You owe me. You promised."

"I didn't promise anything! I've known you both for years, so it's unseemly for me to endorse one of you over the other."

Shocked, Alice asked, "Both? Who else?"

Damn. Catherine was cornered.

She had to say it. "David's in the running too."

Roger was standing in the third-floor hallway, near the far end but facing her as he talked intently to a short boy whose back Calyce didn't recognize. Roger didn't see her as she left the stairwell, but he would when his eyes left the student's face.

She ducked back into the noisy central staircase and planted herself against the painted wall, which was all stars up that high, above the earth's stratosphere that had shaded from palest to darkest blue. But she shook her head at her own ridiculousness and confirmed with herself that, indeed, the only way to the flat roof was through the set of doors just beyond Roger. She would have to either give up on lunch alone outside overlooking the slushy street, on what was the first warm-enough day in weeks, or march past Roger awkwardly, rictus plastered, barely speaking. But her coat was already on and her insulated gloves were already balled in her pockets.

"So let's go," she said to herself as two girls on the staircase looked at her.

She approached as Roger and the boy finished. The teenager slipped into a classroom. Roger saw her and they made eye contact, but then he pulled his phone from his shirt pocket to check it. When she passed, he didn't speak.

Calyce installed her mother in front of the little TV on the main floor on both days of that next weekend. She made sure the remote and a day's worth of food were nearby, and she left to drive to other middle-class Maryland suburbs. She made sure the apartments she saw were close to the tentacles of the D.C. underground metro, however.

She explained to the landlords that her son had sent her. For everything suitable, she obtained rent amount, deposit requirements, lease term and application paperwork. By late Sunday night, when he came in the door long after Effie had gone to bed, Calyce had four solid one-bedroom, clean, rodent-free candidates.

But Damion reacted volcanically, nearly shouting. "How *dare* you use my name to lie."

"You weren't looking. Here, this one's in Beltsville."

"I'm not living anywhere but in D.C."

"You can't afford that. Look at these applications. They don't want your tip income. All they want is your W-2. The only places you can afford on your official salary are out here. Plus, even with your tips, you can't afford an apartment in D.C."

"I'll get a roommate."

"You hate people. This is the second weekend I've spent."

But she smiled after a moment. "I guess that, if you want to live in D.C., you'll have to find a full-time job."

Damion made himself scarce the next few days, so Calyce assumed he was staying at Selene's despite his constant whining about her roommates. Apparently, they didn't like his knocking in the middle of the night after his bar shift.

She and her mother spent the evenings together. Effie said often how much she enjoyed the company, even if they didn't speak while the old woman read and Calyce graded papers and tried to write fiction. Effie had become someone recovering successfully and no longer a post-operative invalid. Her wounds were "healing miraculously," the pleased doctor had told them.

One night, after that day's follow-up appointment, Calyce fixed a special dinner. Over flank steak, she said happily to her mother, "We need to start thinking about your plane reservations home."

⋀⋀⋀

Calyce was checking flights that same night, trying to find a deal for her mother, when Damion came bounding up with flowers in his hands – irises, her favorite. He wanted to thank her, he said. He wanted to say again how sorry he was.

What great news he had, he said. He'd found an apartment, a one-bedroom in D.C. and if she hadn't pushed him, he never would have looked.

"But it's so much money," she said when he told her the rent.

"I'm getting a new job, remember? You were right. And you were right about the tips. They don't count. So you have to co-sign. That's what they all require, but we'll meet at least once a month, I promise. You won't have to chase me down anymore about my job search."

His eyes lit with genuine glee. "That apartment shows me what I can do. I'll be incentivized to get a good day job. Selene doesn't want me working nights either."

It was such an onslaught of joy from her normally sullen son that she felt a shock experiencing it. She couldn't tell him "incentivized" was not a word.

"I have to co-sign? How long's the lease?"

"A year. What's wrong?"

She paused, doing the math. "That's nearly thirty thousand dollars. I don't have that kind of money."

"I'll pay. It's just a formality."

"But I'm on the hook if you don't."

He reared back. "But I will."

"Where are you going to get thirty thousand? And that's not how it works. You get the job and then the apartment, not the other way around."

He was incredulous. "Are you telling me you won't sign?"

Another pause. A much longer one.

"No." She shook her head. "I won't, and they don't all require it. None of the ones I found out here in the suburbs do."

Calyce slammed out the school's front doors without hearing the loud bang. She took in her breath immediately on the outside, then let it out and saw it freeze as she stepped into it, pumping her arms already, heading up the sloped street, then right, then straight and along the block past National Cathedral and still farther, feeling her calves work. Her lungs cut with knives of welcome icy air. Cold sliced her cheeks too and soon dried her lips but she kept on, warm in the knit cap she had pulled over her ears so only the curved ends of her dark hair feathered.

She walked steadily for half an hour, on the first day back from two days off of school for snow, which had already begun to turn sooty on the far neighborhood streets she had never walked before. The lawns and houses, though, were still blurred with white, the trees still clad in stiff ice that wrapped every twig and stubborn withered leaf in a coat of shine, fattening and immobilizing them.

It was beautiful and lonely. The only people outside their homes were huddled in their white-puffing cars, bouncing over icy road bumps, and negotiating traffic lights that still were not working. No one but her risked the treacherous sidewalks.

She felt her body as she walked confidently in her new thick-soled boots. She had greater stamina now and more wind. The new diet and its early-evening time had made a difference. Her reflux would never be cured but it was better. The coughing was only sporadic, more burning but essentially the same as for other people.

As she returned downhill to the school, a group of teenage boys slip-slopped across the street all wearing virtually the same uniform of knee-length shorts, one in that odd salmon color, together with boating shoes and no socks. Every one of them wore the same navy blue down jacket with a fake fur hood, and not one of them was zipped.

She came through the entrance panting, wearing tiny beads of wet on her crocheted scarf near her mouth. She saw Belinda at the guard desk and Belinda saw her too, as Calyce pulled off her knit cap and shook it.

Belinda started laughing.

"I'm sorry," she said in response to Calyce's raised eyebrows. "But you look like a Q-Tip, the top of your head is so flat from that hat."

"Jesus Christ, Calyce. You're driving her out," Simon said over the phone on her long commute home. "Mom just called. You want her to leave already? She's just had surgery."

"I was just trying to get tickets. They're cheaper if you buy them in advance."

Her mother was unctuous to her that evening, asking Calyce all about her day. When that didn't work Effie talked about the slushy roads.

"You know, there's no snow in Florida. If you were down there with me … "

Calyce sent her a sideways look. "I like the snow. I walked outside today my whole lunch hour."

The next week Damion came back to Calyce with another apartment still in downtown D.C. but this one was very different. There was no guarantee requirement.

"But it's so run down," she said as he showed her the place online. "And it's in such a bad neighborhood. You're asking for trouble."

"It's all I can afford, right?"

"But you'll be robbed. And what about Selene? She's going to be there, presumably. Why can't she help pay for a decent place where no one will break in?"

"She's already contributing. She did the last set of repairs on my car. I didn't tell you because I wanted to give you all that money at Christmas."

Valentine's Day came and went without a whimper. This year even Damion forgot to give her his annual card. Maria sent a bouquet of flowers to her and Effie jointly. Calyce gave her mother nothing and Effie gave Calyce a long, squeezing, uncomfortable hug with a gift certificate to Macy's.

The twenty-minute drive from the high school to the middle school took Calyce down the long incline from Upper Northwest to central Georgetown, where the school's combined elementary and junior high campus occupied an entire city block behind an encircling chain-link six-foot fence protected by cameras and uniformed security guards.

As D.C. had grown, the wealth that had initially concentrated at harbor-level in bustling eighteenth-century Georgetown had crept first to higher ground and then up the hill to Northwest and beyond in a straight line to Bethesda, Maryland, though the state border was barely noticeable. The only difference, really, was the age of the houses from which the bulk of the school's parents mailed their hefty annual tuitions. Due north led eventually to Silver Spring, where Calyce and a diverse population lived, while far northeast and east housed communities that were nearly all black. If D.C. were a clock, morning would be white, darkening soon after lunch.

As she drove, Calyce saw no other Camry's. She noticed only one car as old as hers until she turned into the parking lot in front of the middle school, where a few teachers were working late. It had been years since she had spent any regular time there, so she had no idea which vehicle was Javier's. She had emailed him a few days before to schedule the meeting, dressing for it even more formally than usual, head-to-toe in black with black skirt and black opaque stockings. She expected him to dress more casually than she, as they all seemed to do nowadays.

But she was wrong. Javier Contreras wore brown wool dress slacks, pressed and still without a wrinkle at the end of the day, along with a camel's hair blazer and a silky, fine-gauge turtleneck that looked like what Damion bought, only it was the color of wheat in sunshine. He stood for her as she entered his classroom – they had their own classrooms here, with no need to move around – so she saw the matching belt and shoes too, Oxfords with proper laces that echoed the wrapped leather buttons on his jacket.

He smelled good. She got a whiff as he hugged her courteously.

They sat. He said he was glad to see her, and she said she was glad to see him. They danced for a moment, but it was her meeting, for she had asked for it, so finally she mentioned the departmental head-ship. She noticed he didn't sit up straighter or shuffle his body but sat calmly with elegant ease. It confused her, so she pushed on, telling him in detail how the department had been consolidated, so the middle and lower school English teachers now also had a vote.

"We always had a vote," he said. "We had our own department head here."

"You know what I mean."

Not even a fly buzzed. Javier was a statue.

She said in a rush, "So I wanted to tell you why I should have the job. I've worked here for twenty-six years. When I started you were a sophomore in high school. And I've worked at both campuses, in all three schools. I started out in the fourth grade, then eighth, then up to the high school. You'll get there too, I'm sure."

She flashed him a smile. "I'm the only one in the entire department who's taught at all three schools. I'm also the only one who's ever served as Interim Head."

"I understand you asked to be Interim."

"You're misinformed. John asked me, but that's a common problem. This campus doesn't always know what's going on. That's one of the things I want to work on, making sure we send you regular communications –"

He put an elbow on a student chair-desk near him.

" – because the ball gets dropped between the middle school and the high school. I want to streamline the curriculum particularly so we don't have to re-teach, or rather teach in the first place, what should have been taught down here."

"We focus on content, Calyce." His voice was monotone.

"Well, that's wrong."

"It's a progressive school."

"Which as far as I can tell only means the kids call us by our first names. No, what they need is basic English, and that's not being taught well at the middle school."

"So you're giving us a critique now?"

"Damion, it's worse than the last one. It has to have rats."

"But it comes furnished." He pointed to an old, used bed in the photo he had taken.

"It's filthy. Look at those walls. You can't live in a place like that. You'll get sick."

That next Saturday was blustery and cold, with a sky that looked like the sea, it had so many clouds scudding and rippling. But Effie wanted to go out, and not just out but drive three hours across the Chesapeake Bay Bridge and over the farmland of the flat Delmarva Peninsula all the way to the Atlantic, to touch the water again after so long, she said.

She had been asking Calyce for weeks, starting in her delirium after surgery but continuing even in her increasing lucidity so that now it was a drumbeat that throttled Calyce every evening during dinner. By that Friday, Calyce couldn't stand it any longer, so the next morning she bustled her mother in protest at all the layers and plopped her impatiently into the car.

An hour later, over the bay, after they had talked once more about the weather and Effie had re-re-assured Calyce that yes, she still wanted to go, Calyce waited intolerantly in dead-stopped traffic at a canted drawbridge for a cargo ship to pass languorously through. Effie said, to make conversation as they idled, "I really don't need to be downstairs if he'd rather stay."

"He doesn't."

"I like it upstairs next to you."

When Calyce didn't answer, Effie said, "He's only leaving because of me. I could help with his rent."

"Don't you dare." Calyce swung her a look. "He has to learn to do this on his own. I did."

Effie didn't say it, but then she did. "You think that's the best way? Having to always do everything on your own?"

Calyce parked the car as soon as she could, at the end of the first road off 50, at the root of the low bridge, where in season it would have been impossible because of the crowds. She pulled up to two white decorative towers above which a fancy metal *Boardwalk* sign arched. Through it, acres of beach stretched to a muddied horizon indistinguishable from the dark wash of clouds that fell to meet it.

"Is there water out there?"

Her mother peered through the windshield into the opening in the low, sparse picket fence that threw no jail shadows on the putty sand in the dull day. "I can't see it. Can we maybe drive to where it's not so far to walk?"

A closer beach hugged the boardwalk farther north, so Effie finally got out. They stepped off the wood and began across the sand, their winter shoes sinking, their feet heavier with each step. Calyce reached to take her mother's hand.

"How great it is to be together," Effie said, breathing hard but talking easier than she had in Florida. "It means as much as the beach."

But in the sharp wind she tripped, then couldn't retrieve her footing. The old woman's balance was momentarily gone.

"I'm okay," she said but she clutched Calyce's fingers. "I'm sorry. I can't do this yet. And it's cold. Can we go somewhere and just look?"

Calyce brought out her laptop and bade Damion sit next to her. She was Cheshire-cat smiling as she patted the seat of the dining chair.

She made a show of turning the screen to reveal the apartment she had found for him. It was on the corner of Eighth and U, right by the Shaw/U Street Metro station, a one-bedroom in a brand-new building whose front was covered with scattered glass. On one side the façade slipped straight to the street. On the other, it stepped in as it rose to allow a block-long balcony and roof deck. It was urban hip between Florida Avenue and Logan Circle in the coolest, most upcoming part of an historically all-black section of D.C.

"How much is it?" he asked with his mouth open.

"More than anything you've shown me," she told him, then said the lease was twelve months.

He was confused. "No guarantee?"

She sat back. "Yes, I have to guarantee it. I called to ask."

She smiled wider. "I'm willing to do it on one condition. That we meet once a week like clockwork. Not once a month like you said. You come here and I'll feed you, and you prove to me each and every week that you're looking as hard as you can."

"But why?" He was ecstatic.

"It was something your grandmother said. You have her to thank. I would have liked to have had some help myself when I was getting started, but I didn't. Lots of parents help their kids with their first apartments. And this will give you a kick in the pants. It's such a nice place that you won't want to lose it, and I'm definitely not guaranteeing it a second year. To keep it you'll have to qualify on your own."

Simon was in town for the night on a layover. He came all the way from his hotel near the airport to take their mother out for dinner, just the two of them, just Effie and "Samwise," her grown-up little boy.

In the front entryway, as Calyce arranged her mother's coat and scarf and hat and gloves for her, Effie said, "I hate this weather."

"Don't worry," Calyce told her. "You'll be home soon."

Once they had gone, Calyce sighed, listening to the silence. She mounted the stairs, leaving behind Damion's room, from which he had taken the flat-screen TV. He had assured her that he would return to move down the one in Calyce's bedroom, but in the week since he had left with his things he hadn't called, hadn't texted, hadn't e-mailed. His closet and drawers were empty, left open when he departed and closed softly late that same night by a roaming Calyce. Early the next morning she had moved down her mother.

Above her, the house was hers again, and she was alone upstairs for the first time in months. As she went up she felt the smooth banister under the palm of her hand. She inhaled as she crossed to her kitchen, smelling her Chinese takeout in her microwave. She poured herself a glass of soda, then thought, then went to the dining room to dig out from her sideboard one of the two champagne flutes she and Damion's father had received for the birth of their son. She poured her ginger ale into it and raised her glass to toast her freedom. It surprised her, this sudden elation. She hadn't felt her son's confining.

As she laid a placemat for herself, she began to sing. For the first time in years, she sang full-throated, a lofty tenor from her tall frame that filled her house with her happiness.

Calyce made sure to park her car in the underground garage on days when snow was predicted before dismissal. In the cement gloom of the weak lights spaced too far apart, she didn't see DeGroot until he caught up with her. She asked about his brother but he asked about "this dinner meeting at Javier's" for that coming Saturday.

"What dinner meeting?" she said.

"He's invited every English teacher at both the lower and middle schools to his house. Something about egalitarianism, not having the middle school dictate to the lower school but being collaborative from now on. Know anything about it?"

She shook her head. She didn't mention their recent meeting.

As they walked he asked, "Did you read *Persepolis* yet?"

"The comic book?"

"Graphic novel. Dan suggested it for next year."

"Is that how you found out about this Javier thing? From him?" She blurted it.

John frowned. "No. I got an email directly from Javier. He wanted to keep me in the loop."

"We'll see you at six," Calyce said into her phone as she pulled up to her curb. Two large cardboard boxes sat outside her front door, one of them already open, its top flaps wings.

She knocked on what used to be Damion's door. "Mom, what are these boxes addressed to you?"

Effie came out wearing a caftan Calyce had never seen, its fabric black and teal paisley sateen. "My clothes. Can you help me bring the rest in?"

"But you're going home. None of that's changed just because you've got a temporary balance problem."

Damion and Jimmy arrived then, bounding in, uncle and nephew having spent the day together. After Jimmy hugged Gammy and Great-Gammy, the two "men" dragged Effie's heavy boxes over the threshold, after which they tangled like puppies up the stairs with Damion making sure the ricocheting boy climbed safely. Jimmy went on and on to the women about all the cars they had just seen at sooo many dealerships. They had even been on a test-drive.

"You brought his car seat from home?" Calyce asked.

"You bet."

"You're buying another car?" Effie asked him.

"No, but it's fun to pretend, isn't it Jimmy?"

Calyce said, "Aren't you misleading the dealers?"

Jimmy told her, "We even went to Toys R Us and he bought me the same cars. You want to see?"

The child dug in his pockets as Effie asked Damion, "Do you do this often, spend time alone with Jimmy?"

Damion smiled, sincerely, genuinely. "Every chance I get."

Damion came into the kitchen where she was cleaning up after dinner, as Effie sat in front of the TV with her great-grandson, where they were both nodding off.

Calyce asked Damion, "Are you coming back for dinner tomorrow, for our meeting?"

"I've got to work late," he answered.

His mother spun around. "You're blowing me off already? Have you done anything at all this week?"

"What about *you*? You're trying to throw *her* out now too. She just got me alone. What are you going to do, rent out my empty room for extra money?"

"Yes, he's available for work immediately, Mr. Sherson. Yes, I understand you have to meet him. I'll make sure he gets there. Thursday? How about lunchtime?"

When Calyce's phone rang, it was someone who had never called her before, but she recognized the three-digit prefix. It was the only one assigned to every teacher at the high school for each of the landline phones on their departmental office desks. But it wasn't anyone in the English Department, and it wasn't Belinda from her new extension.

"I couldn't stand the awkwardness anymore," Roger said in a voice she had never before noticed. It was honest and wholesome with open vowels. "We see each other every day. We should at least be friends."

She hesitated.

"Friends, right?" he prodded. "Because you don't want to go out with me."

She didn't speak.

"So … if I asked you out again, you'd say no again? And rudely like before, without giving me any explanation whatsoever?"

He paused and let it grow and she did too, neither of them talking as it stretched to become an 'I-dare-you" mutual silence. She breathed, he breathed, and then he breathed harder, a horse snort. She laughed out loud, giving in, and the weeks of oddness flew away.

"You don't give up, do you?" she said.

"I heard you're training for a trip back to Zion over Spring Break. I hear you're going with your sister."

Calyce made a mental note to shoot Belinda. But when she asked who told him, he said, "Dan. I confess, I asked him how you were. I want to volunteer. If you want to head out locally here with me once this weather gets better, we can hike along the Potomac. I know this great trail."

She asked her mother that night whether she had checked messages lately on her answering machine in Florida. Effie asked how she could, since she wasn't there in her condo to push the button on the box next to her telephone. Calyce explained that the phone company had a way to let you access them remotely.

"But I don't have a remote control for that phone. I only have a remote for my TV."

Later, after her mother had gone to bed, Calyce began what became an hour-long labyrinth into new technology. She eventually did it, pressing all the prompts, and she finally heard her mother's hesitant, weeks-old, recorded, pre-operative voice.

"I'll be away indefinitely, so you shouldn't leave a message.

Write to me, since all my mail's being forwarded to my daughter in D.C., where I'll be living. Here's the address."

The next Thursday at 11 a.m., Calyce drove in clotting D.C. traffic to the newly painted yellow curb in front of Damion's brand-new building on Eighth Street. Idling with her flashers on, she looked in both directions on the skirting sidewalk. She called up, but he didn't answer, so she called again. Finally she turned off the Camry and popped out nearly at a run to the elevator inside and up to the door of his apartment, on which she rapped hard and kept rapping.

When he threw open the door with irritation, she startled at his college sweatpants and directed him to change "right now." But he wouldn't.

He said, "I didn't ask for this interview. I'm not interested."

He closed the door. She heard the tongue of the doorknob in the latch, so stunned she couldn't move. She stood at eye level with his peephole, staring at the tiny circle of unblinking glass.

They liked her flash fiction, they told her. The Greek stuff was interesting.

It pleased her. They had to say nice things because she was grading them, but still. She was encouraged.

"Our assignment for the week is to write a Grimm's Fairy Tale. Read a few of them to see how brutal they actually are, then write one for modern times, using one as your stepping-off point."

A girl asked, "Which one are you using for yours?"

She wasn't smiling when she told them.

"The Stubborn Child."

Every moment of every day and every night, her strong, lithe body was covered. There was no one to see her and appreciate her, naked. She had no man to make her lonely skin feel the warmth of touch.

At night, when she couldn't stand it anymore, she drew a bath and slipped into it, sliding in her legs and her rump and her hips, then leaning back so the heat enveloped her. She didn't use bubbles on those occasions, or tea lights. There was no soft music but just the tight hug of the water. It plumped her so that, when she climbed out, the super-rich moisturizer flowed smoothly and rubbed in completely.

She had hidden the baby blue stiff-crinolined party dress at the back of her small closet, keeping it though it ate up precious room. She had last worn it for a cousin's wedding when she was in ninth grade. Her mother had saved it, knowing her child had outgrown her yellow-ruffled elementary school dress-up dress with its white-starched collar and turned-up short-sleeve cuffs, the one she had put on for every ceremonial occasion for years.

This blue one had been her next favorite, with its organza swishy skirt over the full lining whose bulk pinched at the bodice's tight waist that defined her narrow torso and budding breasts. It had made her uncomfortable at first, this chesty emphasis, but she had grown into it as she had grown into being a young woman. Today, though, it was too long and old-fashioned, and it too had become far too tight. The

last time she had tried it on in desperation for a high school dress-up day, the bust darts had stretched and some of the stitches had popped.

Her mother insisted, though, saying of course it still fit. She made the teenager pull the blue swirl from deep in the closet and required her child to model it, sure she could wear it to the first large family gathering since her mother had finally returned. When her daughter, now seventeen and tall, refused to don it, the mother snatched it from the bed and thrust it at her, announcing that no other dress would be purchased.

"Mom, you don't know," the girl said. "You've been gone so long."

"No I haven't. You're just trying to make me feel bad."

"Almost a year. Since August twenty-first. It's June. You bought me that dress for my birthday two years ago."

"But you haven't changed. It ought to fit you."

"I've got these now," the girl said, looking down.

"You're just sensitive. Here. Try it on."

But still she wouldn't take it.

The mother's mouth made two angry lines. "When did you get so stubborn?"

The girl's mouth did the same. "If you'd been here, maybe you'd know."

March

The blue-jacketed young man at the desk knew her well enough already that he no longer made her sign in. He even hopped up that Saturday morning when he saw how over-laden she was and darted around the marble counter to help, unburdening her, and rushing ahead across the polished travertine to push the elevator button.

"He's sure lucky you do all this for him. My mother doesn't."

"I'm just glad I found parking on the street."

She let the guard hold the groceries but held on to a full box of business stationery that she held like a waitress with a tray.

At Damion's new door at one far end of the perfect, long, beige, just-carpeted hallway, Calyce knocked. When he finally answered in his sweats, rubbing his eyes on a face not yet arranged for the day, she bustled in past him, talking as she unloaded the perishables into his brand-new, builder-installed, stainless steel refrigerator.

"I brought your resumés," she said. "You owe me $149.99. That was the cheapest."

He watched her empty the bags. "Nobody uses paper anymore. I don't need them. But I'm glad you're here. I need your advice about something. Let me walk you back down to the car."

She protested that she had more time, but he led her out of his apartment with his hand on her back. As they went, he told her he had a new, scene-ster boss at the bar now, and this idiot wanted him to work a day shift twice a week, with two fewer nights.

"What's a scene-ster?" Calyce asked.

"An asshole."

"Damion!"

"Sorry."

He said he had to cut fruit garnishes now and fill ice bins and beer coolers in advance for the night bartender, who should be him, who was a fat guy in bad clothes now making Damion's good nighttime money. He had to get up early, go in and haul beer, wine, and alcohol deliveries into the basement storeroom when he wasn't pouring fewer drinks for fewer tips for stupid daytime drunks, he told her as they walked out the building's front door. And the bar, he saw now that he lived here, wasn't nearly as chill as the newer ones right on this street, which attracted a much better crowd and didn't require a Metro ride for him to get to work.

"I never did like that place," Calyce said as they stopped at the curb.

"So what should I do?"

She noticed the growing Saturday traffic. Drivers were shooting her angry looks that her parked car was blocking the right lane.

Quickly, she fished for her keys. "The same thing I always tell you. Get away from there."

He nodded. "You're right. You're always right."

At school the next Monday, Calyce scanned the teacher's lunchroom from the doorway. *I'm imagining it*, she told herself, but then she saw it again, people shifting their bodies not to look at her, including a whole table of her English Department colleagues.

She looked at her wrist, where there wasn't a watch, pretending to remember something that time chased. She pivoted and walked away.

"He left his job. He's walked out," Effie reported breathlessly when Calyce arrived home. "You didn't tell me."

"I didn't know. He quit the bar?"

"He says you told him to last Saturday."

They lumbered in like elephants, her glum compatriots as they massed for her mandatory weekly meeting. Even DeGroot, who was in town that day, leaned toward the other teachers and away from her. Only Dan seemed to be genuinely friendly.

"So yes, we'll do *Persepolis* next year," she was saying ten minutes later. "It seems to be a popular choice, though I don't know why. Anything else?"

Shy Amita spoke up for the first time that year. "I had a question. A comment, actually."

The beautiful young woman wriggled tall in her chair. "I don't know how to say this, so I'll just say it. What's with all the oppression? It seems to be the subject of everything we do that's not Shakespeare."

"It reflects the history of the school," Calyce said, "and the families expect it."

"It's depressing. Can't we do something else ever?"

Calyce looked down at her. "What do you suggest?"

Amita said *Goon Squad*, but then other answers came spewing as the rest of them added more in a flood. Calyce heard *The Road*, *The Talented Mr. Ripley*, and *The Things They Carried*, which last one came from DeGroot, surprisingly.

A week later at school a text buzzed her phone: **2 interviews 2MORO! FRT**

Ten seconds later another one: **Ur resumes worked! UFB**

She had to look it all up, then texted back: **Language!**

He replied: **LYSM SRSLY**

Five minutes later, another text buzzed, so happy Calyce dug into her purse again. But it was from Belinda.

Can you meet today at 3:30 in my office?

Belinda was alone at her desk, working, but when Calyce knocked lightly she looked up.

Her face didn't change. It still didn't as she stood and gestured to Calyce to sit. At the far edge of the plastic playing field Calyce could see through Belinda's window wall of glass, the rimming trees were pregnant with their first blooms.

Belinda got right to the point. She had received complaints, she said, from several of the English teachers at the other campus about Calyce's recent meeting there with Javier.

"Why are they contacting *you*?" Calyce interrupted.

Her friend steepled her fingers in a new mannerism. "Because you're Interim Head here at the high school. John's only a teacher now, which makes him your direct report. You're mine."

No warmth, no smile. "John's gotten complaints about this too. When he came to me, I told him I'd talk to you. What happened with Javier?"

Calyce told her. She remembered it all virtually word-for-word. She said she had no idea why there should be a problem.

"You really don't?" Belinda said. "You don't see why Javier's so offended, and why the entire faculty at the other campus, and not just the English teachers, want to know whether they're valued?"

But Calyce didn't. Incredulous, Belinda had to explain.

"You have to apologize to Javier," Belinda concluded. "That's a directive. Do it right away because any longer and it won't make any difference in how they all feel about you. And how the rest of us do here at the high school."

At the door, Calyce asked her new boss, "Why hasn't John said anything to me?"

Belinda already had her head down, shuffling papers. "Because he says he's talked to you time and again but nothing changes."

The third Sunday in March, Damion arrived to move Calyce's flat-screen TV downstairs to his old room, where Effie was now sleeping. He didn't install it, though, on the pivoting wall mount where his own had been. He left the unsightly metal bracket exposed and set the big rectangle instead on the long Lucite shelf below it. Calyce was surprised to see that he had stopped on his way to buy a little molded plastic foot-stand.

Later, in the kitchen, a floor above Effie, who had stayed below to enjoy it, Damion asked when his grandmother would finally be leaving.

"I don't know," Calyce said. "It's a sore subject. Why?"

"She's chugging around this neighborhood twice every day in that eighties track suit. What's for dinner?"

But she sensed something was wrong, and she asked him.

"I've been looking," he answered. "You know I have, but the jobs aren't coming."

"What about those two interviews?"

"On the phone! And then they didn't want to see me. I'm going to have trouble with the rent next week."

It was 3 a.m. that same night. Calyce was up, having awakened from a jostling sleep that had coiled her into her bedclothes. She had to untangle herself to get out of bed, sweating in spite of the cold draft from her open balcony door. Her dream had been terrifying.

She booted her laptop and checked her bank balance, which was $38 lower than it had been at 11 p.m.

She found the checkbook for her dwindling savings account in a drawer and wrote Damion a $500 check to help with his rent, which was nearly all she had left. Thirsty, she tiptoed to the kitchen for ice water, then set herself up at the dining table. She sucked the knuckle of her right thumb as she began researching options. She investigated English tutoring but saw she had to split the hourly rate with the tutoring companies. She went next to SAT instructing, and she was deep into Kaplan's website when her mother's voice right behind her jerked her straight up.

"Are you looking for a new job?"

"Where did you come from?" Calyce closed the laptop.

"I'm a gazelle now," her mother said. "Why did you close that? And why aren't you sleeping?" Effie pulled out a chair next to her daughter.

Calyce put an elbow on the computer lid. "I was looking at jobs for Damion. He keeps telling me how much he's doing, but there's no way for me to be sure he's actually looking. He doesn't seem to be making any progress."

Her mother thought, then said, "Invite Selene for dinner, just the two of you. I'll stay in my room. Tell Damion it's a girls' night. Find out from her."

At six-thirty the next morning, Calyce checked her phone, but Javier still had not responded to the voicemail she had left asking for another meeting at the middle school as soon as possible. It was unlike him. Javier was punctilious.

She didn't want to leave a second one from home, since Effie could awaken, and she didn't want to do it from school, so she pulled over once she had driven away from the townhouse. In her lap was a white sheet of copy paper with the handwritten script she had composed.

When he didn't answer her second call, she launched into her prepared speech.

"Javier, it's Calyce again. I want to take this opportunity to apologize if I have said anything to offend you. I certainly didn't mean to cause offense. If you're free for lunch sometime next week, I'd like to take you out somewhere by the middle school. I can come down. No need to come up. I would be grateful if you would let me know at your convenience."

She then texted Belinda: **I've apologized. Done.**

Within ten minutes, though, her phone rang, but she was driving and had to let it go to voicemail. She couldn't listen until she had parked underground at the school.

"Calyce, it's Javier. Thank you for your message. Of course I accept your apology. Unfortunately, however, I am not available for lunch any time soon. So there's no need for you to 'come down.'"

On March 23rd the gods announced the arrival of a sparkling spring with the clearest, warmest day of the dawning year, so fine that all across a city renowned for its springs, magnolia trees would bend with their wedding-gown weight of new waxy blooms by the end of that glorious afternoon. It had already reached sixty-eight degrees by the time Calyce's Senior Creative Writing Class began, and she was staring out the second-floor window as her fizzy students tumbled in.

She turned to them. "'I meant to do my work today.' Who knows the next line?"

None of them did.

"'But a brown bird sang in the apple tree and a butterfly flitted across the field and all the leaves were calling me.' Class, we're going outside."

She took them all waddling up the slope to a small park that had grown on an unused corner lot. She chose not to sit on the picnic table near a rusted fountain but rather on the still-dormant grass, tossing her coat on the ground and plopping herself down. She kicked off her pumps and swung one long leg underneath herself. Looking up, she beckoned to the kids to surround her.

Once they sat, dumping backpacks and parkas, she told the circle to write a short story that very hour, right then, about what they saw around them. She talked with her hands today, above stockinged toes they had never seen.

"Create conflict and resolution. Go ahead. It'll take your minds off those regular decisions. I know you're worried about what colleges are going to tell you next week."

She opened her own spiral notebook and uncapped her pen. "Come on. Will someone time us?"

In this way Calyce purposely guided them to a safe place in their anxious minds, where everything was still possible, if just for another hour.

We sat here, on this bench, with the old wood splintering into my legs in this newborn spring, and I told you I was sorry. I said the words as I felt that hard needle of wood pierce the back of my right thigh. It snapped off as I moved in my own nervousness and drove itself deeper into me. It was you or my leg, and still I chose you. I apologized, made eye contact, everything, I did it all but you rejected me, said I didn't mean it, said to everyone I'd been robotic.

If I had told you I had been in pain the whole time from that snaggled bench, would it have proven to you that I meant it? Did I have to jab that wood spike instead into my throat, up here where you could see it?

Just because this sun-bleached old bench is smooth to you, where you sit, over there, doesn't mean that sitting here facing you, having to say this, isn't agony for me even before I say it.

But I did, I did say it, so the problem is you now.

"Did you know it waxes and wanes in the opposite direction in South America? In the Southern Hemisphere it moves left to right. Up here it starts on the right side."

As they made salads and waited for the grilled chicken they could smell in the oven baking with olive oil and dried herbs from an Italian Seasonings bottle, Selene was talking about the moon. She had just said it had always fascinated her.

"Did you know a man from NASA is actually buried there? And Buzz Aldrin –"

"How do you know about Buzz Aldrin?"

"He radioed back about the shadows. Because there's no atmosphere, everything throws shadows that are pitch black, and sometimes they have these silvery halos because of the opposition effect. He saw them first. Did you know that people sleep worse during full moons?"

There was a familiarity between them, as well as the bond of their mutual love for Damion, so it was no work for Calyce to transition the conversation to her son's job search, which Selene confirmed had indeed been more words than action and below her wish, too. Any day job was an improvement, she told Calyce, particularly now that he had quit the bar.

"So I'm still your ally," Selene said as they ate. "He's working random shifts in places but I'm paying most of his bills. I've been doing that for months. Thank God I've got a job now."

"You what? I thought all you paid for was that car repair."

"I was paying all the bills you gave him here at the house too. He said he finally told you."

Calyce chewed, trying to cover her surprise. She asked casually, "For how long?"

"Since you first gave them to him. He didn't tell you? But he'll pay me back half eventually. We keep a tally book like the one you have. It was his idea. I figured it was the least I could do, what with him paying you rent to live down there and me staying over all the time. But he said you wouldn't take it if you knew it was coming from me, so we said it was his tips."

A thousand thoughts fired and fought inside Calyce's mind.

"It wasn't?" she said to Selene.

"Nearly all of it came from me. I'm sorry I didn't say anything, but he said he wanted to handle it with you directly."

Calyce asked as calmly as she could, "How much rent did he say he was paying me so he could live here?"

"Twelve hundred, which was a big part of your mortgage."

Selene was chomping, utterly oblivious to Calyce's shock. "That's why he was so concerned about moving out. He wanted to. I'm sorry. But he was worried about how you'd pay your mortgage without him."

She speared another bite as Calyce made herself take a sip of her drink.

Selene said, "But now that he's quit the bar, I just hope he doesn't do that restaurant thing, not if it means he's not home nights. But until that takes off, he's having trouble with the rent, which was already a lot higher, so I gave him a check again today. That ought to tide him over."

She leaned toward Calyce. "I'm moving in with him officially next month so that I only have to pay one rent. I can't keep paying for two places."

Calyce rapped on the downstairs door the moment Selene departed.

Effie was awake with the light on, reading, waiting soundlessly for her daughter's report. What she hadn't expected was Calyce's enraged story about how her grandson had taken Selene's money.

"Maybe he needs it," Effie said.

"He lied to her! He's never paid *any* of my mortgage. He told her that so she would pay his bills here. It wasn't his tips he paid me. It was *her* money."

But Effie kept defending him. "Maybe she misunderstood him. Your mortgage isn't really twelve hundred."

"No, but –"

"Then she got it wrong. That has to be the answer. She's just got it all wrong."

⋀⋀⋀

The next Saturday morning Calyce heard the sandy sound of Effie's slippers on the tiled entryway, then the closing front door. Two minutes later it opened again, but when her mother mounted the stairs still in her bathrobe, she didn't say why she had gone outside in such a hurry. Calyce had to ask and watch her astonishment that she'd been heard.

She had just caught the postman, who always came so early, didn't he? She had handed him the return, postage-paid envelope she had received yesterday. They had sent her two identical originals and she had signed both of them, just like the directions had instructed, and she had mailed back one of them just now. It was legal. She had planned to tell Calyce tonight over dinner but –

Effie clapped her hands. "I've rented out the condo! You know Stephanie. She's always liked my place, and I gave her a deal on the rent so she's even saving money. I've rented it to her for the next year. She's already moved in. There was cash in the package for what she called the pro rata."

Effie was blissful as she looked at Calyce, who was dumbstruck.

"And since I don't have a mortgage anymore," Effie said, "That's all free money, so I can contribute here. Won't you please let me pay you?"

Calyce took a swallow of her coffee, which tasted suddenly bitter. "How long has this been in the works?"

"A couple of weeks." Effie was still smiling.

"You've signed papers? It's official? You can't get out of it?"

"I mailed them back to her just now. But what a great solution, don't you think? I can help you financially and I can stay here. I get so lonely in Florida."

The instant Calyce hit the street she started moving, pumping her arms and pistoning her legs to get away from Effie, from the townhouse, from her besieged existence. She truly saw the other houses for the first time as she strode with her phone in her hand. They were all identical human storage compartments, decorated with plywood matchstick siding punched by small, cheap windows all the same size up the narrow street. Too-small, non-working shutters had been nailed on by the builder, along with identical colonial lanterns on posts planted in front "yards" to make the development seem wealthier than it was. People, hundreds of faceless people, were stacked next to and on top of each other, over garages and driveways lined with cookie-cutter cars too, all about the same number of many years old. As she blew up the street she saw, really saw for the first time, that her old Camry and her nondescript house were standard-issue.

Only the corner houses had extra windows. Not different, just more of them.

She dialed her phone, tossing her head to look up at the sky, which whipped mashed potatoes above the gray roofs. "All gray," she said to herself.

When the voice-message beeped, she said, "Roger, it's Calyce. If you promise to keep your hands in your pockets, I'd like to take you up on your offer to teach me how to hike. Take me somewhere challenging, though. Don't hold back."

Effie's cardiologist pronounced her a "one-in-a-million patient." The deep scar was healing, her mind was "a steel trap," and her lifelong stamina had returned. He said he had never seen such a fast recovery from an elderly woman.

"You're from Florida, I know," he said to Effie in his examining room as Calyce stood in a corner with their two purses. "I know you're anxious to get home."

But Effie shook her head. She looked from him to Calyce, imploring.

"But I am home," she said. "My home's here now. This is where I live."

Mather Gorge is a crack in the bedrock where the Piedmont plateau sloping east from the Appalachians slams into the Atlantic Coastal Plain. Over that crack gravity has pushed the churning Potomac River for hundreds of millions of years, but the hard bottom bedrock won't erode. Sharp cliffs jut and crumble up both narrow sides, topped by a boulder streusel hikers must hop to climb.

On the Maryland side of the river, a trail falls precipitously to the water's edge downstream from Class Five killer rapids that claim experienced kayakers every year. Even on the deceivingly placid shore a hiker can put her tired feet in the shallows and be swept away by currents that trap the unsuspecting under drowned, spiked rocks that mirror the dented ridge tops against the sky.

Section A of the Billy Goat Trail requires a commitment, for once begun there are few points of escape, and once a climber begins one particular, nearly vertical climb up the jagged cliff-face there is no choice but to continue. Even in that day's chilly, dense mist.

Calyce was behind him as he had directed, watching and following his careful footsteps that squeezed themselves between the littered rocks, for there was no path or grass, no dirt to walk on in this segment, where they had to jump from stone tooth to stone tooth. But then it had started spitting, which he hadn't planned for, when the white flat sky turned ghostly pearl.

On a slick incline Roger suddenly slipped back, sliding. He had been in mid-stride up the boulder with his hands in his pockets, but it was too wet. He started skidding. His arms went out, flailing, as he struggled to stay upright while he skateboarded in reverse.

She reached out to him as he scraped down toward her. He slammed into her on the hard rock. He hit her front with his back and knocked her sideways. Both their shoulders hit a wall as a single unit, and they both yelled "OW!" though hers wasn't merely the granite. It was the weight of him too, though he quickly moved off her and turned to grab her with both hands.

"Are you alright?" he asked from two inches away.

She panted. She felt his grip as he said, "Seriously, are you alright?"

Here were the pores of his nose, and the tiny wet dots on his upper lip. The freckles of his face weren't uniform but darker and lighter, and he was handsome close-up and big in a way she had never expected.

She put her right hand on his pumping chest and felt the mass of him. No soft flab cushioned her fingers. She looked at him, eye-to-eye at her own level. He was examining her too, she saw, running his dime-colored eyes over her skin.

She pushed him away. She did it firmly, deliberately, as a decision, then stepped into a chink in the rock just large enough for her booted foot.

"I'm fine. Just winded."

She turned away. "Let's go before we're wet to the bone."

She began to walk as quickly as she could without stumbling. She didn't speak. Even when they reached the towpath and its welcome flat dirt walkway she powered ahead of him, stretching the gap so far that Roger had to raise his voice at her to slow down, but she didn't.

"What's going on?" he called from behind her as they emerged at the parking lot, but she didn't answer.

Finally, ten steps from her car he caught up. He reached to grasp her arm and the sudden forced stop nearly toppled her. She turned.

He was mad with smalled eyes. "Listen."

His words knocked into each other. "I'll never do that again. I can see you don't want anything to do with me. I get it. Okay? I finally get it. But you're acting like I'm some kind of freak."

ᗺᐱᗺ

"What do I need duct tape for?" Calyce asked Nina on the phone as Calyce wrote a list of what to bring to Utah.

She was sitting on the floor of her bedroom with Effie standing above her, waiting. Effie waved a hand in Calyce's face but her daughter refused to look up.

"What's a bivvy?" Calyce said to Nina.

Effie bent over even more, waving now from ten inches away.

"Hold on Nina. Yes? Is there something you need?"

Her mother said, "I'm going to bed."

"Well, goodnight."

Then back to the phone and the piece of paper. "Yes, I got the room reservation."

That next weekend she could not get them off the couch. Damion and Greg had fallen into the college basketball game, one of many that day. Jimmy emulated the men so exactly, yelling at the TV, that Calyce laughed while she strained to hear over the noise to listen to her daughter.

Maria was parked on one of the small ottomans, which she had shoved against a wall to flip through the magazines she had brought for Effie. Effie herself had given up long before and gone down to her room.

At the next commercial, Calyce stood in front of the screen, blocking it.

"Let's take a walk," she said to all of them. "We can go to Wheaton Park and Jimmy can play on the playground."

But Damion announced he was going to sit there all day. "Aren't we, Jimmy?"

Calyce said he was setting a bad example, but Damion disagreed.

"Leave us alone," he said. "Where else is Jimmy going to see so many of us at one time on the screen, with so many people cheering?"

That night, alone, she found herself again, but the man who came to her was white.

"Why aren't you seeing anyone?" Catherine's mother demanded. "You're still comparatively young. You just won't make the effort. You keep asking me what's wrong with my grandson. He doesn't have fire in the belly you say, but what about you? You're just like him."

Catherine searched the second-floor science hall. She had looked for Mike in the faculty office, ducking her head in for the briefest instant, but he had not been there. She had not asked the other teachers in his department what class he had where or when, despite their having all raised their heads from their computer screens.

She found him at last in the chemistry lab setting up for a class experiment. Startled, Mike had to pull off his clear plastic goggles at the flame he had been adjusting. He looked at her without greeting and without speaking, but he was not unfriendly, so she said she had been hoping to maybe schedule a day and time soon that worked for him, so they could go somewhere and he could show her how to hike properly.

"Maybe the Billy Goat Trail?" she suggested. "One Saturday? Bring Marlene if you want. That would be fun."

When she had found his wife's name in the school's online directory, which included the faculty's spouses and children, she had tried not to visualize what the woman might look like. He had never brought her to any school function in all the years he had worked there.

"Marlene's not much of a hiker."

Catherine didn't know what to say.

But he was positive. "Let's wait for the weather to clear. Next month? April's better."

She suppressed a grin. "Sure. April sounds great."

"The Billy Goat shouldn't take long. Only a couple of hours."

Once she agreed with him, he wicked up the flame again and put his goggles back on.

APRIL

He had met a girl, Catherine's son Ryan said proudly.

"And she's pretty. She works at Target too. Her name's Elena. It means "Sun." Mom, I want to ask her out but I'm not good at that sort of thing. Can you help me figure out how to say it?"

Catherine and Mike met at the old white tavern building at the beginning of the walk to the scrambling trail. Catherine had come early that spectacular Saturday morning, so she was waiting, and that made her able to see him as he approached from the distant parking lot. He was tall compared to her 5'4", with the broad shoulders and flat belly of a man devoted to a life outside, which she also saw in his walk that swung confidently in his heavy shoes. He wore a sweatshirt she had never seen, silver gray with purple letters. As he got closer, she saw it said WILLIAMS.

He greeted her from four feet away, and they began. She tried to make it social, but he started the lesson as soon as they reached the first large pile of rocks.

She reached out to him, to help her climb, but he declined. Every foothold and handgrip, he said, she had to find alone.

"But maybe you'd like to come?" she said half an hour later to

the man who for months had kept her awake at night pawing herself with her eyes closed. "You and Marlene? Have you been to Zion?"

The narrow path became choppier, so they had to boulder. He told her to take tiny steps and stand up straight with her arms out.

"Relax," he said. "Enjoy it."

He showed her how to keep three points of contact on troublesome spots, and on the steepest incline that photographers loved, he taught her how to breathe, for cramped panicked gulping in a hunched body tore through energy and would make it impossible to achieve the top, particularly on a cliff as high as Angels Landing.

At one point they stopped to look out over the rushing, forceful river. The day was beautiful, and the hiking elated her. With him near her, guiding her, Catherine felt she could do anything.

An hour later, nearing the end of the trail, they laughed down a path littered with rocks and boulders tossed by some angry god who had made huge piles that they had to climb over with tired feet. At one narrow seam, where there was no choice but to balance down it, he directed her to go first.

She was careful to do exactly as he had taught her, balancing and softening her knees. She made it down the steep face without banging into the stones at the bottom.

But he wasn't so lucky. As he came, his feet slid. He lost his balance and stiffened his knees in reaction, and he came skidding at her. He was slick on the ten feet of slanted hard rock.

He crashed into her, slamming her back against a chunk that cut into her.

"Oof!" he said as he landed against her, pinning her.

Face-to-face, it took him a moment but he finally asked, "You all right?"

Catherine wasn't talking. Mike was on her, pressing against her. She felt the size of his chest and how it flattened her breasts against him.

She looked at him, closer than she had ever been to him. Her mouth opened.

He had been drawing away from her but stopped.

He looked at her mouth and she watched him do it.

She kissed him. She closed her eyes and reached him and pressed her lips against his.

He kissed her back. Full on.

She felt the softness of him and the parting of his mouth.

He leaned his body harder against her as she leaned herself against the hard rock.

Calyce was fully prepared for the first day of school after the seniors received their formal college decisions, as she was every year the first school day after April 1st.

She made sure to tape a sheet of paper with the words "DO NOT DISTURB" in black Sharpie over the slit window in the classroom door, as she directed the shell-shocked young adults to pull their chairs into a tight circle so she could tell them in depth, at length, about her own failure. Those who had been accepted by their number-one-choice schools would be distracted, day-dreaming about their rose-petal futures, but those who now had to re-adjust their plans might listen and be buoyed. At least, that's what she hoped.

She told these former children that she had tried to write. She had always dreamt of being a novelist. In high school, she said, she had written in the very early mornings and late at night when she wasn't studying or tending to her two younger siblings for an entire year. When her mother had returned, though, Calyce had discovered that her voice had been buried by that crushing day-to-day load. Now, decades had passed and she was sure she would never regain it.

"So, hold onto yourselves," she told them. "Some of you are hurting because you didn't get into the schools you wanted. People will tell you it'll all be fine, and it will be eventually, but I'm here to tell you that not getting what you want will deepen you. Don't let where you go to college define you. That's true even for those of you admitted to your first-choice school.

"And don't be me. Don't lose your voice. Don't ever become … regular. All of you, every one of you is so much more than some 'regular decision'."

It was everything Maria could do to get Jimmy to sit back down in front of the TV, where the Disney Channel had been primary coloring already for half an hour. The fidgeting boy was long past the end of his attention span.

"So go," Calyce said when her daughter returned to the kitchen. "It's the chance of a lifetime. Jimmy's so young still. It won't affect his schooling."

Maria had climbed onto the countertop again, her neck to the wall cabinets above her, which Calyce remembered was how her daughter had had every serious conversation since grade school. Maria swung her legs and banged the lower cabinets with her heels. "But I'll miss you."

"This is what Greg's been training for. This is what you wanted. I'll be here when you get back. And I'll come to visit."

"But Grandma … "

Calyce snorted. "She's strong as a horse."

Maria cocked her head to indicate the powder room around the corner. "So, what's with the new sign about turning off the water?"

Jimmy called out, "Mo-om! I want to go home!"

"She forgets sometimes. It's nothing, I wish I could travel too but I'm stuck here."

Jimmy began pounding like a pile-driver on the corner table.

"But Mom, where's you?" Maria hopped off the counter to head out to him. "You take care of everyone else. When will you start taking care of you?"

Five minutes later, Calyce watched her daughter scuttle behind Jimmy lugging a bagful of toys brought from home to keep him occupied. The boy strutted as he paraded down the stairs, trailing his servile mother. At the bottom, as Calyce watched from above, Jimmy announced that he wanted to stop for ice cream. He refused to step outside until she agreed, all while she held the front door for him.

Even after Calyce heard the car pull away, she stood staring at what she had seen.

Alone in her living room that evening, Calyce phoned Simon to very calmly raise with him for the first time the idea of putting their mother in a nursing home.

But he refused to consider it.

She said, "What happens if she forgets a pot on the stove? Or trips on the stairs while I'm at school? We're alone here and I work all day."

She lowered the voice she had raised, and she kicked herself for not having called him from upstairs in her own room. She strained to listen and thought she heard movement on the floor below her.

No, he said again. He wouldn't agree to a nursing home.

"You mean 'assisted living,' anyway," he corrected. "She's not sick enough for a nursing home."

He also wouldn't help with the cost of it because he had no money to spare.

"Plus Mom's got her own assets," he reminded her. "Dad left her everything. He left us zero when he died, remember?"

All the rest of that week, Effie talked about the beautiful weather coming on Saturday. "A picture postcard day. That's what they're saying."

On Friday night she said, "Let's go out tomorrow. That canal you like."

Early Saturday morning Effie gave Calyce no choice, calling up to her fully dressed already from the entryway.

By 8 a.m. they were already walking along the C&O Canal towpath, with shafts of early light gilding the new leaves of the high, densing trees. Calyce was pleased to see for herself how much better her mother really was physically as they strode easily, toward Georgetown. The sun followed them, touching the mossy green belt of water that was still as a pond.

Effie even lengthened her strides to match her daughter's.

"I hate being cooped up," Effie said. "See how well I'm doing? You don't need to worry about me. I can walk miles now."

ᴧᴧᴧ

Belinda had texted Calyce: **Meet me in the dance studio at 3:20.**

Calyce descended into the lowest bowels of the high school, down forty feet and four sets of wide stairs, with two landings, the first of which led to the weight room, the fitness-machine room, and the top of the basketball court, where a full-sized track looped around the rim above the bleachers. Another set of stairs took her down to the small recording studio and the professional dance studio with its sprung floor and rows of birch ballet barres surrounded by three walls of mirrors.

Belinda was already there, alone, pacing over the shiny pine-plank floor under strong overhead lights that made two dark crescent shadows under her deep-set eyes.

"You look tired," Calyce said, but Belinda charged right in.

Javier had come to the high school to speak with Belinda personally earlier that afternoon. He had made a special appointment to tell Belinda that he had tried but he could not get beyond the way Calyce had treated him. The artificiality of her apology had haunted him, he had said, because it had demonstrated an even greater flaw in Calyce and more generally in the English Department at the high school, for the upper school had seemed to condone for years a perpetual disdain that now amounted to contempt for the contributions of the English teachers at the other campus.

"What the hell, Calyce? What the hell?" Belinda's hand gripped the barre. "What did you say to him *this* time?"

"I apologized!" Calyce insisted.

"Did you? Or did you do that wooden thing you do when you don't agree with what you're saying? I've known you a long time."

Calyce's eyes narrowed, and when they narrowed they disappeared. "You made me. You know I didn't want to."

Belinda spoke very slowly. "I don't know who you think you are."

Her friend started counting on her fingers. "You presume to be Head of the department already. You're so self-impressed you don't even consider John, and you don't ask for his endorsement until it's too late. You dictate to teachers like they're your servants. You condescend to Javier. There's been a parade of people in my office since the first day I became Vice Principal, telling me about their problems with you. I tried to tell you, but you won't hear. And now you've made me so angry I've had to meet you down here so no one could possibly see me."

Belinda wasn't willing to gift-wrap her words anymore. "Do you know that every single English teacher on both campuses has seen what you wrote about dictating the lower and middle school curricula? Hell, I think the *whole school* has seen it by now. Do you know how arrogant that was? They all avoid you at lunch, Calyce. Have you noticed?"

Stunned, Calyce said, "Of course I have."

"You've got to change how you interact with people. I've spent all these months defending you. I can't anymore. I look ridiculous. From now on, this is all on you. You're hurting yourself and your department and even the school. If you don't change how you deal with people Javier is going to pass you by. He's *beloved*."

Simon called her the next day at school. He was oddly hesitant, searching for words.

"Nina agrees with me about the nursing home, but she said you might have some … some need. Do you want me to chip in for a piece of whatever she's adding to your costs? A couple hundred a month maybe, to help cover the light bill?"

Tersely, Calyce said no, she didn't need his help, thank you.

But then he did something unexpected: Simon apologized. It took him a moment of fumbling, but he thanked her sincerely for taking such good care of their mother. He even said Effie wasn't easy.

He told her, "I've never been able to get used again to her telling me what to do. That was always you, from that year you were our mother."

He laughed, awkwardly at first but then relieved. "You know Sandra can't stand the way she chews? That smacking, it drives her crazy. Even my girls imitate it."

"Have you never been to Bryce?" Nina folded the paper map to the precise rectangle where they were driving.

Calyce had been navigating all afternoon, and they now approached Zion's unassuming East Entrance on a two-lane road. Fat grass waved already in the April spring, contrasting with everything dry and barren Calyce had ever thought about Utah.

"No," Calyce said. "When do you leave for Chile?"

"Next month. You ever heard of Punta Arenas? It's the closest city to Torres del Paine."

"Don't they have enough English-language teachers there already? You're thirty years too old."

Nina turned to her. "I rented this convertible for a reason. Why did you close the top?"

Calyce kept her eyes on the pavement. "I don't need my hair messed up. It doesn't matter to you with all that up there, but I like to keep mine organized."

They passed the old wooden hanging park-entrance sign, then started subtly descending. Furred spring shoots gave way to hardened white sand dunes that grew until they thrust high above them in layers of rust red and lighter chalk farther skyward. Around them soon on both sides, pitted formations made mounds like some filmmaker's vision of the moon. Over the millennia the wind and ice and rare but brutal rain had carved striations in them. Even the road wasn't asphalt any more but red-paved.

Soon the land changed to outcroppings of peeling layers, then to a hardscape of undulating wrinkles in pink-stacked coils.

"My God," Nina said, pointing left. "There it is."

Towering next to them was a soaring cone of white rock so cut horizontally that it looked like a million stacked dishes. Calyce slowed to find the top of it in the flag blue sky. Down the sides of it a thousand long lines were deeply carved too, running so distinctly parallel they looked chiseled by a conscious hand.

"Checkerboard Mesa," Nina said. "Holy shit. What caused that?"

They arrived at the entrance hole to the tunnel, which was so tight it looked like the wire arch over a croquet ball. Calyce drove into the unlit cavern feeling the tons of deadly mountain poised just above their heads. Inside, in the ink-dark, she saw to her right a flash of light, and seconds later two more together, followed by two more individually. The tunnel then opened completely on the right for a fleeting instant to a view of rugged cliffs bathed in daylight.

She plunged into the tunnel again at the same instant she realized that the portal windows had been blasted into the mountainside intentionally, for the views.

They exited to a canyon of stone in slabs higher than anything she had ever witnessed, extending as far ahead of them as they could see. The walls were copper and streaked in places as if they were crying. Along one dented cliff stretched a vastly wide natural arch, still attached to the rock face behind it, still being etched by the carving power of erosion.

Calyce pulled over without saying a word, steering to the lip of one of the looping switchbacks falling from the tunnel. She got out, gawking. Speechless too, Nina came around to stand next to her. They looked up, then far right and far left downward into the monumental canyon, following the forced perspective of the two soaring ridgelines. Hard earth rose a thousand feet all around them, with vertical lines and cuts that caught the blazing sun to cast charcoal shadows.

Calyce listened but heard a silence unbroken even by wind.

"I've never seen this," she said quietly. "Last year we came in the other way." Leaning toward her sister the smallest bit, she added, "Thank you for coming. I know it was a lot of effort."

"That's okay." Nina too was awe-struck. "Thank *you*. My God, this is amazing. Now I see why you wanted to come back."

They were touching shoulders as Calyce said, "But why did you offer? You've never done that before."

Standing on the looping curve, staring up at the endless chiseled cliffs, Nina turned to her. "It was the first time you ever said you wanted something just for you. I figured it had to be spectacular."

Nina insisted that they catch the very first shuttle the next morning, which departed north into Zion's main canyon from the Visitor Center on the dot of 7 a.m. A jointed bus with an accordion middle, it pulled out from the collection curb with only the two middle-aged women in it.

Nina dumped her fat daypack on the aisle seat of the row next to them. After the first stop she said suddenly over the pre-recorded voice talking, "Shit. We both look like dirt. If we get separated, we won't be able to see each other. I didn't wear anything bright."

They passed a band of mule deer startled by the shuttle. Their out-sized ears twitched on heads uplifted from grazing, the gaining light outlining just one set of antlers.

Calyce pointed up out the window to the top of the eastern cliff-face. "These aren't mountains, you know. It's flat behind there because it's a shelf. That's ground level up there, and we're in the basement."

They alighted from the bus, which then gunned north without them. In the quiet morning they heard its engine far longer than they saw its square white tail.

On the other side of the footbridge, spring trees canopied over a sinusoidal path. It meandered up and finally revealed after ten steepening minutes a far-off pinnacle of rough rock whose front edge facing them looked like the curved bow of a massive ocean liner viewed from the surface of the sea. But it soared much higher than any ship that had ever existed. Standing alone proudly as its own promontory, it thrust itself into the porcelain sky well above the top of the shaded canyon where they stood. The morning sun was already firing the top third.

They stopped.

"That's it?" Nina said with the back of her head on her shoulders. "All the way up there?"

Calyce nodded.

"Then I have to pee and maybe poop," Nina said. "This'll take a minute."

"Is that allowed?" Calyce called after her but Nina had already stepped off the trail. "There's a bathroom back at the shuttle stop."

"Why?" Nina called to her. She had already disappeared downhill, away from an outcropping of rocks that hung above them.

As Calyce waited, she smelled a smell it took her a moment to locate. Something had died to her left and it was newly rotting.

She saw a narrow way through the boulders and stepped off the path to follow it, balancing with her hands on the thick rocks to a secluded spot with branches and underbrush in a pile. Sticking out of it she saw two hooves, then legs and suddenly, two more little baby hooves spooned next to them and facing outward the same way.

"Oh no." She put a hand on her mouth.

She knelt. There, under the twigs and leaves were two bodies of mule deer, a mother and a newborn fawn.

But not newborn. Unborn. And partially eaten.

She crouched, transfixed.

"Calyce," Nina said behind her, purposely calm.

Calyce looked over a boulder between her and the path to where her sister stood facing her. Their eyes locked.

"Don't move," her sister said. "Don't even turn your head."

Calyce saw Nina look up then at the rock ledge directly above Calyce.

Nina looked back down at her sister.

A growl started in a throat above her. It grew. A deep rumbling noise.

The hairs on Calyce's arms lifted.

The motor-sound came again, louder now.

It stopped.

Calyce was between whatever it was and its kill.

Below it, facing it, Nina stepped towards it. She stared at the thing eye-to-eye. She raised both arms and waved them up and down. She lifted on her tiptoes and waved huge half-circles.

She boomed at the cougar. "Get out! Calyce! Don't you move!"

She jumped up and down and continued flailing.

The mountain lion screamed and she charged it. Nina came at a run, tearing across and onto the rocks toward it as she shrieked like she hadn't since they were children.

Nina was still holding Calyce five minutes later, both arms tight around her. Calyce was shaking and couldn't stop.

"I want to go down now," Calyce said. "I want to leave. I don't want him coming back."

There was nothing Nina could do. Calyce got up and galloped down the trail and into the trees and over the metal footbridge spanning the river. Nina yelled after her but Calyce wouldn't listen.

At the shuttle stop Calyce gripped the metal sign at the curb. "How did you know what to do?" she asked Nina.

"I've seen them before. They're all over the Americas. You know they go for the neck? That's what scared me. You were crouching with your back to him. You looked smaller, and you looked like you were going to eat his dinner. This is all my fault. We weren't wearing anything neon that would have told him we weren't prey."

"But you went *towards* him."

"The key is to make yourself look bigger. They back away if you're lucky."

"Nina, you saved my life."

Calyce said she wouldn't go back to Angels Landing ever.

"But you've come all this way," Nina said on the bus. "I don't get it. We scared him. He's moved on."

"But how do you know?"

That warm spring night they ate at a hilariously bad Mexican restaurant on Springdale's main street, and they had a blast. The food was all right but the margaritas, which were Nina's goal, were mixed by such a blessedly generous bartender that Nina soon found the bumbling Keystone Kops routine from the clueless wait staff infinitely entertaining. The two women sat on bistro chairs at a round table on the front patio watching the four servers walk in and out the front doors in alternating confusion. They brought checks to tables that had just sat down. They parked appetizers in front of diners who hadn't ordered them, while those who had gestured frantically. One group of diners they ignored for a full half-hour. Even Calyce began laughing.

Dry evening fell to a clear nighttime and stars threw themselves across the crystalline sky. Nina drank and both sisters saw the traffic diminish outside the restaurant's front half-wall of stucco. Across the street dozens of tin whirligigs, some of them enormous, spun on poles and caught the floodlights in the front yard of a shop. Concentric circles turned and spoon wheels rolled.

"It's not the mall, Calyce," Nina was saying. "It's dangerous outside sometimes."

She licked the salted rim of her third margarita. "It's like this thing you have about not drinking. You don't want to lose control, but it's just a defense mechanism. You need to relax. When was the last time you got laid?"

"Excuse me?" Calyce darted her eyes to see if anyone was listening.

Nina didn't care. "Any luck with that white teacher?"

"Are you done with this?" An errant waiter thrust his arm between them over the top of the table, reaching for Nina's half-eaten plate.

"No," Nina said to him.

"No," Calyce said at the same time. "I'm not interested."

The young man left to bother another table.

"You're not attracted to white guys?"

Calyce shook her head. She didn't stop, so she looked like a bobblehead gone sideways. "No. No, I'm not. No."

The next morning Calyce was sitting on the second-floor balcony of their shared room. She sat in one of the two Adirondack chairs as she held a steaming mug of hotel-room coffee she had made on the tiny plug-in machine in the bathroom while Nina still slept. Slid back into the wooden chair contentedly, Calyce had both her elbows on the flat arms and the ankle of her right leg posed on her left knee. She sat overlooking the shining ribbon of ebullient water winking through the cottonwood trees. Above them was a white glimpse of rock-littered mountain still in shadow, its back to the climbing sun. Immense and solid, the rough cliff faced west toward her. She felt its hard, forever certainty.

There was nothing, finally, but the chiming of the creek and the gossiping rustle of the hemming trees, the painter's light kindling the mountains, the sensation of the mediocre but welcome coffee in her mouth, the heat of it in her hands, and the tender touch of the smallest breeze on her left shin below the pajama bottoms she had hiked up to her knees to feel it.

A while later, the door opened and Nina stuck her head out. "You sure you don't want to go back? We've got time before we have to be in Vegas."

Calyce said with sureness, "No. I'm too old now."

Nina stepped out quietly and sat with her sister next to the brushing trees and the soft wind that ruffled them. Just like Calyce, Nina put her right ankle on her left knee, then waited silently, sensing her sister's sadness.

"I'm stuck with her you know," Calyce said after a while. "Did she tell you she rented out her condo?"

"Not until after she did it."

Calyce looked out at the little river that was giggling as it hopped over sharp rocks. "Sandra hates her, so Mom can't stay with Simon, and you're month-to-month in a one-bedroom."

Nina laid her hand on the wide arm of Calyce's chair. "I'm sorry, but I need that job."

Calyce nodded. They hadn't been so amicably in each other's company in years.

"Mom looks out for Mom," Nina said. "That's what she does. You were the one who looked out for us. Dad was flying all over the country that year. You put us first. Mom still doesn't."

Calyce turned to her a minute later with her dark eyes shining. "What do I do about Damion? He's just like her."

Nina made her hand into a fist and pumped it on her sister's chair arm. "You tell him to get his damn ass in gear. You don't have to be stuck with him too. But why are you asking me? What do *you* want?"

"I want him to succeed."

"You think he won't? Because if you ask me that's what you're telling him with all this hovering."

"He had trouble in school. I was getting my degree then, and I was working and going through that divorce."

"You've been saying that for years, but that little boy is gone. He's a grown man now but you're still treating him like he can't do it without your help. It's like what you said about Angels Landing. You're not too old, but you think that, and your thinking it makes it true. It may be that all he's doing is living up to the message you're sending him. Or down, rather."

Nina watched Calyce regret leaving Zion. Her tall, slender, stunning elder sister kept looking up and looking back to the rims of the sunset-colored cliffs as Nina pulled out of their hotel at noon with the convertible's top down, finally. Calyce moved her whole body and craned her neck seemingly to record everything forever, as if she were never returning. Nina saw it all and slowed, then stopped at a curb.

"I have an idea," Nina said. "Didn't you say there was a northern road with a view of the park?"

"Fourteen," Calyce said. "But it's way out of our way."

"Wouldn't you rather do that than sit at the airport?"

Nina exceeded the speed limit on the interstate while Calyce held her flapping hair with both hands. Nina took an exit toward Cedar City, which brought them along the lip of a high shelf as Calyce kept clutching her head.

She yelled at Nina over the car wind, "There's a lava field around here with chunks of black rocks. Can you believe it?"

Nina yelled back, "You look ridiculous. You won't sleep with a white man but you wear white hair."

"Who says this is white hair?"

Nina spotted two motorcycles parked on the roadside ahead. Four riders stood staring over the cement barrier that protected them from the deadly drop-off. She drove until she could make a U-turn that had Calyce protesting, "What are you doing?"

Nina wouldn't tell her as she drove past the motorcycles and turned left onto a dirt track that was barely a road. She turned off the engine.

"Go," Nina said as she pointed at the people. "See what they're looking at. I'll stay here with our stuff."

Calyce climbed out and walked carefully along the perched edge of the road. Ahead of her the riders mounted up and drove away east. The only sounds became the bumblebee of their engines on the old highway and the crunch of her hiking boots on the gravel shoulder. She was still wearing them and planned to wear them on the plane, though there was no need to.

When she came upon it finally, she stopped cold. Far away below her, down many discernible steps of descending earth and veins of trees, deep vertical gouges were carved in the land. Huge, sharp, connected canyons ran twenty miles southeast with bottoms she couldn't see, but she saw the white cliffs of their walls like movie-theater curtains. Their tops were as flat as hatboxes stacked on a closet floor. One rose taller than the rest, pure white all the way up without a single tuft of fuzzy green. It was an altar, the Great White Throne of Zion, scratching the blue-jay sky higher than everything around it, shouldering above, resting unconcerned and unchanging for eons.

Calyce lost track of time. She moved her feet apart and put her hands on her hips. She stared, unmoving, at the cathedral of stone.

At last she spoke, but she didn't realize it, so no one heard her, not even herself.

"This," she said to God's handiwork. "I want this."

They made it to the airport just in time for Nina to run to her flight, but Calyce's was long-delayed. The inbound plane from Baltimore had had some equipment "thing," the counter woman said unhelpfully as she paged through a bikini catalogue. Calyce had two extra hours to sit and think.

Eventually she grimaced as she rehashed for the tenth time her awful meeting with Javier, realizing at last that she had done what she always did. She had bulldozed him, and then she had given him a disingenuous apology.

She walked the perimeter of the gate area, keeping her rolling bag in sight. Out the wall of windows she saw her boarding ramp still without a plane.

It was after 9 p.m. in D.C., so she began by apologizing for phoning so late. Once she knew Javier had time to listen, though, and was willing to, she told him she was deeply and truly sorry for having treated him chronically with such disrespect. She was a bull and a tunnel-visioned person, and he had been far more gracious than she deserved.

Javier remained silent as she went on for more than a minute.

"I'm so very sorry," she said sincerely. "It'll never happen again."

At no point did she ask him to forgive her. There was no attempt at absolution, just guilt and genuine remorse. But he did forgive her, and he did it immediately, telling her he was stunned and struck by her humility. He assured her that yes, they were fine, they always had been, though he had indeed been angry. But he wasn't any more. He was impressed, he said.

They talked for a while about their families. Finally, they circled back to what they both shared: DeGroot's departure for the troubled brother who had necessitated it, the school-wide consolidation of the English Department, and the need for a new Head, who would be voted on the next month.

Suddenly, and without her asking, Javier told her that he didn't want the job – that he never had wanted it.

"Really?" she said.

"Really." About that rumor to the contrary, maybe the teachers at his campus had started it in an effort to draft him.

Javier told her, "I've seen how hard it's been on John all these years. I don't need to have to handle the high school teachers. I've got enough thirteen-year-olds as it is."

Effie stayed up with her, padding behind her around the main floor the night Calyce returned home, even standing next to her when she opened the refrigerator door to search for a snack when her body refused to ramp down. Calyce was still on Zion time.

Effie had been chattering without taking a breath since Calyce had come downstairs after her shower. She told her daughter every morsel about Damion and Selene, and about little Jimmy and his parents. As part of his upcoming placement, Greg had had to list all the foreign service posts on the planet in ascending order of his preference, Effie said, and more than half the names she had never heard of.

"Like Oo-waga-somewhere. It's in Africa."

Calyce moved things around inside the refrigerator. "I made all this and you didn't eat any of it. And all the yogurts are still here, and the rotisserie chicken."

"You left too much."

"This casserole I made. Look, the whole thing's gone bad."

"It's no fun if I don't have anyone to eat with. When can you and I take a hike, just the two of us, like you did with Nina? I'm fine now. I'm up to four miles a day."

MAY

"You've been out of work for months," Calyce said angrily to Damion, who was just as furious. "You keep talking but you haven't done anything but fill in at bars."

"You know what I've done? I met a guy last night who says he maybe wants to sublet my apartment. That way I can come home and save some money while I go back to school."

"Yet another pipedream," Calyce told him.

Effie stepped into the space between them, to say to Calyce, "Be civil."

Over the top of Effie's head, Calyce said, "I will charge you rent if you dare move back here. You're a grown man."

"You don't charge *her* rent," he said. "And she's not paying for utilities either, like I did. She told me."

"Like Selene did, you mean. *She* paid all your bills here."

"Quiet!" Effie said to Calyce. "You don't charge family. You pay *for* them."

"You've got *her* on your side now?" Calyce said. "Tell me, is Selene still paying towards the rent on your fancy apartment?"

He stepped forward, pushing against Effie, who had to move backward. Her shoulders pressed Calyce's chest.

Damion said from a foot away, "You're a dinosaur, Mom. You know that? It would be sexist if she didn't contribute. She lives there."

Before school the next morning, Calyce was deep into her computer, fat chunks of moist blueberry muffin in her mouth as she typed a long email. She had arrived early, just as the sun had summited the tops of the houses along the school's property line, when the day was already rapidly heating. She was so hunkered she didn't notice Dan, not even when he thunked his backpack twice on his desk to get her attention. He had to call her name finally and say Good Morning before she looked up.

"You look possessed," he said, so she told him she was typing up an entirely new proposed English curriculum for the lower and middle schools. She had been up most of the night working on it.

"I just took the bull by the horns, but I've integrated everything and there are no overlaps or holes. I want to get it out today." She plopped in more muffin as punctuation.

"Is this because Javier's not running?"

But she was gone again. She didn't hear the next thing he said so he had to say her name, "*Calyce*, do they know he's not running?"

"I don't know. Why's that important?" she asked distractedly.

"Because if they don't know he's not running, they'll think you're doing this because you're competing with him, and that won't go over well. Has he told them? I found out through you. I haven't gotten anything in writing from him."

"You're right. I'll tell them right here at the top."

"Wait! Stop." He had raised his voice.

She looked up again. Dan was trying to help her.

He said, "Don't you want *him* to tell them?"

She stood in front of her class an hour later in taupe pants stained umber where her lap was soiled with muffin grease. She didn't notice, though, nor did she register that she had placed her right foot on top of her left instep in the new flats she was wearing.

She told her seniors that only two class periods remained before they left on their Senior Quests. Tonight, she wanted them all to vote on their favorite pieces written by the class during the year. They would talk about the top ten winners once again during those last two meetings, moving backward, starting with number ten.

"So if you want to know who the big winner is, you need to be here the last day. I'll bring homemade cupcakes. But there's no final, and nothing more you need to write. Congratulations, everyone, you're about to be done with me."

On her way up to the second floor, Calyce turned into the central stairwell and set her sights on the flying pterodactyl. The senior artist had painted it with its mouth open, so its tearing teeth showed as it searched for prey. She didn't see Belinda and Dan in a back niche of the main level where the maintenance staff stored folding chairs. She heard them first, then somehow knew to keep her head straight ahead and continue upward as if she hadn't. But she strained her ears as she slowed her climb.

Behind her, Dan was talking in a low staccato stream so dense he wasn't taking breaths. She thought she had seen Belinda nodding.

Ten long seconds later she arrived at the straightaway under the shark. She gave it three steps, then looked down as she slid her hand along the railing casually.

They were both gone.

The next week, Damion sang as he arrived in her kitchen.

"I've got news," he said happily. "I met this guy and he's opening a four-star restaurant and he wants me to be the manager. He likes the way I look." Damion gestured to himself, model-style, his long fingers sweeping down himself as he posed comically.

She snagged a dishtowel and began drying her hands. "Where?"

"Shaw. It's going to be upscale."

"In Shaw? I doubt it."

"This is a real opportunity. I'd have a salary. I wouldn't be unloading deliveries. They would all work for me."

"Starting when?"

"He's still trying to find space."

She made a face. "There ought to be a lot in Shaw."

"It might be somewhere else. I don't know for sure." He walked out to her living room and turned on the TV.

She called to him. "What about your rent next month? Selene's not paying all of it this time, is she?"

He yelled back to her above the noise. "Don't worry about it. I've got it covered."

She didn't hear him say quietly to himself, "Bitch."

It kept bothering Calyce, niggling her in the middle of the night. She couldn't explain it to herself, so the next Friday she waited like a supplicant for Belinda outside the faculty lunchroom, hugging a wall as she folded herself smaller, feigning to check her cell phone. She was bad at it, though, and looked like a howitzer trying to be origami.

When Belinda finally exited, Calyce fell in quickly beside her, asking for "a brief minute," which Belinda said was all she had.

Calyce tugged her into a corner and said she needed to know what Belinda and Dan had been discussing so guiltily in the stairwell.

"'Guiltily'?" Belinda's chin pulled back. "Why is that any business of yours?"

"If it affects me, it *is* my business."

"I'm not sure I agree, but yes, it was about the vote. Dan is running too, and I think he'd be good. He's collaborative. That's not your strong suit."

It's four days from now. Calyce was texting with Javier that night as she searched for the rest of the pastry-shop chocolate fondant cake that Damion had brought for dinner earlier that week as a surprise. But she couldn't find it. A broad wedge wide enough for two slices had still been on the cake stand an hour before when she had gone upstairs to shower.

Don't. Javier replied. **Let him be**

From the kitchen, she raised her voice to be heard through the closed door of the powder room, where her mother was making bodily noises. "Did you eat all the cake that was left?"

Why? she texted.

"There weren't any names on it," Effie yelled back.

Don't trust him

"Both pieces?"

You don't? Or I shouldn't?

"There was only the one big one."

Yes

Calyce said, "You never asked!"

She texted, **Before the meeting I need to know what he's thinking**

Effie said, "I can't read your mind. If you don't want me to eat something, you need to tell me. I'll be out in a minute."

He wants dept head. That's all you need to know

What's he been saying about me? Calyce asked as her phone rang on the counter.

"It's Nina. What's up? You left a message."

Calyce spoke to her sister quietly, in a hurry. It was Damion. He shouldn't have enough money to pay his rent, or rather, his half of it that Selene didn't cover, but he seemed to have a lot of disposable income.

Calyce said, "He came for dinner this week in a new V-neck pullover, and he brought a cake for Mom from one of those fancy new stores on his street. It came in a pink box with a ribbon."

"For Mom? Not for you?"

"For Mom."

Imagine the worst

She steeled herself to talk to him, finding him alone in a classroom at the end of the next day, collecting finished tests from the desktops.

She had never looked for him before, and she had no idea where he would be, so she had had to check his class schedule before she had left the English Department office. She also had to plan when to arrive, exactly as the bell rang and the door flew open in front of a wave of fifteen ninth-graders. One tiny girl was so prepubescent still that she looked like a fifth-grade boy, which was a full grade older than some of the short boys tumbling out behind her seemed to be.

Dan was surprised to see her. She saw it in his wide face before it closed. He cast his eyes to the papers, squaring their edges with his fingers, but she started in nonetheless, telling him in a word-rush how much she wanted it. She had waited years. Decades. Since Dan was in grade school. She had waited that long for John DeGroot to leave it to her so she could be Head of the department.

He moved the pile of tests to his teacher's desk.

"It's not personal, Calyce. It's just that you and I have different visions for the department. I think it's good for people to have a choice."

"You can do it next time, when I'm done with it."

He let a beat pass. "It's not yours to own. It's not a hereditary position."

His calm unnerved her. She said, "There's never been a black Head of the English Department before. It's time we had one."

"Do you think it's still 1968?"

"You weren't even born then."

He countered, "No one cares about numbers anymore."

"I've waited twenty years!"

"During which time we've elected a black president. What are your accomplishments? What have you done for the department? What are *your* plans? That's all that matters these days."

He was combative, and ready. He had a tone she had never heard.

To Calyce, no answers came.

"You could win this," he said. "But not if you talk about your being black and all your years of waiting. We get it, but that's not relevant to me or the others. We're not standing behind you in line at the Safeway. It's not your grocery store, Calyce, and we don't have to wait our turn."

The day of the departmental vote, Calyce ran into Roger at 7 a.m. Her hands tingling with anxiety, she tried to avoid him once she saw him, slowing as she walked from the garage, but she couldn't stop altogether on the sidewalk, all alone, so she had to smile gamely and catch up with him as he waited for her, watching.

He insisted on holding the front entrance door. "Today's the day, huh? I can see it on your face."

They nodded at the men at the guard's desk, who were all former D.C. cops. Every one of them was black.

"Can I do anything to help?" Roger asked.

"You can talk about something else."

Then in a *non sequitur*, she blurted, "I'm learning how to fall. I was practicing on my bed, standing on the mattress. I saw it on YouTube."

But then she turned right for no reason and left him as she headed down the wrong hallway. He watched her get halfway along it before she realized she was walking by math classrooms.

They all assembled from both campuses in a conference room hidden under the first-floor auditorium's slanted main riser-wall. Desk-chairs had been pulled into a big donut square. They created an uninterrupted surface of fake wood tops broken only once near the single door, which was glass in a wall of glass to make the claustrophobic space seem more open.

When Calyce arrived early, four other teachers were already

seated together. They saw her but didn't wave her over. She claimed the center spot in the precise midpoint of the side under the whiteboard.

As the others filed in and took seats but not the two chairs on either side of her, DeGroot arrived. He didn't like that she had taken the head position. She was a candidate today, not Interim Head, he said when he bent down to whisper.

She got up with all her papers and moved to another side, pulling out a lonely chair between two groups chatting. It wasn't until everyone else had settled in that Dan blew in and took the last free seat remaining, next to DeGroot, who sat where Calyce had first been sitting.

DeGroot led the jammed room of twenty-five people in a routine discussion of unimportant initial agenda items for this, the first formal meeting of the combined department, then announced that it was finally time to hear what Calyce and Dan each had to say, then vote.

"I've already received proxies from Michelle and Brian," De-Groot said about the only two absent faculty. "We'll do this alphabetically. 'Tate' comes before 'Waggoner,' so Calyce you're up."

Calyce talked from her seat as she touched her prepared pages with the soft tips of her trembling fingers. She saw Javier in the crowd but her eyes fixed on gorgeous Amita directly across from her, so she spoke only to the young woman.

Calyce started with all she had done during her years at the school, the changes she had spearheaded that had now been in place for decades, the suggestions she had made for books the school now used perennially, the fact that she had taught a quarter-century's worth of students.

"And," she tried to smile. "None of them failed."

She had been a student advisor for twenty of those years, and she had served on countless school committees, chaperoned innumerable dances, tutored probably two hundred students, taught at every level from elementary to seniors and at all three campuses. She had covered for the other teachers likely a thousand times when someone had been sick or needed time away. She had the finest attendance record of any teacher in any department in the school's history. Ten years ago, she had even won a teaching excellence award that had been reported in *The Washington Post*.

She then talked about her efforts recently to learn what the faculty wanted.

"At the high school," one of the middle school teachers interrupted.

"Let her finish," Javier said.

Calyce said, "I'd be happy to hear what your needs are too."

"Dan," DeGroot said when Calyce eventually ran out of words. "Your turn."

She had not once mentioned her race.

Dan got up, though Calyce had remained seated throughout her presentation. He walked behind DeGroot, touched DeGroot's shoulders, and stepped into the open area at the center of the room. He had no notes as he stood silently for a full five seconds, letting people size him up before he began speaking. Calyce saw him in profile, and she noticed his newly shined brown shoes, his dark jeans and the baby blue buttoned collared dress shirt below his moon-pie face.

He started by thanking everyone at both the lower and middle school campuses for having met with him one-on-one over the prior three weeks.

Calyce looked around the room and saw all the nodding.

He had heard their concerns, he said, and he knew from them that collaboration must be their motto moving forward. It was now a consolidated department, and that was done for a reason he had endorsed because it made for a unified, focused mission. He turned away from Calyce as he said that he had purposefully not drafted an entirely new curriculum because that should be done together, with representatives from the lower, middle, and upper schools on one joint committee.

"And I wouldn't choose them," he said. "That too we should all do collaboratively."

It was still only May. Changes could certainly be identified and implemented by September. The point was that heading the department would be peer-to-peer and not some top-down, kingly position.

"Or queenly. But there's something else I have to say, which I think is vitally important."

He was making deliberate eye contact with each person around the room, except her, quarter-turning as he did it. "As many of you know, I'm gay. This school has never had an openly gay department head in its history. Not a single department, and there are no gays in senior administration either. None. Not one. One hundred percent of the school's management at all levels objectively appears to be straight."

He began ticking things off. "We have white people. We have white men and white women. We have black people, both men and now even our black high school Vice Principal, Belinda. As you know, I personally led the charge to get her appointed. So black women are represented, even older black women like Belinda, if grandmothers are a separate group."

He smiled. "But there's not a single gay man or lesbian woman despite the school's declared goals of diversity and acceptance. No one who's nonbinary, or trans. Not one person from anywhere in the LGBTQ community, at any level of management at either campus. So I ask you, isn't it time?

"I want to say something else that's difficult. We as a school emphasize our roots in the Jewish and black communities, which is great, but that means there's an ethos of oppression that's always in the air. It's a one-down, underdog sort of atmosphere that permeates. Amita mentioned this recently."

He turned to face Calyce as if on cue. "There's this sulking sense of wrongs that still need to be righted, like we're continuing to fight only the same battles we had fifty years ago. I'm sorry but it's true. But my story isn't that. Sure there's oppression and violence, but it's ultimately a story of attainment, of celebration even. It's about empowerment so it's uplifting for our department and the school. And I say, let's celebrate a new beginning, and let's have that positive attitude imbue our new collaboration as an integrated department."

He then turned slowly, all the way around, looking at each voter before he sat down.

Calyce held back until all of them had left, which meant she had to sit and watch DeGroot depart with Dan, throwing his arm around the younger man as they moved down the hallway. She saw them bonding through the plate glass.

The next day was the first of her creative writing class's final two sessions. She didn't want to distribute all the five stories, though, that had made the winning top ten through six.

"Why not?" a young man now headed to Brown asked her.

"I've made copies of ten through seven but not number six."

"Why not?" a young woman on her way to St. Andrews said.

"It's mine, that's why. The Greek flash fiction about Aeolus on Angels Landing when his children have left him."

"I love that one!" a young woman going to the University of Virginia exclaimed.

"We all do!" they said. "Make copies of that one too, so we can keep it."

Calyce asked her ducklings-turned-to-swans bashfully, genuinely wanting to know, "Is my story really that good?"

Dan was in the tiny conference room/coat rack/storage area at the small round table grading tests with his back to the open door. All Calyce could see was his gray crewneck sweater.

She knocked. Dan turned to look at her, but he didn't motion her inside.

"I wanted to extend my sincerest congratulations," she told him from the doorway.

He didn't speak. He was observing her like a specimen.

"Well … that's why I came by. They obviously wanted you and not me."

Nothing.

"So, congratulations."

She waited, got nothing, then turned to go.

She took a single step, but then he said it.

"You were too easy, you know."

She stopped.

"All I had to do was let you be you," Dan said. "Your way is all you see. All I had to do was stay under your radar and not do anything in front of you and you never noticed. You were so arrogant about your own entitlement that you didn't see a thing.

"There's nothing sophisticated about you, Calyce. Nothing unusual, so it wasn't even interesting. You're just a grandmother treating us all like we're eleven."

As a last salvo, he said she'd have more time now "for your hiking. That was easy too, to remind them of all the times you've talked about Zion. And they saw the walks you were taking at lunch. All I had to do was nudge them into thinking that by electing me they were doing you a favor. That, plus saying that Javier wanted the job, which of course he didn't, but it distracted you from seeing me."

Effie insisted on taking Calyce out to dinner at a famous old time-y seafood restaurant in the next suburb over. Unchanged since the 1940s, the place had two narrow rooms. A large lunch counter curved in one of them, and bare tables and chairs filled the other. Effie told the waitress they wanted one of the tables for two on the "restaurant" side, where they were seated near the clattering front door.

Calyce wasn't interested in eating, or in eating out with her mother, but she couldn't make up a reason fast enough to avoid it, so she came, and she drove them. There was a great deal of Friday night traffic, so parking was hard to find.

"Don't worry," her mother said. "I can walk miles now."

All through dinner, Effie had smiled with some hidden knowledge. She had charmed the waitress and flirted with the young male manager, who had come by to see how they liked their clam chowder and crab claws with a hot dipping sauce that Effie had always found addictive. She licked her lips as she wiped her fingers, reaching for yet another paper napkin.

"It's casual," Effie said over the din and the banging front door that blasted late-May humidity onto their shins. "But it's good."

Calyce said, "This dinner will cost you a fortune. Seafood is expensive."

When their coffees arrived, Effie leaned over to pull something from her purse on the floor, which she then handed to Calyce with a big, game-show-hostess gesture. "This is to make you feel better."

It was a brochure for a Caribbean cruise, to start the Saturday after the Friday that school ended in early June. It was an exterior stateroom, with two twin beds and a balcony. The colorful brochure showed the sea viewed from two balcony deck chairs angled toward each other. In them, a gray-haired couple held hands across the air, their love knot of fingers centered perfectly in the frame.

"That's us," Effie said. "Only we're mom and daughter. But this is the beginning, now that that awful school has given you more free time. I know you needed the extra money from being Head but since I'm here you don't."

Calyce looked at her, nearly speechless.

She asked her mother, "You can afford a cruise? For two? You have that kind of money?"

∧∧∧

Calyce asked Effie the next question in the car, in the dark, before she started the ignition. They had parked two blocks from the restaurant, and the question had dawned and brightened into certitude as they had walked.

"You're paying Damion now, aren't you? You're helping him with his rent. He's unemployed. He can't possibly afford that stuff he's buying."

"He gets jobs."

"Not enough. Are you paying his other bills, too? How much are you giving him?"

"I don't think I like your tone."

"That's why he brought that fancy cake. It was for you."

Effie crossed her arms but didn't deny it.

They drove silently toward home.

Finally, at a stoplight, Effie said, "He needs the money."

But in the townhouse driveway, after Calyce pulled onto the cement, Calyce took in her breath and said, "I know why you're doing it. I've figured it out. You're paying him so he doesn't try to move back here. You don't ever want to go back to Florida, do you? You want to stay here with me, and he's taking your money because he's in on the whole thing."

To: Senior Creative Writing Class
From: Calyce Tate
Re: Extra Credit Opportunity

If anyone wants/needs extra credit, please read *The Lottery* by Shirley Jackson and write me a personal essay of no more than 250 words describing how someone you love has betrayed you. Deadline May 31.

Once Calyce had sent the email, she checked her bank balance again, as she had done twice a day since the vote.

She then began researching assisted-living facilities for her mother.

Overwhelmed with data an hour later, Calyce phoned Damion, who said he didn't have time to talk. Selene was coming to cook dinner and she had just left Whole Foods with two lobsters. She had some good news, he said. "Something about her job. What did you call for?"

"You were keeping this a secret from me, both you and your grandmother."

"It was none of your business."

"Everything about her is my business. And it's not fair to Maria that your grandmother's giving you money. Your sister's not getting any, and it ought to be equal."

"How do you know she's not?"

"Is she?"

A pause. "Not that I know of."

He told her that Effie had insisted. Effie had said she knew he was in a bind because he didn't have a regular job anymore to pay his big new monthly rent bill as long as she continued to live with Calyce and occupy "his room."

Effie said he would be doing her a favor, really, that it would be a privilege if he accepted money every month for his "kindness" – her word, he said – in allowing her to stay with her daughter, in a part of the townhouse where she would cause Calyce the least trouble.

"She was nearly crying," Damion said. "She begged me. What was I supposed to do?"

But Calyce would not be diverted. "How much is she giving you?"

"She said you'd ask, but she says she wants that to stay between us. I don't feel right violating her trust."

To: Calyce Tate
From: Dan Waggoner
English Department Head-Elect
Cc: John DeGroot

Re: Extra Credit Opportunity

The parent of one of your Creative Writing seniors has already sent me your email from earlier this evening. You know you can't give assignments during Senior Quest, even for extra credit. I want you to send out an immediate email withdrawing your prior, and copy me on it.

Also email me in advance about any future changes you propose to make to the set curriculum, including any new assignments/extra credit. All changes from now on will need my advance written approval.

Calyce read Dan's email, then checked for cheap flights to Las Vegas, the closest airport to Zion. When the search window asked how many travelers, she clicked "1."

Her phone rang.

Maria was calling to report giddily that Greg had just gotten his first, directed assignment from his career development officer at the State Department. They were leaving in two months for a consular post in Tanzania, which was a country Greg had put high on his bid list, so he was ecstatic.

"It's not as dangerous as you read," Maria assured her. "Come see us now that you have more time? We'll have a couch for you."

On the final day of May, Calyce took a long shower. She felt the hot water course over her with its dialed pulsations from the yellowing showerhead that was old but still worked perfectly. As she was climbing warm and moist into bed, her phone chimed its incoming-phone-call song, though the sound was muffled in the depths of her satchel, where she had already buried it for the night. The white charging cord kinked out the top and made its way to her wall outlet.

She ignored the caller, who was violating don't-call-after-ten etiquette. A minute later, though, she realized that the lateness of the hour might mean something serious had happened, so she climbed out of bed.

Damion had called but had left no message. She cocked her head at the strangeness of a call from her son, rather than a text. She dialed him back, but then he didn't answer until the fourth ring.

"I figured you'd be asleep," he said without alarm, so she relaxed.

"I just bought plane tickets for Zion."

"With Aunt Nina?"

"She's back in Chile. I'm going alone next month, right after school lets out."

Calyce propped herself against her headboard and tucked her feet in with her free hand. "God knows how I'll pay for it. I charged it all, including the hotel for three nights. And I –"

"Mom. Selene's pregnant."

Catherine couldn't stand it anymore. Mike had been avoiding her since the Billy Goat Trail. Every day she had waited at lunch but he had walked past her, and no one else had come to share her table. Day after day she ate alone, right here at the front of the lunchroom by the doorway where everyone could see her. She could have approached other tables and asked to sit with them, but she hadn't the whole year as she had yearned for him, turning them down until they had stopped gesturing for her to join them, and now she did not know if she would be welcome. So she paged a book and ate in silence.

That day once more, she smiled at Mike as he entered but he ignored her.

"I have to talk to him alone," she told herself with her head down as he squeezed by toward his friends.

David was all smiles after the departmental meeting, hanging at the door as the others filed out congratulating him. He motioned for Catherine to exit ahead of him, so she had to. He joined her in the hallway.

She swiveled her head to look back through the glass door into the conference room, where Alice now sat entirely alone at the vast table. In that moment, Alice was she, with Catherine's same expression from the lunchroom every day now watching Mike ignore her. On Alice's bombed face Catherine saw the same total devastation.

"You were coughing all during our meeting," David was saying. "Do you have something wrong with your throat?"

"Tonight I want you to read The Lottery by Shirley Jackson," Catherine told her class. "It's a modern example of third-person *objective point of view, which isn't used much nowadays. It's also called the cinematic point of view because we don't go inside the characters' heads but receive the story through action and dialogue. It's my favorite POV because it really makes the writer have to show and not tell. After you read it, I want you to write a piece with this point of view."*

Ryan's new girlfriend Elena from Target was nice enough, and now she was pregnant. That, at least, he could accomplish.

JUNE

Calyce couldn't remember the last time Damion had come to the high school voluntarily to visit her, the last time it had been his idea without her prodding. In fact, she couldn't recall that it had ever happened. Even when he had been a student there, Damion had never sought her out. When they had passed in the halls, he had ignored her.

Once he graduated he was gone, and he had stayed away until his five-year reunion, when he had drunkenly told her at the end of the night that he'd gone to the bash only because "I'm hot now. I wasn't back then."

But he had called that Friday morning, the first of June, to ask if he could take her out for lunch at the French bistro he still remembered on Wisconsin Avenue.

"The one with the cat," he said. "On me. My own money."

Calyce had been delighted.

Over mussels in garlic broth and bowl-glasses of wine, he said Selene was ten weeks along already when she had told him the prior evening. She had wanted to be sure, Selene had said, and she had wanted to be sure first that she wanted to keep it. She had decided she did.

And so did he. He had made that decision immediately, he told his mother.

Calyce asked him gently, "Do you love her?"

He ducked his head and nodded and he was a boy again, bobbing his head about something happy that embarrassed him.

"When did they paint this?" Damion asked half an hour later as they entered the earth and stars stairwell.

And then, "We're thinking of Cisco. Cisco Tate. Sort of Western. Do you still get the family discount on tuition here if you're the grandmother and not the mother?"

"As long as I teach here."

But then she stopped. "Tate. Are you getting married?"

He smiled deeply then, his joy running to his eyes.

Near the top, he asked as three teenagers angled by them, "When are you going?"

"Tomorrow morning. They're giving me a tour of the facility."

"You're still not telling her?"

"Hey, Calyce."

They turned to see Roger coming up behind them. She introduced the two men, who shook hands. Damion then said goodbye, descending quickly as the other two continued. When Damion got to the bottom, he shrugged with both palms up in a playful gesture. Even from thirty feet above him, she saw his "guess who's got a boyfriend" smirk.

As Calyce and Roger exited into the third-floor corridor, she said, "I'm going back to Zion next week. I'm going to get to the top of that thing."

"You want company?"

He had surprised her, and she looked at him.

"I'm serious," he said. "I'll go with you."

She inhaled. Then exhaled slowly. "Have you got a minute to talk somewhere privately?"

Calyce found them an empty classroom. She didn't sit and she didn't motion that Roger should, so he stood as she moved her fingers inside her clasped hands nervously.

Finally, she told him. She said he had always been nice to her, and patient. He was a good man and he deserved her honesty.

He responded by clasping his own hands behind his back as he waited.

"I like you," she said. "I do, but I don't date outside my race. I'm sorry."

She took a breath and corrected herself. "No, I'm not sorry. I don't date white men and I never have, but I am sorry if that hurts you."

A pause happened then that was so long the class bell rang and ended. As they stood, silently, the hall began to fill with charging feet.

"No way to change that?" he asked simply.

She shook her head but her tone was kind. "People say I should be more open-minded and modern, but I'm not. These are my values and they don't change."

It was a high-rise in Wheaton, a short drive from her townhouse, with a surface parking lot behind the tall structure. On the front side of the assisted living building that faced the busy street, a thin strip of grass skirted four low-rise trees planted in regular intervals, their mulched brown circles cut precisely. Facing one another along the cement walkway to the businesslike front doors were two metal benches, both fully occupied, three each, by elderly women, who watched wordlessly who came and went. All the old women were white.

The forty-something marketing woman shook Calyce's hand too eagerly. After a brief meeting in the woman's office off the dated lobby, which was paneled seventies-style in floor-to-ceiling wood, they began a tour first in the communal dining room in a windowless corner of the first floor, beyond the bank of elevators. Under a low ceiling the servers, all of whom were black, were setting up "for luncheon" in the artificial, romantic-dining light cast by outdated, dangling-crystal wall sconces and overhead can lights in the popcorn ceiling.

The air was unmoving. The round tables, Calyce saw, each had place settings for six on the green tablecloths.

"We change them with the seasons," the woman told her. "Do you see the napkins are cloth too, and they match?"

No, there was no assigned seating, though "the residents" usually quickly chose their preferred spot and friends "with whom to eat, though family is always welcome." Several of the tables were partly occupied already with ancient ladies waiting, one of whom at last was toffee-colored. The three meals a day, the marketing woman said, met all the residents' dietary needs, for they had been established in a set rotating order by their on-site nutritionist.

"Certainly nothing spicy," the woman said. "Only American food. Nothing exotic, and we try to keep the salt down. Most of the residents don't like seafood, so we have sole sometimes but nothing fishy. Let me show you the tenth-floor unit we have available. You said your mother would be the financially responsible party?"

As the elevator rose she described the levels of care they provided. From what Calyce had said over the phone, her mother would still qualify for independent living, though she was on the cusp of needing some assisted care. The available unit was for their most ambulatory residents. When the time came later, Effie would have to move to a lower story.

The woman unlocked a door down a shadowy interior hall of identical facing paired doors, one of which still wore an Easter egg wreath, in June. The corridor smelled lightly but distinctly of Clorox.

They entered an empty one-bedroom unit with a small sitting area. Along one short wall was a mini-kitchen with a sink and a two-electric-burner stovetop, but no dishwasher or oven.

"Too dangerous," the marketing woman said.

She then pointed out the small fridge, explaining that the building had a little commissary on the first floor, which she would show Calyce on the way out. "As for furniture, the residents usually prefer to bring their own, to remind them of home, though we can arrange for rental things if you need them."

There appeared to be one large window where heavy blue pinch-pleat curtains were pulled back on each side, over white sheers that covered the window. Behind the sheers, a Venetian blind was pulled all the way down and closed. As Calyce walked over, the woman said, "It's not the modern taste, but our residents like their privacy."

"From what?" Calyce moved a slat of the blind to peer outside.

The window was smaller than the coverings suggested, beginning halfway up the wall. The view was down to the roofs of shorter commercial buildings and 1940's homes.

"No balcony?"

"We would consider them unsafe. There is plenty of room outside, though, on the benches out front."

Calyce asked, "Doesn't the window open? I don't even see where it can slide."

"But what will you do?" Catherine kept asking her son Ryan whenever they talked about the cherished baby, who had changed everything even now, still months before its birth.

"Where will you live?" Catherine repeatedly asked him.

Calyce toured three other places over the next ten days but never told her hummingbird mother, who hovered, asking repeatedly what the odd forays were to the outside world. Calyce kept changing the subject. Finally, it was a Sunday evening and Damion arrived for dinner with a nauseous Selene, whose body still had not gotten used to the idea of a baby. The young woman wasn't eating much, she wasn't sleeping, and she asked Calyce and Effie if she'd be sick for the entire pregnancy. Effie assured her no, this would pass, but Calyce answered frankly, that it really depended on each woman. Everyone was different.

"I think I've lost ten pounds." Selene's pale skin was wax.

Sitting together in Calyce's small living room, where Effie claimed her usual spot on one loveseat, Calyce wondered out loud whether she should still go to Zion.

Selene answered, "I'd hate for you to miss it because of me. My mother's coming from Minneapolis anyway. Damion's going to meet her next week."

The air was filled with the smell of baking pork chops, zucchini and diced tomatoes.

From under her backside, Effie pulled out an envelope.

She announced, "I have a surprise for my Number One Daughter!"

"Another surprise?" But Calyce opened it.

As Effie beamed, Calyce pulled out a check signed and dated that same day, made out to Calyce for $4,000.

"I'm going with you to Zion!" Effie trilled. "That should cover both our tickets and the car and everything else. I booked us into the Bellagio. You didn't seem to like the cruise idea so I thought we could do this instead. Don't you love it?"

Damion watched from the other couch, where he sat with Selene. Calyce had seen him lean forward once the check appeared, to listen to every word.

"And when I talked to Nina," Effie continued, "she told me you really liked that convertible you had before, so I reserved one." Her wide grin nearly sliced her face in half.

"Grandma," Damion said. "Do you think I can go too?"

"What?" Selene said.

Damion ignored her. "Is that enough for me to go too?"

"But what about Selene?" Effie said.

"She's got her mother," Damion said quickly. "And with the baby, who knows when I'll have the chance again."

To Calyce he said, "We never got to go anywhere when I was little. You were always working. This will be that vacation. Selene will let me go if I tell her how important it is to me."

Selene jabbed him. "I'm sitting right here."

But still he didn't look at her. "Please, Grandma?"

The next Friday was the last day of the school year. Calyce was heading toward the main entrance lugging a cardboard box with her desktop things when a graduating senior called her name. Calyce stopped to wait for her.

She congratulated the teenager, who was now a poised and confident young-woman version of the anxious girl rooting deep in her backpack at the beginning of first semester.

"Are you sure we can't get that extra credit, like you posted?" the college-bound senior asked.

Calyce shook her head. "These things aren't mine to decide anymore. Dan said no, so it's no. He's the one in charge now. I only work here."

Simon's daughter graduated from high school that next Saturday, on the same day that Calyce had to attend the graduation ceremony for her own high school, whose administration dictated that all faculty and staff sit compulsorily through a ritual unchanged for twenty years, but for the identity of the new Headmaster. The former square-chinned Episcopalian perpetually in buckled flats had finally been forcibly retired. She had been replaced by a well-intentioned late-forties man whose one child attended the middle school. He better fit the school's demographic but had an odd habit of gesturing for emphasis with his right pinkie in the air. Calyce in her stiff seat played an internal parlor game of Count How Many Times during the man's platitudinous speech, which flowed over them like warm bath water. His predecessor had been the same soothing way, an occupational requirement in a world of over-educated, easily outraged, combative professional parents who keep constant score.

That evening, they all called Simon's daughter to congratulate her. She in turn thanked Calyce for the Amazon gift certificate.

"Are you excited about Tulane?" Calyce asked her.

Calyce congratulated Simon too, when he got on the phone.

"The last one," she told him. "Your house will feel empty, at least until they move back in."

Because Effie was paying for everything, they could afford to take a private minivan cab to Reagan National Airport.

Calyce was ready a full half an hour before she had scheduled it to arrive. She had stuffed her new backpack with everything she needed for the climb, times two, since Damion had insisted he wanted to accompany her to the top of Angels Landing. He was perfectly capable of it, he had told her. He said the hike couldn't be nearly as tough as she described.

She wore cargo shorts and the same stiff high-top hiking boots she had worn when she had gone with Nina. They felt like old friends, as she felt the renewed hug of wool socks against her ankles. On her head she wore a rust-colored billed cap with sequins, which Nina had bought for her at the airport in Las Vegas. It flattened her hair, the fit was so tight. Her curls flipped like dolphins at her shoulders.

"You look absurd," Damion told her at the front door, which she had propped open with her rolling bag so she could watch the street.

She scanned her meticulously groomed son's black knit shirt and charcoal knife-pleated slacks. "You can't hike in that."

"It's Vegas."

"We're only in Vegas one night."

"I forgot how much I *love* spending time with you." But he

was smiling, and it was real, and it traveled between them unfiltered.

"You two look like you're already having fun," Effie said as she appeared in her pristine new white tennis shoes and broad-rimmed cloth hat with a neck flap that made her look like she was on safari.

"I forgot the mail," Calyce said. "I'll just be a second."

In the box was a small padded brown envelope addressed in a hand she didn't recognize. The minivan had come, so she threw it in her satchel purse and didn't give it another thought until they were waiting idly at the gate. She told them she had to use the airport bathroom, then found a stall and tore the package open to find a one-line note and one last carved stone star. This one was Carrara marble, milky white with veins of dove gray. She turned it in her grateful fingers, where it was cool to the touch and smooth to her thumb. She flipped it, the points familiar as all the others had become over the six months since Roger had given her the stars at Christmas.

She read the note.

I'm sorry I'm the wrong color. If I could change that, I would.

It took Catherine several more weeks of public humiliation, but she finally stormed into Mike's classroom after yet another ostracizing lunch. She had walked by the door's slit window twice to make sure he was alone.

She did not knock but simply entered. As she came across the short carpet, he said, "What are you doing here?"

"You ignore me. Can't we talk about this?"

He was instantly angry. "I'm married. Happily, in case you didn't know that before you threw yourself at me. Get a life. You're like a puppy waiting for me in there every day."

"I am not!"

"You're a sad woman who spends all her time inside her head. That damn poncho with those trinkets. You look like a bag lady."

"Then why did you eat with me?"

"I felt sorry for you."

"All those months?"

"You had no one else to eat with. Not once."

"But you kissed me!"

"No I didn't."

"You kissed me back!"

"That's just another story you tell yourself inside your head."

They headed north out of Las Vegas the next morning with Damion driving. He insisted even though Calyce was the one who had driven the route before. Tiny Effie of course got the convertible's front seat next to her grandson. It took them five minutes to open the top, which Calyce thought was a great idea.

As they left the eerie early-morning neon and reached the flat pre-heating desert, Calyce's knees in the miniature backseat were shoved to her chin. Crammed next to her was her backpack piled on top of her mother's rolling bag, its four small hard wheels punching her side. Damion's one suitcase had claimed the miniscule trunk.

"The air's so dry!" Effie yelled back to Calyce.

Damion yelled too, as the wind whipped. "Never had heat without humidity before."

Calyce leaned forward to shout to him in the bright sunlight as they passed a motor speedway fifteen minutes later. "Did you put on sunscreen?"

After an hour they approached what looked like a weather front of barren grey mountains that rose like a sandstorm nearly vertically off the flat plane of endless sand. There was no visible entrance for the highway, yet they drove inexorably toward them. At the last moment, the highway curved into a hidden passage that began the rise northward on two narrow lanes of asphalt with hard cement moveable barriers protecting them from the southbound cars, semi's, SUVs hauling jet skis, and boxlike rigid RVs, some of which seemed as long as the tractor-trailers but all of which matched the grays and browns of the dirt and jutting naked cliffs that thrust next to the highway. Above them as Damion took the sharp turns, ships of rock with striped layers rose 500 feet and slanted as sharply as sinking Titanics.

Calyce watched her son glance up, then stare up at the five-hundred-million-year-old hardscape like nothing he had ever seen.

"Virgin River Gorge," she yelled up to him. "You know how much this road cost? A hundred dollars an inch! Ten million a mile, and that was back in the seventies."

"Where are you taking us?" Effie asked that evening in Springdale as they walked north toward the touristy restaurants and shops. Cars and RVs choked the street in both directions, and they had to negotiate through a stream of pedestrians.

Calyce answered with a smile, "A Mexican place I know."

"I love Mexican food!" Effie exclaimed.

Damion said, "I hate it. Makes me fart."

Effie said, "Let's take a walk after dinner. How far is the entrance to the park?"

Damion had changed clothes. His slacks were gray now and his new polo was purple. "They're all white," he said about the other tourists they were passing.

Calyce looked to the cloudless sky and saw the canyon walls, not because she could actually see them in the darkness but because the glittering stardust above them ended suddenly in utter blackness on both sides of her field of vision much higher than it would if there were a flat horizon. What at home was a bowl of shining sky was here only a fat pie slice, but that slice was so much brighter. Directly overhead a million holes were punched by straight pins through black construction paper held in front of a spotlight.

"Isn't this beautiful?" she asked them.

Damion pulled the front of his shirt away from his chest, flapping it. "I'm still sweating. It must be ninety."

Calyce turned into a stucco courtyard that faced the street. On a wall, *Mexican Village* was painted in turquoise. "This place is fun, you'll see."

"But I told you. I hate Mexican," Damion said, but Calyce had already stepped in, trailed by her happy mother.

At 5:00 a.m. the next morning, the Utah sky was inky still, for creeping dawn would not begin for another thirty minutes. By 6:30 the sun would rise, but it wouldn't reach the top of Zion's western rim until Calyce and Damion had already climbed to Scout Lookout, if her time estimate was correct. They would take advantage of the early light at the cool of the day to hike that first 1,000 vertical feet.

But now, as Effie readied herself in the bathroom, humming, Calyce stepped onto the Lincoln-log balcony of their hotel at the south end of town, on an exposed hillock on the west side of the main road. Arranged in long two-story buildings, every double-queen room had a rustic décor and a matching balcony that faced the psychedelic canyon.

Outside, the birds that would welcome the dawn had not yet awakened. There were no sounds but the infrequent swish of a passing car breezing through as it moved south toward Hurricane.

Calyce put both elbows on the rough-hewn top log of the balustrade, gazing west to where the sky was still dark velvet. There, was the falling full moon that had journeyed across the night for hours. She blinked as her eyes fixed on it, for it was so sharply focused that it surprised her. A perfect ring circled it so closely that there were no stars between the ring and the paillette disk.

She turned and called through the open sliding door. "Mom, are you ready?"

The three of them parked in the huge dirt parking lot at the Visitor Center, then walked the short distance to the display boards on posts near the entrance, across from the bathrooms and the outdoor water faucets. As her son and her mother waited in the warming morning, Calyce filled the three liter-sized water bottles from the tap.

"Is one for me?" Effie asked.

Calyce shook her head. "You'll be at the Lodge. They have water there. Did you bring money?"

Calyce pointed at Damion's feet. He was wearing ratty,

stained, half-tattered old running shoes whose pitted foam bottoms were detaching.

"Are you sure you won't trip?" she asked him.

"I don't need all that water." Damion was stiff in jeans so new she had never seen them. "This isn't the first time I've taken a hike, you know."

Calyce said, "We need to check the board inside for flood conditions."

"Why?" he said. "We're going up."

As Effie looked reflexively at the clear sky, Calyce said, "Flash floods can happen, and when they do, they have to close the Narrows to rescue people. I don't know what it does up there on Angels Landing, on those rocks."

At the shuttle bus stop, there was already a line of early hikers, all men and one woman, confirmed as serious by their sturdy shorts, no-nonsense hats and boots and, for two of them, including the woman, thick coils of rope looped over their muscled shoulders. Damion was their age, but Calyce was thirty years older. Effie beat them by more than fifty years, yet the old woman charmed them all, chatting amiably.

"So here's your stop," Calyce said to Effie as the motoring shuttle approached Zion Lodge and its wide front lawn's huge, ancient cottonwood. A little boy and a little girl were playing under it already.

"But I'm going with you," Effie said as the bus pulled in. "I can make it."

"No you're not," Damion told her firmly. "It's too hard."

"But I walk more than you do."

"Mom, I only bought vests for two," Calyce said. "And you're not going up there without some bright color on."

At the Lodge, Effie still refused to climb down. Damion made a face, waiting irritably for her to leave them.

Calyce talked to Effie like she was a child, as the shuttle headed north again. "The bus will let Damion and me off at the next stop, then turn around eventually. It'll loop back to the Lodge, so get off there. No arguing. There's food, and you can sit in the lobby. It's nicer than waiting for us up there. There's nothing but bathrooms and benches at this next bus stop, and we'll be gone for hours."

"I can't even come partway?" Effie said. "I can do it. I want to show you."

"No," Damion said.

"But I –"

"No!" he said. "You'll stay at the Lodge."

"Alright. Alright," Effie said. "I'll go back there and wait."

The instant they stepped off the shuttle and the doors closed, leaving Effie inside, Calyce said to Damion angrily, "You told her, didn't you? You told her I'm looking at nursing homes. That's why she wants to show me she can do this."

But he was crossing the street already, striding toward the metal footbridge over the winking river.

"When do we get to Angels Landing?" he said over his shoulder. "This is easy."

A mere fifteen minutes later he was so out of breath he had to lean on a boulder in a litter of rock-fall ten stories above the canyon floor. As he sank back against the stone, Calyce saw that under the neon-orange, plastic, road-construction vest she had brought and made him put on, his taupe shirt had armpit stains already.

Calyce unhitched her backpack and fished out one of the three water bottles for him to carry, but he wouldn't. He took four long swigs as he bellows-breathed, then gave it back to her to lug for him.

They stopped every five minutes to regain their wind. Under the open vest front, his shirt soon became wet in a pyramid, and the half-moons under his armpits grew to meet it.

"Are you really going to put Grandma in a home?" he asked during one of their breaks, to cover his gasping.

She nodded. "More water?"

Ten minutes later, "Mom, you watch Jimmy sometimes. Would you do that for us too, with the baby?"

"Of course. I'd be happy to."

"Because," he said between breaths, "Selene is thinking she may want to make extra money by being on-call at night in addition to her day job, and I'm thinking about going back to school."

"Are you serious this time?"

"Really? Is that what you say to me?"

She saw that, even exhausted, his insolence never stopped.

At the Lodge, Effie visited the lobby restroom, then climbed the stairs to the Red Rock Grill. It was too noisy and crowded, though, with breakfasting families of very loud small children. She found the snack bar instead near the gift shop downstairs and bought a cinnamon bun with a cup of coffee. She sat at an outside table until all the other tables quickly filled and a family with a bumptious seven-year-old asked if they could "join" her.

"It's great you'll have more time now," Damion said when they stopped at a tight loop in the trail, which had turned rose-colored as it cut under an outcropping and tilted upward in an endlessly long run like the initial climb of a rollercoaster.

He looked at it and asked, "How much farther?"

She adjusted her backpack. "Still far. We're not even at Scout Lookout, up there above that cut-out. This is the easy part. Do you want a protein bar?"

She fished it out, feeling past the hard side of her cell phone.

He took his time chewing, chewing and breathing.

Across from them now, hundreds of feet above the riverside trees below them, the laser sun had risen over the eastern rim of the canyon. Its heat reached the top of her head. As they rested, she stretched her arm above her hat to feel it.

She said, "It's going to be very hot soon."

"You know," he said, "she's not working as much now because she's been so sick with the baby. She's had to cut her hours. And she's had those doctor bills, and she's got this high deductible."

He paused, but Calyce didn't say anything.

He added, "And at the moment, I'm not working full-time either."

As he handed her the empty wrapper, she realized suddenly that she had bought the bar, she had carefully packed it, she had lugged it all the way from D.C., and she had hauled it up the mountain for him. She was now expected to carry the foil all the way back down.

She said, "You know I don't have any extra money. You know as well as I do that I didn't get that raise when I wasn't elected."

But he surprised her then. He reached out and said, "It's my turn to carry that backpack."

He circled around to the subject again a few minutes later as they arrived in refreshingly cool Refrigerator Canyon. She thought they had resolved it, but they hadn't, apparently.

The level grade helped him regain his lost breath as they walked between walls soaring vertically hundreds of feet above them. The sun streamed overhead but didn't reach them and never would, the little canyon was so pocketed. The heat would blast again, though, the instant they left it.

"The thing is," Damion said. "She may have to run out quickly to a call at night, and I might be working."

He let it hang, walking alongside until she got it.

Calyce stopped and turned to him. "You're kidding. You want to move back in, don't you? And you want to bring Selene and the baby."

"Just until we get enough money to get a place. And she's already found someone to sublet my apartment in D.C. It's a guy she did some work for."

"So you want to move back in right away? Immediately?"

He nodded. "And until you can get rid of Grandma, we thought she could move up to the guestroom again. She's fine now. She can do the stairs. Selene and I will pay our share of the bills, and two-thirds of them, for sure, once Grandma moves out. And you'll be able to see your grandson all the time once he's born."

"Grandson? You know it's a boy?"

He smiled. "And think of all the gas you'll be saving not having to come down to the D.C. apartment. Don't you want to be near him as he grows up?"

They left the sheltered canyon, heading toward the whiplashing, stacked switchbacks.

"'Grows up,'" she said into the furnace-blast of sun. "How long do you plan to stay?"

He exhaled audibly. She heard his annoyance.

"What?" she said.

He tugged on his orange vest. "I don't know what you expect. If you make her pay for her own nursing home, she'll be using all the rent she's getting from Florida."

"How else would it be paid for?"

"That puts it all on me and Selene, to pay the rent in D.C. But that's what you want, isn't it?"

"What does *that* mean?"

"These vests are stupid. I don't know why you're making me say this." He was mad now. "With how sick she is with the baby, she's not making enough to cover her share of the rent. You're the one who made me rent that."

His rage was growing. She felt it bloom.

"No thanks to you," he said, his voice louder, "I've found someone to take it off my hands. You'll be off the hook on your guarantee. You ought to be thanking me instead of criticizing."

But Calyce was angry now too. She marched quickly ahead of him, starting up the steep switchbacks that were so narrow as they snaked up the sheer vertical face that helicopters had had to fly in cement when the Park Service restored them in the 1980s.

Calyce didn't look back until she reached the cerulean blue hundreds of searing feet above them. Far below, she could see

Damion struggling as he pitched forward, gulping for air with his hands on his knees on a switchback that still wasn't the last one. Her son could barely move the grade was so unrelenting and he was so badly out of shape, she realized. Her own legs were tired but not shaking this time. All the walking at home and at school at lunchtime had made her stronger.

"You alright?" she yelled down to him.

He waved her forward but she waited until he finally arrived, his chest ballooning and collapsing. Another hiker originally far behind them now passed them, giving her son a concerned look, lingering on Damion's chest as it accordioned.

Slowly, they walked to a sign a thousand feet above the valley, on the cusp of a flaking, porous sandstone mound that blocked their view of the final, far-off, harrowing fin they had to climb, which neither of them had ever attempted.

Since 2004 six people have died from falling.

The 1.1 mile (1.8 km) round-trip route from Scout Lookout to Angels Landing is a strenuous climb on a narrow ridge over 1,400 feet above the canyon floor. This route is not recommended during high winds, storms, or if snow or ice is present.

"Is that for real?" Damion asked.

They walked forward, to the sharp left edge of the lookout, where the plates of hard-sponge rock ended suddenly in a straight red cliff with a sheer drop higher than a skyscraper. There was no rail. There was nothing to stop a fall. One step and they would be free-falling.

She pointed way, way down to the sinuous road that looked like embroidery thread it was so far below them.

"Right here is a thousand feet up," she said. "That's the road we came in on."

He tried to lean over but she shot an arm across his chest as if he were five years old again in the car at a stop sign.

She said, "Someone died right here when they stood up. She had her feet dangling over the edge but when she got up she lost her footing and went backwards."

He craned to look down. From their left, from the north, the same white shuttle bus appeared with its kinked center, but it was so small now it looked like two Tic-Tacs connected.

They drank again in the drying sun, preparing. He was exhausted. She could see it. His disordered face showed the blazing heat and the extreme effort of climbing, which had been steadily uphill for longer than he had ever ascended. His puddled face dripped sweat from his hairline to his eyebrows. His feet didn't look planted, for he moved them tentatively.

She could see he was breathing hard too, still, after several minutes of rest, but it wasn't bringing much recovery. The water he was chugging didn't help.

She wanted to ask him again if he could do it, but she dared not. Instead, she chose to say, "I'm proud of you," to encourage him.

"Don't be condescending," he snapped.

She reached for the empty water bottle in his hand and stowed it once more in the backpack, which she now insisted on taking from him.

"This way," she said, turning to her right, toward the rising slope of blush rock.

She wouldn't have seen them anyway, even if she had been

looking skyward, for they were still miles away, but hidden in the vast sky, far above and well west of the north-south cut where they were, mountainous storm clouds were assembling.

One of the first support posts sunk into the porous rock had been pulled out by the force of climbers depending on it with their full body weight. The dangling post was still attached by its needle-eye to the thick metal links, though, as it swung uselessly.

Damion didn't know what to do. "The chain stops," he told her.

Calyce had never made it beyond that point before, but she said, "Let me get past you."

There was nowhere to put her hands. She had to climb up without touching anything because there was nothing but smooth, naked slope under her shoes and air between her body and the far valley. She hunched as far forward as she could so as not to fall backward. She talked him up too, extending her downhill hand to help him.

They continued along a narrow ledge weathered into a soft, uneven lip. Sometimes more chains assisted, but otherwise nothing helped them over the pancake-stacked stone. Everywhere, the path was so severely eroded that their right, outside, feet slanted dangerously outward toward the deadly fall-off.

They reached a spot where the chain itself had dug so far into the left wall of porous sandstone that the links had cut a groove into it, created by the strain of hikers. Calyce stopped when she saw that it had carved itself into a stone corner around which the walking ledge had disappeared. There was nowhere to walk. To get to the next foothold she had to hang on, swing her body, and hope to land her right foot into a square flat spot just eight inches wide that had been manually cut into the rock opposite. Below her, the void opened.

She swung and landed, then smoothed her vest as she turned back to Damion.

On the far side, though, he held the chain and shook his head. He wouldn't hop it. Straight down hundreds of feet ran the cool path they had taken through Refrigerator Canyon.

"You can do it," she said to encourage him.

He made a face. A teenage boy's face embarrassed by his mother, but he swallowed hard and swung.

His foot slipped the first time because the carved square was so eroded, but he found it at last and straightened.

Once they reached the more level saddle in the ridge, they slowed on the stacked boulders, ending at a protruding diving board of layered stone they were supposed to walk, like walking a plank. They stopped, looking at it, both struck mute with awe.

The photographic view before them was the one in every photograph of Angels Landing: the thin back vertebrae of a long-necked dinosaur facing away from them, whose bony spine started far below them and rolled up in a curve to somewhere beyond them they couldn't see yet, an arched hump that extended hundreds of feet forward into the very middle of Zion's wide central canyon. To their right were chiseled sentinels of colored stone. On their left were close-in cliffs that changed from rust at their eye level to white-as-chalk above.

Damion pointed up the dinosaur's back as the sun beat down on them. "We still have to do all that?"

But it wasn't sun, she noticed, as much as glare from white clouds that were finding each other to form a solid plane too close above them. Far in front of them, off to the east, the sky was still blue, but overhead – she looked up – a ceiling of white was being painted.

"How much farther?" he asked, spent.

"I don't know." And then, "Do you want to turn back?"

All his pretense had climbed out of him. Calyce saw his chest working as his eyes said he was regaining nothing, no strength. No energy was recharging.

He nodded. It was all he could do. "Maybe we should."

"You go back," she said. "Wait for me at Scout Lookout."

He blurted, "You want me to go back alone?"

And then, "It's okay. Let's stay together. Keep going."

They were as high as the World Trade Center towers had been as they walked carefully forward and descended slightly to travel along the left side of the vertebrae. This was the sheer side of the cliff with no chance of survival, with no trees or sloping shoulder to break a fall. The whole spine they still had to climb curved now to their left, in a bowed curtain of dents and rusty streaks swept by a soft wisp of new breeze. It had been still before, but now the air was moving.

They stopped again. The thin fin had suddenly narrowed to only two feet wide.

On both sides of it, twelve hundred vertical feet plunged so precipitously that a single wrong step would be fatal. On the left the river-ribbon far, far below was dull with silty run-off. On the right, Calyce couldn't even see the bottom.

Before them was a single step carved into the stone. A foot wide, the cut block could have been an altar, it was so solitary and exalted, held aloft in mid-air. There was no choice. There was no other path possible around it.

"The Step of Faith," she said.

"That's got a *name*?" he said, staring.

"It's in all the pictures. I'll go first. Be careful."

"You're not really going to do that."

But she already had. She had taken the step, then believed in another. She found the chains again on the other side.

To keep him distracted, she told him again how proud she was of him. In response, she was relieved to see again that sullen-teenager expression, which meant he was focusing on being annoyed at her rather than dying.

"I'm not just proud of you about this," she continued as he was crossing it, "but about the two-thirds. You're offering to divide the bills at home by the number of people, with you and me and Selene sharing equally. You're being fair to me, and it also shows you're thinking of the two of you as a couple, because you're claiming two-thirds of the costs."

Damion made it, but as they were breathing a group of three hikers approached, to pass them going down.

"Excuse us," the front man said, pointing impatiently for Calyce and Damion to move over on the narrow ridge.

She nudged Damion to inch him sideways, but when he stepped he lost his balance and threw out a hand. She had to grip him until he regained his stability.

When they continued, he made sure she went in front, in order to guide him.

"It's not a headcount," he called forward as she led them.

"Then what is it?"

"Space."

"I don't understand," she said over her shoulder. "What's the two-thirds then?"

They had reached another narrowing. No carved step was there this time but only smooth, sandy stone the width of her forearm.

To her back, he said, "Two floors."

If Damion had been looking skyward instead of at his tattered sneakers, he would have seen that more clouds had been hiking in too. They were thickening as they tufted to gray where he and his mother were fully exposed on the narrowest bones of the dinosaur's spine, open to the air now on gritty slabs without handholds.

He said, "We need two bedrooms, and the kitchen. There's no kitchen downstairs and we don't want to wake you up at night with the baby. And once Grandma leaves, Selene wants to make the guestroom upstairs into a nursery."

It took Calyce a long moment, long enough for the wind to blow in around them.

But then she turned.

"You want me to move downstairs? You want me down in *your* room?"

Suddenly his vest flapped and he pressed it flat again as he said, "You can use the kitchen of course. And once Selene figures out this work business, we can contribute to the mortgage, at least until I need it for tuition. If that's what I do."

Calyce's hair blew in a gust. "You want me to move downstairs, but you want me to pay *all* the mortgage? You're only offering to pay two-thirds of the *utilities*? Is that what you're saying?"

"Until I go back to school, if I do. Then it might have to change."

She looked at him in wonderment, then said incredulously, "So if you go back to school, you want to still live there with Selene and the baby, but you want me to pay for *everything*?"

And then, as the rain began, it dawned on her.

She said, "You only want me there so I can babysit the baby. You want my free babysitting. In exchange, you'll allow me to live in the basement of my own house while I pay for your entire family."

"It's your family too, and you pay for family, like Grandma said."

The sky was pelting now. Damion cast his eyes downward at the wetting stones.

He motioned to her, rolling his hand. "Let's go back down. Give me the backpack. I'll carry it but you go first, so you'll have to come around me."

Calyce didn't move.

She said, "You came here to get me to give you my house. That's why you came. Not to be with me, not to share this. But so I'd agree, and I would agree to pay for it."

Lightning jolted, not too far off.

"Give me that." He began pulling at the backpack as the rain hardened on them on the exposed ridge top.

"No!" Calyce held onto the shoulder strap. "You played me. Like you play everyone."

They were in a tug-of-war now, fighting over the backpack, though the loaded bag wasn't their real battle.

He got it from her at last as the rain rat-a-tatted around them, his orange vest wet now as he looked back where they had come, at the charcoal clouds that Calyce saw too.

"It's going to storm," he said. "Come on."

But she wouldn't budge. "You're taking money from all of us, even your grandmother. And Selene. You cannot be like this. I won't believe it."

He leaned toward her then, ignoring the sky.

He shouted at her as the rain began blasting and sheeting.

"Surprise, Mom. I am *exactly* like this."

He yelled over the noise. "This is me. This is who I am. You just don't like it and want me to change, but you know what? I chose this. I chose to be exactly the way I am. I'm not even going to act anymore like I'm interested in whatever stupid dream you have for me."

The water was soaking them as the wind growled.

"You keep trying to make me into what *you* want, Mom. You do this to everyone, and not just me. Ask Simon. You know what he says? He says, 'No wonder Dad left.'"

"Damion!"

"You know what they call you, Simon and Nina? The Dictator!"

He brought the pack to his chest, then twisted around and hurled it with all his power, pitching it far out into the air.

The sack launched, arcing over the canyon. It flew, and curved, and then plummeted straight down, disappearing.

But the toss was so violent and required so much strength that the centrifugal force turned Damion on a wheel. He had twisted to throw it and he kept twisting after it was gone. He couldn't control it. He stumbled backward.

Desperate, he reached out to Calyce again, his arms windmilling this time.

She cried out and grabbed him.

She flailed but she caught him.

They bobbled. They had to shuffle their feet to stay upright.

She held onto him in the rain despite his wobbling, wrapping both her arms around him. They would both fall together if he lost his footing.

Below them the bag hit somewhere with a crash, then hit

again, then not again as it dropped to the bottom fourteen hundred feet below them.

They recovered their balance as one, as a single unit, for she did not let him go. Her mothering arms would not let her.

But then he moved his own arms to reject her. He shrugged her off him once he was safe, then turned his back to her in the driving water on top of the mountain.

"I've got Selene," he said. "I don't need you."

He faced downward on the trail back to where they had come.

"Let's go," he told her. "You in front of me."

He waited for her to inch around him and lead him home.

Mine are not the only children in full rebellion.

Calyce didn't speak. She didn't move.

For the briefest moment, the sky inhaled. The wet retreated into the soot-gray above them and the storm lost its breath.

But then she spoke in a voice he had never heard before.

"I'm going to the top of this without you."

Damion didn't turn, for turning would be taking her seriously. He kept looking forward at the slick, wet rocks around him and down again at his treadless, dangerous tennis shoes. He peered ahead again at the path, slippery now, where the glistening sandstone couldn't drink the pouring water fast enough.

He yelled back at her. He shouted without turning.

"But what about me?"

He couldn't see it, but Calyce shrugged.

She then shouted back at him in the tempest, which had begun again more strongly, with a purpose.

"It looks like you're on your own."

Come, Aeolus said to her. Come to me my daughter.

Once Effie arrived below them on the shuttle, having taken it north from the Lodge where she had quickly run out of things to do, she had watched endless busloads come and go dispensing and swallowing their increasing cargo. Seated on a bench under the tall trees, she had watched group after group get out, collect themselves in a tight circle, then cross the street in upbeat anticipation, energy high, so high any youngster along would be skipping. The earlier trickle of single and dual hikers returning with arm pumps had become at mid-day raucous platoons of day-trippers celebrating. She saw one group of giddy girls high-fiving barefoot.

Along with this stream came a trickle of can't-do's – those too old, too unfit or too scared who had tried but turned back far from the top, wherever that was. Effie didn't know. Their heads were low, their body language defeated. Too hot, too dusty, no fun, ran out of water, damn sun, too steep, too far, goddamn impossible. By mid-morning Effie had heard it all many times over.

"Only for the young," she kept overhearing. "You can get killed up there."

But then the weather changed. The trees began rustling and their leaves started beating. She felt a slight drop of temperature then a scatter of rain, not enough to darken the road but sufficient to palomino it. In the heat the first few drops that found her were soft and welcome.

She looked upward, trying to figure out where her family was through the branches, but her view was obstructed, even if she had known where to find them on the topless mountain that lurched skyward. On each of the last three shuttles, more people got on than alighted. Those crossing the road toward her from the footbridge were wetter and wetter, soaked and scurrying like bugs toward the protection of the trees by the bus stop.

Damion looked around himself, remembering the climb up.

He turned toward his mother again, yet again, as he had just done three times previously, but she kept her back to him as she walked away. He saw that she had climbed fifty feet already. Above him, where she was reaching out to a rounded boulder, the path sprang even more steeply. With both hands she lifted herself up and out of his sight.

No one else was climbing upward toward him in that moment, and no one was heading down. He was alone and vulnerable to the elements on a slippery ridge, balancing just barely on a sharp slant of smooth slab that vectored into mid-air. His legs, his tired legs, were rattle-shaking.

"Don't move," he told himself, but then he realized that doing nothing would not serve him. He couldn't remain frozen there forever. The sluicing water soon would carry him.

"I have to move," he said out loud to no one.

But he couldn't.

"How far is it?" Effie asked a forty-ish woman.

"I didn't do it. I got to Scout Lookout and that was far enough."

"Could I get there?"

"In this rain? Alone?" The woman eyed her. "You in good shape?"

The winds surrounded Calyce, swirling. They circled to hide the far top she still couldn't see. There was nothing but piles of boulders being hit by drowning water, as was she.

Her knees trembled from fatigue. They hadn't before and not until the fight with Damion, which had taken the rest of her strength, and now she was on an upsurge of rock that wouldn't stop. There was no break in it, nowhere she could stand levelly on the littered stone. All she could do was climb, climb it or turn back, and so she went on, making mistakes now that she was so tired.

To her in her exhaustion, though, the path felt more stable in the rain, which seemed to have washed off the sandy powder that coated the sandstone and otherwise would likely have sent her feet skidding.

On a steep uptick, she had to step aside suddenly into a small indent for a couple coming down toward her hunch-shouldered and speeding. They were shocked to come upon her.

"You're staying?" the sopping young man yelled as he negotiated by her, his green Utah Jazz hat stuck to his head.

"Really black clouds are coming fast," his female companion told her. "You can see them from the top. And bad lightning."

They scrambled to get beyond her.

She considered, then pressed on, believing that the growing wet gave her searching fingers more grip on the sandstone.

Calyce my daughter of my wife Ephimedia who left us for Poseidon. I see you below me, climbing to reach me. The winds that force me to crouch here where you cannot see me resent you. These gales, my children too, shrieking in their fury, do not want you here, for they mean for me to dwell alone, yearning for but never again holding them as they spin and taunt me. Take care my daughter, mother of Endymion, for they intend to kill you by throwing you off this cliff and I can do nothing but watch them.

Rain poured as Damion looked at the deadly slope and the torrent that flowed over it. He was stuck, or he risked his life trying to scale downward. Along the front of him, water ran slick on the shiny neon plastic.

"Fucking vest."

He unzipped it and yanked it off himself, then balled it with his fists. He threw the wadded orange thing as hard as he could into the rain, up and rocketing. It unfurled. As it arced, it caught the water. A wounded bird, it twisted down. It dove and was gone.

Calyce clung now to wet chains that stopped anyway above a blind drop deeper than her legs could reach. Was she meant to turn and face the rocks to skitter sideways? Was there a place for her toes in the darkness of that cleft she couldn't see? To her left, just there, was the plunge.

Effie had crossed the footbridge and was hugging the western bank as she walked on sudden beach sand so thick it ate the bottoms of her sneakers.

As Damion maneuvered over steep rocks, the thunder came. It clapped and banged as rain cut sideways. He had no idea how to move safely through the lightning, so close it strobed like a broken ceiling light.

"Where are they?" Effie said out loud as the hard rain hit her along with the wind.

Calyce stared up and up as wet shards stung her face. There wasn't another person on the climb. No bright colors, no hikers, no other idiots dumb enough to still be on the mountain.

A boom of thunder clashed above her.

There were no chains now in this spot where the barrage had stopped her. She struggled to balance, her feet at two different levels. She tried to lean into the wind that crowded her, for there were no handholds here but only the deadly-smooth, shining stone she was standing on with her vest flagging.

She twisted around carefully to look back behind her, and her tight hat flew. It left her head to soar like a bird.

Backwards, where Damion had gone, the path was even steeper and wet-slick.

"Stop!" Aeolus cried to his wind-children, but they bark-laughed and Calyce heard them.

What Calyce didn't know was the chemistry. Sodium bicarbonate binds sandstone, which is just compressed sand, and in water sodium bicarbonate dissolves. Rocks impossible to break in the arid desert snap easily in a driving rain.

She didn't know, so she put out her right foot. She stepped on the wet ledge and it cracked. It broke under her weight.

She fell.

She tried to grab something but she couldn't. There was nothing for her hands, so she slid. She flailed her arms but she was on the ground on her right side now, sliding, ripping quickly. Gaining speed, she was feet-first and there was nothing to break her fall.

"Was that a scream?" Effie said to the wind that whipped her.

Calyce rolled, screaming. She tumbled on the wet rock toward the side of the cliff, slipping and yelling, unable to use her empty fingers, which were bleeding now along with her arms and her right hip from the desperate friction.

Tumbling, she tried to tuck her body.

Another five feet and she would leave the earth.

He stood up straining but he couldn't help her.

"Was that a man or a woman?"

Effie couldn't tell because the storm distorted it, but she began to run.

She didn't know where she was but she knew she was below her family.

Calyce hit a cutout. She slammed hard into a boulder in a dip that stopped her tumbling thirty feet down. Mid-roll, her twisting back crashed into the trunk of a pine tree on the steep slope.

The trunk held and it braced her and kept her from flying.

Effie saw the trail spike upward on the canyon wall but it didn't stop her.

"My Lord!" Catherine had finally raised her voice at her son. "Do I have to tell you even when to use the bathroom? Can't you do anything on your own? Stop thinking and do something. Do you want to be at Target all your life?"

Ryan cringed. His thin shoulders hunched in shame. He dropped his chin so she wouldn't see him.

"I'm sorry," she said immediately. "I'm so sorry. I didn't mean it. What kind of mother am I?"

She hugged him close with his head on her chest. He wrapped

*one arm around her and hugged her tightly. The other hand he thrust
into his mouth, to bite a bitten nail to the quick.*

They rocked together, mother and son, for more than a minute.

Over the top of his head, she then whispered, "Heal thyself."

"What?"

I was talking to myself. I said, "Physician, heal thyself."'

Calyce lay inert for a full minute, then opened her eyes at
dirt-level. The rain kept coming but didn't drown her. She realized she was on her side and hurting but still alive. Then she
realized she was in a chink and that chink and the tree there had
saved her life.

She sat up, then scooted herself back against a boulder. She
stretched out her legs gently and felt them with her bleeding
hands, then pressed her arms, her neck and both sides of her face
to look for damage. She assessed her bloody fingers. Her legs in
her wet shorts were torn up and bloody too and covered with
brown debris, but they were solid.

Her right hip hurt and she felt a sharp pain under her chin.
She held up her hands in the rain, which washed them, and she
saw the cuts. But everything was still attached.

She inventoried her brain, forcing herself to rehearse what
had happened. As the panic slowed and her breathing moder-
ated, she realized she was injured but still capable. Maybe she
could stand, and maybe she could locate a way up the unmarked
and rocky mountain dumping rain.

Eventually, she realized as she sat that no one knew where she
was. Then she registered that they would never find her. No one
walking the trail would ever see her, not even in good weather.
She had flown over a hump in the slope and was hidden from the

trail she figured had to be somewhere above her, but she couldn't see it.

It took her long minutes to get to that one clear thought.

Calyce crawled. She never left her hands and knees but depended on them like a baby, seizing the sharp rocks with her ripped hands where she could, then onto the tree roots as her body screamed.

Standing at last on the trail again, at the same point where she had fallen, she had to make a final decision.

Above her, her father Aeolus said, "Come now. I want to hold you."

"No," Calyce said out loud, "Damion wants me to chase after him, but I won't. Not anymore. I've come this far and now I've paid this price."

Effie hastened despite the panting, wheezing, pumping of her chest.

Calyce tackled each next vertical run of chain and each next chainless exposure. She put her feet sometimes not seeing where they would go or if the ledge she chose would hold her. She moved without knowing whether she would lose her wet grip or her balance or whether her weighty boots would slide on the molded surface. She hauled herself, lifting her legs and her body weight higher than she had ever done, all while she judged with every step the lethal angle of the sandstone.

The last approach was a series of links and posts and open spaces straight up forty feet, every coming moment visible to the eye.

She took another deep breath, then grabbed the metal. As she did she talked to the top of the mountain she saw only as an ending against the sky. There was no way to know it was the roof, but it was, at last.

"I'm nearly home. I can do this."

The overlapping slabs came to a sharp peak like a pointed gable, only the sides weren't even. On the short left side, to the north, a woman could barely lay full-length outward without her boots dangling 1500 feet above the far thread of the distant river.

The storm abated the slightest bit as Calyce crab-walked on the right instead, but the rocks never leveled. One wrong foot and she would tumble off, but she knew the end wasn't there. It was still out in front of her at a far tip she could not yet see.

As she moved she never looked beyond her hands. She didn't see at ground level the south-running Narrows gorge that was now inflamed with flash-flooding rain, and she didn't see the water streaking the white-topped cliffs to her left, on the north.

But there they were, finally, marking the end of her journey. She didn't know they would be there but of course they belonged.

Cairns. Handmade stacks of little stones like a tower of precarious dishes placed by hikers to mark their achievement, to say thank you to the gods who had delivered them safely.

Cairns like the rock piles on Three Sisters Islands in the Potomac on the way to National Airport, only these at the top of Angels Landing weren't thrown by God but assembled by people. She counted one that was seventeen pieces tall, while another had two funny arms like a cactus. At another spot, a dwarf forest grew. There must have been twenty of them, each still as upright as when they were first constructed by nameless pilgrims now far from this place, this temple of Zion.

She sat down cross-legged carefully on the wet stone.

She looked beyond the cairns at the sweeping view. She was up as high as an eagle soaring, as she saw a green valley bounded on both sides by monumental rock-teeth that widened to the south. As she breathed, suspended, it seemed the winds too died for as long as she willed it.

She was not alone there on the top of the world, and she did not feel she was. She could feel strong arms around her even before she realized she was hugging herself.

A siren.

Coming toward Calyce from her right, from the south where the shuttle bus came and the Visitor Center was. She knew it was approaching because the sound of it was raised. Past her and it would lower, but it hadn't yet, so her hearing could place it grossly but not specifically, not yet.

She peered far, far down to the thin gray wire of road but saw little, so she stood slowly, inching up and straightening. Still not enough, so she took three steps and re-balanced with her right foot twelve inches lower than her left. She couldn't see any movement in the fuzz of rain below her, but then she did.

She saw flashing red and blue lights on a speeding white roof making the turn, as she heard its shriek not continue around the great bend of the river toward the rushing Narrows, where it should have been going, because a flash flood there was a certainty.

She saw a bit of the tiny parking lot below her. She saw the white flashing SUV pull in.

Then she saw two Park Rangers running toward the metal footbridge.

She gasped. She put her hands to her mouth.

An instant later, she had already turned to run but couldn't because running there brought certain death. She crab-walked back where she came as fast as she could.

Damion heard it too.

The shrill noise began as he was halfway through the slot canyon. In the tall, tight groove the siren reverberated. It cycled round and round, echoing loudly.

He covered his ears, so he didn't notice the siren getting closer and more insistent. But he did notice when it finally stopped. He took down his hands and kept stomping through the overflow from the gushing creek bed.

He got to the mouth of the squared-off hanging canyon, then turned right on a steep down-ramp into the distant valley.

As he did, he ran into Effie. Literally. Coming up, she didn't see him. She was winded yet still trying to run, and she startled, then cried out when she saw that she had slammed into him.

"You're alright!"

She grabbed him. She was panting but he wasn't.

She took in huge gulps of air. "Where's your vest?"

She held him with both her hands on his upper arms. "So it's her. It has to be her. They saw her."

Then she passed by him in a rush. "Come on! We've got to get up there. The police are coming. They called them on the way down."

"Who did?"

"They passed me. A couple. They're meeting the police and coming back up. All I heard was they saw someone in an orange vest fall over the side of the mountain."

Calyce saw the flash of orange. It was halfway down, straight down, fluttering on a rock beak on the sheer cliff below her. It hadn't been there before, on their way up.

She screamed and began running.

Damion watched Effie race off upward, but he didn't follow her. His eyes calmly scanned the valley below, then the white sky above him as he thought.

From where he stood hundreds of feet above the canyon floor, the rain was relenting as it moved southeast away from Zion, where it would peter out eventually over the desert. In the receding torrent a far-off jolt of lightning sparked.

He sidled close to the cliff, where it was driest, and he began descending on the path.

As he walked with his right hand on the moist wall, he said to no one, "Fuck her. She turned her back on *me*."

"Damion."

Calyce kept saying her son's name over and over as she scurried. She grabbed chains and gripped rocks and inched her way.

She stumbled but caught herself. She slipped and slopped but kept going.

Coming upward, Effie made it finally to the stack of short, steep switchbacks and began up them. She looked to the top but couldn't see where they ended.

She asked herself inside her mind, to save her energy for breathing. "Does this ever stop?"

They were running up as Damion was walking down, the two hikers and the two Park Rangers not in olive green but corn-yellow t-shirts and black backpacks. The couple, a woman and a man wearing a Utah jazz hat, struggled to keep up with the rescuers.

The front Ranger said to Damion. "It's closed. We're closing the trail. Can you stay at the bottom and keep people from starting up? You can leave as soon as the other vehicle gets here with the sign."

And they were gone without waiting for his answer, all four of them rushing up, turning left around a kink in the trail.

Calyce finally got herself down to Scout Lookout. There she gained speed on the level ground as the dirt trail jerked through the brush.

Suddenly, Effie sprang out at her.

Effie leapt from a turn in the path, and reached upward to her towering daughter.

But Calyce jumped back. Surprised. Shocked to see anyone.

Without thinking she shook her head and thrust both arms high in the air.

She jumped up on both feet, up and down, up and down, waving her long arms in big half-circles.

She yelled, tearing her lungs, "Get back! Get back!"

"Calyce, it's me!"

"Get back from me!"

Effie shouted, "You're okay!"

Effie grabbed her and held on tight. "You're not hurt! You're alright."

"Mom, Damion's fallen. I saw his vest."

"Honey, I –"

"The sirens, I heard them."

" – just saw him. He's fine. He's right here, right behind me."

But then Effie turned and he wasn't there.

She told Calyce, "I don't know where he is but he's fine. I just saw him."

Calyce bent over double then. She fell to the sand-mud on her knees and started shaking. Her breath hitched and caught and finally hiccupped into tears. Her insides broke loose.

Effie went down with her, on her knees, and held on, holding her.

Calyce cried and tried to breathe, and then it all came out in rush as she pressed her her streaming face against her grateful mother.

"Mom. Mom, I'm sorry. I'm so sorry but I don't want you to live with me. I don't want you there for the rest of my life. I have a life, Mom. I want my own, like you had yours. One that I choose, that belongs just to me."

Effie clutched her and patted her and thanked God she was alive.

Calyce said with her head buried in her mother, "Can you understand that? Can you forgive me?"

Effie stroked her child as she hadn't since before she had left her. Like a child, Calyce kept her head under her mother's soft hand.

"Of course I do," Effie told her. "Of course. I would never want you unhappy. Or to do anything you don't want to do. All I care about is what's best for you. And I'm so sorry. So sorry for everything."

The two women sat together shoulder-to-shoulder, far away from the lethal cliff edge. Around them the thirsty sandstone was drying already, turning pink again.

"I'll think of something," Effie assured her.

Calyce leaned her head on Effie's shoulder. She had had to scrunch down in order to do it.

Effie said, "I know. I'll live with Simon."

Calyce laughed out loud. "You hate Sandra."

"No, she hates me. But they have room now that both the girls will be gone."

A moment later, after they had sat in quiet, just loving each other, Effie asked, "So what was all that jumping and screaming and arm-waving? That was scary. I thought you had lost your mind."

Calyce laughed at herself.

"I thought you were a cougar."

Catherine made it too, finally, when she returned to Zion alone.

Every foothold and hand grip she found herself, having learned how to take tiny steps and stand up straight, with arms out, and how to take micro-breaks by straightening each leg after each step so her skeleton could absorb her body's weight.

When she at last arrived at the top, she tiptoed carefully along its pitched roof to sit on hot stone so high that birds flew below her. She hugged her knees. Spread beyond her was the deep, wide, green canyon floor bounded by rock candy chunks with sharp peaks in a widening V. They were washed with color in bands and cut with streaks of rust and they rose higher than any pyramids, pointing the way in the same arrow shape for hundreds of millions of years, an arrow that could only be seen from this height, an arrow of cliffs that led northward to this place, to this church of God.

Here, she had become someone who had climbed Angels Landing. She would do it again tomorrow or the next day when her aching muscles hurt less. She would remain in Springdale so she could do it, unguided and easily, because she could. She knew how.

She was someone who had done what others had died not doing. She had achieved. Within her now was a certainty, an abiding sureness in herself that no external assault could rob her of. It left a solidity she had never felt before, a confidence that, at last, she could attempt anything.

"At least, that's how it felt to me," she tried to tell her mother when she visited the old woman three days later, the first Saturday after her return.

"That's nice, honey," her mother said from her bed in the nursing home, where she had gone after complications from open-heart bypass surgery. They had known the operation was especially risky because of the diabetes, but her intransigent mother had insisted on it anyway.

"How was the weather out there?" the frail woman said.

"*Mom it was really something to climb that. I started at the –*"

"*Can you tell me next week? Read the paper to me now. It's right there.*"

As always, she did exactly as her mother directed. Catherine had to cough, though, before she began. Something burned in her throat that wouldn't go away.

"*It was amazing. You have to go and –*"

"*Mom, the baby's crying, and Elena's at work, so I've got to take care of him. I tell you what. When you get home tonight, come on upstairs and we'll talk. And could you bring home some carryout? I'll sit up here in the kitchen while you tell me all about it. At least 'til I fall asleep. Oh, and can you get some laundry detergent? I checked down in your room, and there isn't any left.*"

A week before Catherine had boarded the plane alone to Las Vegas, she had led her last Senior Creative Writing class for the year. It was the Thursday before their Saturday graduation, and they were discussing the winners of the student writing pieces. They had arrived at last at the top of the list, at the very best work according to the kids, who were all leaving her.

The number one, they said, they had voted on without her, secretly. The winner? Not a student work but a portion of her own first novel, which she had given them, about a black English teacher who tries to climb Angels Landing.

"*Write the whole thing,*" they told her. "*And keep the Greek stuff.*"

The next December, Calyce walked over the metal bridge

again at the beginning of the trail from the bus stop. A sixty-ish man who was very tall and thin with long strides soon caught up with her. They were strangers, but because no one else was making the climb on that winter morning, they fell in step together.

He was a professor from SUNY Binghamton who had seen Angels Landing on YouTube and had to try it. In answer to his question, she told him yes, she had climbed it before, many times, though this was her first December. Yes, she lived nearby. She had just moved to Hurricane to teach English at the private school there.

As they mounted the steepening path, she told him she had sold her townhouse in the D.C. suburbs and moved lock, stock and barrel to Utah. Her kids were grown. Her daughter's husband was in the Foreign Service so they lived in Africa with her grandson. Her son was recently married and expecting a baby in a few days, and if it was a boy they planned to name him Cisco.

"What does my son do?" Calyce repeated the man's question. "Last I knew he was a bartender. His wife's an electrician. Isn't that something?"

Later, as they traipsed Refrigerator Canyon, he asked if she had family "out here."

"My mother lives in Texas with my brother and his family but I'm the only one in Utah. I'm here alone, but it doesn't really feel that way. There's something comforting about this mountain."

To take the nice man's mind off the extremity of the next stacked steep switchbacks, she asked him about his work at the university.

He answered, then parried with, "So what do you do when you're not teaching?"

"I write. I'm working on my first novel."

They made their way panting to Scout Lookout. After a long moment staring down from the left lip-edge where the woman Calyce was writing about sees a condor gliding, he said, "It's sure different from back home, isn't it?"

But she shook her head.

"This *is* home," she told him, and then to pay him back for hearing her story, she guided him safely all the way up Angels Landing.

Author's Note

I was fascinated by Calyce, who in Greek mythology is the daughter of Aeolus the god of winds and the mother of Endymion. Her son was so worthless and vain that he made a pact with Zeus to sleep for all eternity in exchange for Zeus granting him eternal youth. There's a statue of him in the British Museum and a Keats poem called *Endymion* that starts – you've probably heard this – "A thing of beauty is a joy forever."

Before Endymion makes that deal, he fathers a child with Selene, the goddess of the moon, who visits him nightly after he falls asleep, so she can gaze upon him and adore him. You know who their child was, this boy child, Endymion's son and the grandson of Calyce? Narcissus. Yes, that one, the one who stares at himself in the lake. This is a grandmother who will all her life blame herself for that happening.

I also wanted to write a book about a mature woman who finally chooses herself. When given the impossible choice between her elderly mother's needs and her adult son's, she picks Door #3 – her own life, and she does it without being punished by death, poison, drowning, having to throw herself under a train, etc. Interestingly, as I described this decision to every woman I know, every single one of them refused even to contemplate such a story line. Every one said no, that wasn't possible, a loving daughter/mother would never do that. She would serve her son and her mother and deny herself, of course. The visceral-ness of their reaction and its uniformity told me that we as women of a certain age have indeed been inculcated with an assumption of endless service. It is so successfully ingrained that any other hypothesis is expelled. That reaction also meant that if I retained the Calyce story line I had to include an equally plausible parallel one about a woman who concedes and does the expected. Hence *Alternate Ending*, with each protagonist the author of the other's story.

ACKNOWLEDGEMENTS

I am immensely grateful to everyone who graciously gave me their time and expertise to help make this story and my writing better. All factual mistakes are my own.

Perry Amati

Plateau District Ranger Andrew Fitzgerald, SAR Coordinator, Zion National Park

Michael B. Fowler

Gene Gerstner at the Zion Canyon Field Institute

J.J. Jefferson

Dr. Melissa Kerley

Sara Lofti

Camille Masse

Dr. James Metcalf, geologist at the University of Colorado, Boulder

Also helpful was Bryan A. Garner's article, "A Bizspeak Blacklist," *Harvard Business Review*, March 21, 2013

On my third attempt up Angels Landing in Zion National Park, I met an actual angel. Francois-Xavier Gagnon, founder of *Alta Expedition*, happened to come up behind me as I was struggling at the first gap in chains. He gallantly spent the next two hours patiently getting me to the top and back down again, teaching me how to hike the deadly slope as he sacrificed an afternoon alone on the cliff with his girlfriend Lee. I am in their debt.

www.ingramcontent.com/pod-product-compliance
Lightning Source LLC
Chambersburg PA
CBHW020331120726
47904CB00002B/366